Hold on Tight

SHELLEY SHEPARD GRAY

Hold on Tight

BLACK STONE
PUBLISHING

Copyright © 2019 by Shelley Shepard Gray
Published in 2019 by Blackstone Publishing
Cover design by Alenka Vdovič Linaschke
Book design by Blackstone Publishing

The characters and events in this book are fictitious. Any similarity to real
persons, living or dead, is coincidental and not intended by the author.

First edition: 2019
Printed in the United States of America
ISBN 978-1-5384-4091-9

Fiction / Romance

1 3 5 7 9 10 8 6 4 2

CIP data for this book is available
from the Library of Congress

Blackstone Publishing
31 Mistletoe Rd.
Ashland, OR 97520

www.BlackstonePublishing.com

Hold on Tight is dedicated to this series' street team, the Bridgeport Book Club. This group of ladies read the novels, posted reviews, gave me suggestions, and were all around exactly who I needed whenever I needed a little boost. So, thank you, Annie, Patti, Michelle, Liz, Kristi, Connie and Connie, Cindy, Cathy, and Carrie!
I hope this book does y'all proud.

Letter to Readers

Thank you for picking up *Hold on Tight*! I hope you like Dani and Jackson's story. I enjoyed writing this book so much. There was something about having all four main characters in the novel be survivors of one kind or another that hit me hard. I found myself rooting for each of them—and working a little harder to do justice to their wishes and dreams. I hope at least one of them strikes a chord with you as well.

Writing this book also brought back fun memories of when our son, Arthur, played baseball. For a couple of years, my husband, Tom, was one of the team's coaches, which meant I spent most of every spring and summer going to Little League baseball games. I'd sit in my canvas chair for hours at a time, bite my nails whenever Arthur came up to bat, and pull out lots and lots of snacks and toys for our daughter to play with while I promised that the game was "almost over." Tom and I made friends with all the other parents, too. We sweated together in the July heat, complained about the amount of laundry we did at night, and ate too much pizza.

Then, all too soon, Arthur grew up and those years became just a jumbled memory.

Maybe you can relate?

I have to admit that my favorite part of this series is still the thing that inspired me to write the series in the first place: the Bridgeport Social Club. I enjoyed having the club evolve a bit into an organization that tries to help out when they can. I have a feeling the BSC is going to continue to grow and prosper—and maybe even welcome another couple of newcomers into town.

Until that happens, I wish you sunny days, good friends, and time to enjoy both.

With my thanks and blessings,
Shelley Shepard Gray

CHAPTER 1

FROM LES LARKE'S
YOU, TOO, CAN HOST
A POKER TOURNEY:

*Hosting a neighborhood poker tournament is
a great way to get the guys to spend more time
together. It can be a lot of fun—if you follow
some basic advice.*

Saturday Night

"I'm really glad you're here," the slightly tipsy blond announced as Jackson Koch placed a third glass of merlot into her hands. "Until you came to town, I knew everybody. Having you around has shaken everything up." She paused. "In a good way, I mean." Leaning forward, she smiled while giving him an eyeful of cleavage.

Jackson knew that eyeful was a promise of a whole lot more— if he was inclined to take her up on the opportunity. He wasn't. Even if he was interested in a night with a pretty blond, he wouldn't pick one up where he worked.

"Glad I could help," he said at last. He turned and started on a pair of gin and tonics for the couple sitting next to her.

She frowned before getting up from the barstool. After a

second, she smoothed her knit dress along her hips and stepped away. No doubt, she would be smiling brightly at someone else before the hour was up.

As he poured Bombay and filled the rest of the glasses with tonic water and added the lime wedges, he couldn't help but mentally finish his reply to the woman. He was glad he'd moved to Bridgeport, too, but she didn't know him.

Didn't know him *at all*.

If he was going to be real honest, sometimes he didn't even know himself anymore. Bartending at the Corner Bar in Bridgeport, Ohio, had never been in his plans.

The fact of the matter was that he'd never imagined that he would be living outside of Spartan, West Virginia. He had been settled there. His family had been part of the landscape for generations. He had a group of friends that he'd known since kindergarten and a thousand memories on practically every corner of that one-stoplight town.

He'd also had a good job.

He'd liked mining. Liked the camaraderie of the men he'd worked with. Liked feeling like he was providing something useful for the rest of the population. Something necessary to help them run their businesses and lives.

But two years ago, he and everyone else at Spartan Mine Number Nine learned that *they* might have thought they were doing something good, but the rest of America thought they were ruining the planet. Nobody wanted to use coal anymore. And though there were no doubt a hundred other reasons his mine had needed to close, Jackson had given up trying to figure out what they were. All he knew was that he—alongside four hundred other men—was out a good job.

He'd been laid off, given a severance package for his twelve years of hard work, and left behind. Forgotten.

"Hey, Jackson?" Genevieve Schuler prompted. Her voice was laced with concern. "You all right?"

Damn it. He'd done it again—let his mind go to places it shouldn't.

"Sorry, Gen." Luckily, she'd already passed the gin and tonics he'd poured to the couple who had been waiting. He turned, ready to help the next customers, but only saw his boss, still standing by his side.

Realizing that they were experiencing a momentary break, he looked around, already anticipating what Gen needed. "What do you want me to do? Wash glasses?"

Gen shook her head, the slight motion causing the tail of her long blond ponytail to brush along her shoulder blades. "I was thinking you could go on home."

After glancing at his phone, he looked at her in confusion. Gen was a couple years younger than him, had started this bar two years ago, and would have been able to put any worker at Spartan Mine Number Nine in his place with one withering look. She also seemed to have a soft spot for men down on their luck. She'd hired him even though his only bartending experience was sitting at one with his buddies.

"It's only midnight." It was also a Saturday night. They didn't start shutting it down until one at the earliest. More often than not, two a.m. was last call. Given that the crowd was having a good time, he was pretty sure that that was going to be this evening's scenario.

Still staring at him through gold wire rims, Gen explained further. "Kimmy's working tonight, and she just got on at six. Brad's working the door and Melissa's doing just fine out on the patio. You've been on since four. Go on home. We've got this, Cookie."

"I'm starting to wish I never told you about my high school nickname."

She laughed. "You might as well wish for something else, because it's cemented in my mind now." Making a shooing motion with her hand, she said, "Go on, now. I'll add up your tips and have them for you after you wash up."

He nodded again as he slid out from the gate and headed toward the back rooms. As he walked, the blond he'd served earlier and her two girlfriends smiled up at him. One of them might have said something, too. He wasn't sure. All he knew was that he'd be out of there soon.

As soon as he got to the back room, he washed his hands and arms with soap, as thoroughly as he could, and switched out his T-shirt. He hated to walk into his apartment smelling like stale beer. After he changed, he grabbed his backpack and strode back into the main bar.

Gen handed him an envelope, his portion of the tips for the night. "See you Tuesday night. You're on from seven till close."

"Yep. See you then." He pocketed the envelope then headed out the side door and started his five-minute commute home.

The minute he walked outside, the dark silence soothed him like a balm. Though mining wasn't the quietest job in the world, a lot of his old job had been spent in relative silence. Some guys had worn headphones, needing something to distract themselves from the repetitive sounds and hard labor. He had never been one of them. He'd gotten used to the sounds and had even come to rely on them. Plus, he liked being able to hear if one of his men had a problem.

Like an old friend, memories of being something more than a mediocre bartender flashed through his mind. He'd been a crew leader, responsible not only for his team's output but their well-being. He'd enjoyed it. Just as he'd enjoyed being responsible for his women at home.

Before more painful memories surfaced, he shut down that train of thought. Tight.

"That part of your life is over, Jackson," he reminded himself as he walked down the sidewalk to the entrance of his apartment building. He needed to stop thinking of his old life. Stop thinking of Beth. Stop thinking of how things used to be.

Using his key card, he let himself in the main door, then headed up the one flight to the apartment he shared with his daughter, Kate. He really hoped she'd had a good night with Dani.

His key clicked softly as he turned the lock and then shut the door behind him. Waited.

But he didn't hear anything.

Concern snaked through him. Suddenly, he was torn between looking through the two-bedroom apartment and pulling out his cell phone. Damn. When was the last time he'd checked it? Maybe around eight or nine?

Over three hours ago.

He cursed himself again as he started toward Kate's bedroom door. What if something happened? What if Dani had been trying to get ahold of him and had finally given up and taken Kate to the hospital? What if—

"Jackson! Oh my gosh! You scared the heck out of me!" Dani exclaimed. Looking like she'd been caught doing something bad, his babysitter shot to her feet.

His neighbor—and part-time babysitter—had been sitting at the little nook in the back of his kitchen. He hadn't even noticed her. "Sorry, Dani. I guess I should have let you know I was getting off early."

She was looking down at her phone. "Did you text me, and I didn't see it?"

"Nah. I forgot. Like I said, I'm sorry about that."

"It's okay. I think I fell asleep reading anyway." She pulled a pair of headphones off her head and then shook her hair slightly.

Her curly dark-blond hair bounced with the motion. "So, you got off a little early, huh?"

"Yeah. At first, I was kind of bummed about losing the money, but I got over that real quick. It's good to be home early for once."

"I bet."

She studied him carefully, her concern making him warm inside—reminding him that he might be lonely here in Bridgeport, but he wasn't alone. Seeing that she was gathering her books, he grabbed her backpack and started putting her laptop and notebooks inside. "How was Kate tonight?"

"Perfect." She smiled, her brown eyes conveying a wealth of information with just one look. "We played princess, then watched *Frozen*, then read her bunny book. She went to sleep around eight."

He chuckled. "You getting tired of playing princess yet?"

Pulling out her keys, she gave him a look of mock horror. "Are you kidding? Not on your life. Jeremy had me playing trucks for hours when he was four. I was constantly sitting in the dirt. Bugs got on me! Playing dress-up and acting all girlie never gets old."

He smiled at her, thinking that she was one of the most feminine women he'd ever met. Her long blond hair. That pretty smile. The kindness that radiated from nearly everything she did. There was something about Dani that he couldn't seem to ignore—no matter how hard he tried. "I'll take your word for it. I still can't imagine you being all that pleased to be playing in the dirt."

"Well, Kate tells me she likes to play princess with me almost as much as she does her daddy." She raised her eyebrows. "I think that means we're all doing things we never intended to do."

She had him there. "Do me a favor and don't picture me in a tiara."

"What? You afraid you'll ruin your street cred?"

"Absolutely."

Dani chuckled as she walked toward his door, her bright-red backpack slung over one shoulder. "Don't worry, your secret's safe with me. How about we simply agree that good parents will do just about anything for their children instead?"

Thinking about his sacrifices, and the ones that both of their former spouses had made, Jackson swallowed hard. "Agreed."

Turning back toward him, Dani paused. "I'm sorry. Did I say something wrong?"

"Not at all. What you said was everything right." Just as he opened the door for her, he realized that he'd been so busy bantering with her that he'd forgotten to get out his tip envelope and pay her. "Dan, crap. Hold on. I forgot to pay you."

"Don't worry about it. You can pay me next time you work." She paused. "When is that, again? I know you gave me next week's schedule … but I didn't look at it real good. Are you working on Tuesday?"

"Yep. I work seven till close."

"I'll come up around six thirty then."

When she yawned, he realized that she'd been standing there holding a heavy backpack. Where the heck was his head? "Let me walk you up."

She waved him off. "No need. I'm good."

"Dan …"

"Please, Jackson. If you don't mind, I'd rather go on my own. I'll see you later."

"See you." He let her go but stayed in place as he watched her walk down the hall and then take the stairs up to the next flight. Even when she was out of sight, he stayed there. Remembering.

Suddenly overcome with memories of when he walked

another woman to her door. Then, years later, walking her to *their* door.

All after making vows before God and everyone—they all knew that he'd never let her go.

It was too bad Beth's cancer had had other plans.

CHAPTER 2

FROM LES LARKE'S
*YOU, TOO, CAN HOST
A POKER TOURNEY:*

*First off, make sure you have the proper poker
supplies on hand. You're gonna need a deck of
cards, chips, and a table to play on. If you have
these three things, you're on your way.*

All Danielle Brown cared about was entering her apartment as quietly as possible.

Jeremy was the only fourteen-year-old on earth she'd ever heard of who didn't sleep like the dead. She'd learned the hard way the dangers of microwaving a snack in the middle of the night or watching a movie on television without headphones. Even slight noises triggered an instant reaction.

When he was little, he would pop right up out of his *Star Wars* sheets and come find her after the slightest noise. That greeting would be followed by at least another hour of conversation and gentle coaxing before he went back to sleep.

Now he didn't bother waking her up, which was almost worse, as far as she was concerned. He stayed in his bed and read or played on his computer or phone for hours, only to be groggy in the morning and running on empty by the time he was halfway through his school day.

Jeremy's light sleeping habits were the exact opposite of her own. Unless her alarm blared or her boy pushed her shoulder, Dani slept through practically anything.

At least she didn't have to worry about waking him up tonight. She'd gotten home earlier than expected, and since it was a Saturday night, it wouldn't have even been a serious issue if she had disturbed him. They could sleep in until nine. Church didn't start until a quarter after ten. Getting the chance to sleep past six or seven in the morning always felt like a gift.

Just as she opened the refrigerator, contemplating the pros and cons of having a glass of icy chardonnay, her son walked into the kitchen.

"Hey, Mom."

"Please don't tell me that I woke you up."

He looked insulted by that idea. "I wasn't asleep. It's only twelve thirty."

"It's a legitimate question. You were yawning around three this afternoon."

In typical Jeremy fashion, he smirked but didn't say anything about that. "You wanna watch *Ice Road Truckers?*"

"Sure. Let me get a glass of wine and I'll meet you on the couch. And then I want to hear about your night."

He turned away without replying, sending a shiver of warning through her as the questions started to race in her head. Was he avoiding the question … or just avoiding answering because the answer didn't matter?

Half the time she never knew. About a year ago, he'd started pulling away from her, which she knew was natural but hard for her heart to accept.

After pouring herself a half-glass of wine, she joined him on the tan suede couch that she hadn't wanted to spend the money on, but Brian had insisted was worth the investment.

"So, what did you do tonight?"

He shrugged. "Nothing. Just hung out."

"Oh, Jackson gave me his schedule for next week. He's off next Saturday night!"

Jeremy shrugged as if it didn't matter to him.

"That means you can make some plans, Jer." Like it was a new idea, she said, "Hey, maybe you could invite someone over to spend the night. You haven't done that in a while."

"I'm a little old to have sleepovers, Mom."

"Oh. Hey, I know. We could do something fun, just the two of us," she continued, hoping her voice didn't sound as eager as she felt. "We could go to the movies."

"On Saturday night? I don't know, Mom."

Obviously fourteen-year-old boys did not want to be seen out on Saturday nights with their mothers. Thinking back to when she and Brian were a high school item, she realized she should have known that.

No, she should have remembered that.

"Sorry. I was just thinking it would be fun to spend time with you instead of a three-year-old for a change."

"How was Kate?"

There is was. The first warmth and interest in his voice. She would never have guessed it, but the first real spark of life that had appeared in his eyes after his father's death had been brought on by a dark-haired, blue-eyed little girl.

Dani smiled. "She wanted to play princess all night and watch *Frozen*."

"Ugh."

"I know. I think I now know every word in that movie."

"Kate's so silly."

"She really is," she murmured, though she was thinking that little Kate was a blessing, too. Jeremy's eyes had lit up. There really wasn't much that girl could do that he didn't seem to find appealing. "She did ask if you could come over to play, by the way."

The smile that had been playing on his lips turned into a full-blown grin. "What did you tell her?"

"The truth. That you had other things to do besides play princess."

"Uh-oh. What did she say to that?"

"What do you think? She asked again if 'Jimmy' could come over to play soon."

As she'd hoped, Jeremy chuckled at Kate's butchering of his name. "Do you think Jackson does all that girlie stuff?"

"I know he does." She smiled at him. "Kate's got her daddy wrapped around her pinkie." Seeing the wistfulness in Jeremy's eyes, she added, "Just like you did with yours. Your dad could never tell you no."

And just like that, all of the warmth that had been settling in his expression evaporated. "You know what? I'm getting kind of tired. I'm gonna go to bed."

"But what about *Ice Road Truckers*?"

"It's just a repeat. No reason for us to watch a repeat."

"All right." Feeling disappointed but trying hard not to show it, she stood up and pressed her lips to his brow. "See you in the morning. We'll leave for church at ten."

"I know. Night, Mom."

After she heard his door shut, she leaned back against the cushions of her couch and picked up her untouched glass of wine. Took a tentative sip before setting it back down.

This wasn't how it was supposed to be. When she'd married Brian back in their little Indiana town, they'd had all sorts of plans. They were going to both work hard, move to Cincinnati or Indy and buy a house. Have another child after Jeremy, who'd been the reason they'd had to get married so early in the first place.

Then, one day, when there was finally a little extra money, she was going to go to college and get her degree in early childhood education.

Letting the memories continue, she took another sip. Boy, she'd had big dreams. She used to dream about one day owning her own a little daycare and preschool. She was going to name it something cute and concentrate on helping working families. Families that needed good care but couldn't afford to pay an arm and a leg for it.

After a while, though, a lot of those dreams started to fade. Brian's quest for a *really good* job had taken them to Jeffersonville, Indiana, for two years, then up north to Findlay, Ohio, for three. Two more moves followed, much to all of their friends' and families' dismay.

When they'd moved to Bridgeport four years ago, Dani had finally put her foot down. She'd needed some stability, and Jeremy did, too. Brian had grumbled but had found a pretty good job at a factory up in Middletown.

Unfortunately, he still hadn't been happy. Almost every conversation had centered on how he was next in line for a promotion at his job. How one day he was going to do something important, something better than driving a truck for a uniform company.

He'd ignored her reminders that they already had a lot to be proud of. They had each other and Jeremy.

Instead, he'd clung to his belief that one day his managers would trust his judgment enough to listen to him, maybe even put him in management so they'd have good insurance. It was all going to be so good.

And maybe it would have been if he hadn't gotten in that car accident.

Some days, the hardest part to come to grips with was the fact that there was no one to blame. He hadn't gotten hit by a drunk driver or a kid texting. It was just an accident on the freeway, one rainy night on his way home.

But that one night changed everything. She'd learned that Brian had saved even less than she'd imagined, and she'd had to come to terms with the fact that they still didn't have good insurance, they'd never bought a house, and that she hadn't ever started on that degree. For months she'd mourned Brian, the dreams that would never come true, and the fact that she didn't have a whole lot to speak of except for an eleven-year-old boy who didn't smile much anymore.

After a tough meeting at school, where Jeremy's teacher had shared that Jeremy's grades had fallen and he'd drifted away from his friends, Dani had known it was time to wake up.

So, she'd stopped wishing things were different and started their new life. They'd moved out of the rental house she couldn't afford and into an apartment. She'd stopped working part time at the grocery and started cleaning other people's houses full time. A year ago she'd started taking one online class at a time.

And two months ago? Jackson Koch had moved in.

One Saturday morning, she'd met him and Kate while getting her mail, started talking, and, somehow, she'd started babysitting for him at night.

Now, she was constantly busy and working harder than she ever had in her life. But for some reason, she realized that she wasn't as sad as she used to be. Some days, she was almost happy.

And every once in a while, she even found herself not aching for Brian but thinking of a sandy-haired, blue-eyed man instead. A man who was a couple of years younger than her, but who also knew what it was like to have the majority of one's dreams shatter. A man who had dimples, was model-handsome but only cared about a little girl who was his world.

Finishing her glass of wine, Dani waited for the feelings of guilt to hit her like they used to. Like they did just six months ago. But instead, she only felt a seed of hope.

She'd now completed three online classes and had gotten As in all of them. Jeremy's grades were better. She had clients who appreciated her efforts and even tipped her from time to time.

She was making enough extra money babysitting Kate that she had been able to add to her savings account. She and Jackson had even become pretty good friends.

All of those things were blessings and they certainly helped her sleep better at night. If it sometimes crossed her mind that she was actually doing pretty good on her own, she told herself that she was only doing some of the things that would have happened if Brian was still alive.

She just wasn't sure if that was a lie or not.

CHAPTER 3

FROM LES LARKE'S
*YOU, TOO, CAN HOST
A POKER TOURNEY:*

Don't forget the snacks and drinks.

Sunday Afternoon

"Are we gonna go see Mr. Ace and Finn now?" Kate asked as Jackson pulled his truck out of the parking lot on Sunday afternoon. After they both slept in and went to the children's service at a country church down the road, he'd made her grilled cheese squares for lunch and then did some laundry.

Now they were on their way to Ace's house. Ace Vance was an old friend from Spartan and was one of the reasons he'd even heard about Bridgeport, Ohio.

He'd run into Ace's parents in the middle of the frozen-food aisle of the grocery about four months earlier. After they'd looked at his collection of cheap frozen dinners, Mr. and Mrs. Vance hadn't wasted another minute's time telling Jackson how happy

16

their son was in the southern Ohio town. Their enthusiasm for the place had led to a couple of phone calls with Ace and two other guys he knew who'd moved there. Then, after he and Kate had spent a really good weekend with those guys, Jackson had decided to move to Bridgeport.

It had been one of the best decisions of his life. He'd needed to get away from all the reminders of Beth and the mine. Even his parents had encouraged him to go, saying he needed to take care of himself and that Kate would be just fine, especially if her daddy wasn't moping around the house any longer.

Bringing himself back to the present, he answered Kate at last. "We sure are going to see Ace and Finn. And don't forget they have a puppy now, too."

"Touchdown?"

"Uh-huh. That's his name, all right." He smiled as he sensed her wriggling in her car seat directly behind him. "Miss Meredith will be there, too."

"They're my friends." Just like always, she sounded delighted by the statement.

"They sure are, honeybee. They're our friends. Good ones, too."

She clapped her little hands. "Yay! Is Mr. Ace gonna have some ice cream for me?"

"I'm pretty sure he will. He knows you're coming."

"Mr. Ace and me really like ice cream."

"That's a fact." Jackson smiled as he stopped at the first of three stop lights they had to go through before they got to Ace's recently remodeled house.

By now, he'd met enough people in Bridgeport to know that most of them considered it to be a very small one-horse town, a suburb for everyone who worked in Cincinnati, a safe place to raise a family. It was all those things.

But for guys like him and the other guys from home, it was

a world away from Spartan. That town was small, rural, and filled with men and women who worked hard and tried to make a decent life for themselves, even when they didn't have much money to make that life with.

Even though it had only one stop light instead of these three, it had been home. He still couldn't quite figure out how so much of his life had ended. It was like the rug had been taken out from under him, leaving him barefoot on cold tile.

When Kurt and Ace had been home back in March and talked nonstop about Bridgeport, Jackson knew he'd had to make the change. He just wished he hadn't had to leave his whole life when he did it.

"Daddy?"

"Hmm?"

"Are we almost there?"

Correction. He hadn't left *all* of his life behind. He'd taken along the most important part. His heart. "Nope. We *are* here."

"Yay!" she called out again.

He chuckled as he got out and started toward her door. What had he done before Kate's claps, *yays*, and all-around exuberance?

"You need a hand, Jackson?" Ace's sophomore son called out from the yard.

"Yep. You can help me get my girl out of her seat."

"Yessir."

Upon hearing Finn's voice, Kate's mouth opened into a sweet little O. "Finn?"

"Hey, Kate," Finn said as he opened the cab's door and leaned inside.

Kate threw Finn a bright smile as he reached in to unsnap the car seat's straps. "Hi, Finn!"

As Finn's smile widened, Jackson chuckled and pulled out Kate's backpack. "What's going on around here today?"

"Nothing much. Meredith was over at her studio teaching, so Dad and me spent the morning cleaning her car."

"Fun."

"Yeah. No," he said over his shoulder as he led the way into their house, Kate on his heels.

When they entered the kitchen, Jackson spied Ace sitting at his kitchen table eating a sandwich. "You ready for this?" he joked, just as Kate barreled toward yet another one of her favorite people.

"Hi, Mr. Ace!"

Chuckling, Ace reached down and swung her into his arms. Kate squealed in pleasure as he twirled her twice and then set her gently down. "Look at my best girl," he murmured. "Looking so pretty in pink, too."

Kate's eyes widened in happiness before her expression turned mulish. "Mr. Ace, I'm not your best girl anymore."

Ace's gaze flickered over to Jackson before he focused back on Katie. "You're not? Now, why is that?"

"'Cause of Miss Meredith."

"What? I can't have two best girls?" He knelt down on one knee.

Shaking her head, Kate's voice was adamant. "Nope."

Jackson shook his head as he approached his tiny terror. "Kathryn Koch, you mind your manners."

"Nah, she's okay." Winking at Finn, Ace said, "Kate, if I can only have one best girl, does that mean you can only have one best man?"

While his three-year-old seemed to seriously contemplate that notion, Finn grinned. "That's me, right, Kate?"

"No, I have Jeremy, too."

Ace raised his brows at Jackson. "Who's that?"

"He's Dani's son. He's fourteen and has the patience of a

saint." Looking over at Finn, Jeremy said, "Any chance you've met him? His name's Jeremy Brown. He's in eighth grade."

"No, sir, but I don't know a lot of guys in other grades," Finn said. "Does he play ball?"

Finn was a star football player on the high school team. "Baseball."

"Then I really don't know him. Coach McCoy has been having us work out with a couple of eighth graders, but only the ones on the football team."

"He's a nice kid. I'll introduce y'all sometime."

"Looking forward to it."

Obviously impatient for Finn's attention, Kate stared up at him hopefully. "You wanna watch *Scooby-Doo?*"

Jackson stepped forward. "Kate, remember what I told you? Finn might have other things to do. That's why we have your backpack."

"I don't mind watching Scooby. He's cool," Finn said. "But Allison was wanting to come over, too. Is that okay, Dad?"

"You know it's fine with me," Ace said. "I'm hoping she'll help you manage Touchdown." Suddenly, looking alarmed, he said, "Where is that dog?"

Finn shrugged. "I'm pretty sure he went down to the basement."

"You're pretty sure?" Ace groaned. "No doubt he's taking advantage of being alone and tearing up the couch or something. You better hope that ain't the case."

"Yessir."

Looking at Jackson, Ace's voice gentled. "Don't you go worrying about Kate here. We like spending time with her."

Jackson knew Ace and his boy were good people, but his daughter was only three and at times acted like she was on the fast track to thirteen. "Let me know when you need a break."

"I will. Come on, Kate," Finn said, holding out a hand. "Let's go down to the basement, turn on *Scooby* and find Touchdown."

Like a big girl, she hoisted the purple backpack on her shoulders and followed him through the living room and down the stairs.

The missing dog, who none of them had noticed sleeping, got up from under the kitchen table, yawned, and padded down the stairs after them.

Motioning to the six-month-old shepherd puppy, Jackson said, "Looks like your couch hasn't gotten torn up just yet."

"That's a miracle." Ace shook his head. "TD is cute as all get out, but he makes three-year-olds seem like responsible adults. He's into everything."

"Bet Finn loves him."

His expression softened. "He really does. Meredith, too. Now, have a seat, buddy. Want a sandwich or something?"

"I'm good."

"Get a beer or iced tea if you want."

Jackson poured a tall glass of sweet tea, before sitting down in the chair by his side, enjoying the easy camaraderie that was always between them. "I didn't know your basement was finished."

"That's because it wasn't until about two months ago. I did some remodeling for Meredith. Figured having a place for Finn to go with his friends and half the football team when they come over would be a good thing." Looking a little pained, he said, "They can get real loud."

"We were, too, back in the day."

"My mother reminds me of that constantly." Stretching out a foot, he said, "Anyway, that basement has been a godsend for all of us."

Ace's girlfriend was not only a Pilates instructor who owned her own studio, she was also really girlie. So much so that, at first glance, most people wouldn't see how the mechanic and the delicate redhead could be a good match. "How's she doing, living in with you boys?"

He smiled. "Real good." After glancing down at the empty staircase where Finn and Kate had gone down, he lowered his voice. "We just found out that she's pregnant."

Jackson almost choked on his drink. "What?"

Ace grinned. "I know. Crazy, huh? I'm still trying to wrap my head around it."

"Was it a surprise?"

"Oh, yeah. We had a couple of slipups, but neither of us was too concerned."

Jackson grinned. "Is that what you've been telling your son?"

"Heck, no. As far as Finn is concerned, he's liable to get a girl pregnant if he even breathes on her wrong. I keep telling him that abstinence and patience are now his two best friends."

"Sounds like you might want to take a bit of that advice."

Ace laughed. "Too late now." His voice softened. "I wouldn't want to change a thing now, anyway. I'm excited."

"What about your boy? Does Finn know yet?"

"Nope. Meredith was a little weepy and shell-shocked about it. I thought we should wait a bit."

"She's been crying?"

"Yes, but in a good way." He shook his head a little. "I had forgotten, but Finn's mother Liz was a crier when she was carrying him. I guess hormones are hormones."

"Beth cried all the time, too. I practically had to forbid her from watching Hallmark commercials," he said before remembering that he usually didn't like to mention her name.

"I forgot about sappy commercials. I'm gonna warn Meredith about them."

"Don't think that will do much good. My advice is to buy more Kleenex."

"Will do." Looking pleased, Ace said, "I'm glad you've just been through all this."

"Kate's three, not three months. Most of my memories of all that have faded." He also tried not to think about Beth's pregnancy too much.

"But still, that's a lot more recently than fifteen. Plus, you know I never lived with Liz. I can ask you questions."

"Ask me anything you want, though I don't know how much I'll be able to help you." Realizing how little he did remember about Beth's pregnancy, Jackson felt a lump form in his throat. "I was so freaked out about bills that I was hardly ever around. I took every extra shift that I could."

Ace's expression sobered. "I remember that. You about killed yourself."

Usually Jackson loathed that expression, but in this case he figured Ace wasn't wrong. He'd ended up spending the majority of Beth's pregnancy exhausted, eventually getting some kind of bug that almost took him to the hospital. And for what? Two years after that, she was gone. "It was stupid. I was so worried about staying out of debt that I forgot how much I had to be grateful for. If I could live those nine months over again, I'd do things a lot differently."

"I know that, buddy," he said quietly. After a sip of tea, he said, "Anyway, we're telling Finn tomorrow night."

"How do you think he's going to take it?"

"Probably the same way as you, me, and Mer did. He's going to be a little shocked."

"Maybe a little more than that."

Ace grinned. "Maybe. Or maybe not. Finn's pretty busy with football, Touchdown, and his girlfriend right now."

"Y'all planning a wedding?"

Ace nodded. "If I had my way, I would have taken Meredith on down to the courthouse the day we found out."

"Let me guess, Meredith wasn't down with that?"

"Not at all. She wants a real wedding, one with all the bells and whistles. Since this will be both of our first weddings, I told her she can plan whatever she wants—as long as it takes place soon."

Thinking of his wedding that had started out being plain and simple but had ended up including half of Spartan, Jackson chuckled. "Be careful. Before you know it, you're going to be paying for fancy cakes and more flowers than you ever believed possible."

"If Meredith smiles at me when she walks down that aisle, anything she wants will be worth it. I want her happy." Standing up, he gestured toward the door leading out to the patio. "Want to come out back and tell me about you?"

"Sounds good. Let me check on Kate."

"Check on her if you want, but I think we both know she's sitting with a puppy and Finn and watching *Scooby-Doo*. Plus, Allison will be over shortly, and she's good with Kate. Your little girl is in good hands."

"I guess you're right." He didn't want to take advantage of Finn, but he knew that Ace had a good point.

"I know I am." Opening the door, he said, "Come on out, it's finally warm enough to be comfortable."

Jackson followed Ace out, feeling slightly guilty about leaving Kate in Finn's hands but knowing that Ace was right.

The moment he sat down, Ace leaned forward and rested his elbows on his knees. "So, how are you doing?"

"Good enough." When Ace still eyed him intently, Jackson added, "Relax. Things are all right."

"Sorry, but 'good enough' and 'all right' doesn't sound that good."

"Well, it is. I mean, it's good enough right now. I've got a job and place to live and Kate's happy. That's enough." It was sure a lot better than it had been a year ago.

"I know Kate's happy … but what about you?"

Jackson was getting a little tired of being psychoanalyzed on a Sunday afternoon. "What do you mean? I just told you how I was. I'm fine."

"I mean, are you on your way to being happy?"

Jackson didn't know the answer to that question, but he sure didn't come over to bring Ace down. "Maybe."

"How about you be honest with me?" Ace rested his elbows on his knees as he looked at him straight in the eye. "Remember, I only moved here seven months ago."

"Not to be a shit friend, but you and I both know my situation is different. You came here with a lot of money in the bank and turned a good job into an even better one. You own a company now. You own a house. I lost my job doing the only thing I knew how to do well. Now I'm working at a bar for a whole lot less than I used to and trying to take care of a little girl who lost her mother."

Ace winced.

Jackson sighed. "Sorry. I didn't mean to unload on you."

"Cookie, Kate is okay."

It had been a while since he'd heard Ace call him that. Hearing it made some of the tension he'd been carrying lessen. "Kate's doing as good as can be expected."

Still looking pained, Ace said, "Buddy, I was with you when Beth got sick. I was with you the day she died. I helped carry her coffin. Almost two years have gone by, but I haven't forgotten."

Neither had he. "She was my wife. I loved her."

"I know you did. Just like I know that she never blamed you for working so much. There was no one more proud of you, man. Beth used to tell people all the time about how lucky she was that you wanted to give her and Kate a good life."

Jackson felt tears form in his eyes and blinked them away. Hating that he could still cry at the memories, he shook his head. "We're not talking about this."

"What I'm trying to tell you is that Kurt, me, and the other guys have all watched how you've been handling things. All of us have been ready to step in if you needed it. If you needed anything."

"I know that, and it was appreciated."

"What I'm trying to tell you is that you should be proud, Jackson. Kate is a sweet, happy little girl. I know she lost her momma, but she didn't lose her dad."

"God has been watching out for her." *Maybe even Beth from heaven.* Kate was amazing.

"I'm sure He has, but you should also be proud of *you.*" Still staring at him intently, Ace said, "You're doing okay, Jackson. Maybe not great, but from where I'm standing, you're doing damn good. Be proud of that." He lowered his voice. "Man, you went through something horrific but are still standing upright. That says it all."

Since all the words in his head were feeling like they were about to choke him, Jackson just nodded. That was probably just as well, too. He appreciated Ace's sentiment, but he wasn't real sure that his buddy was seeing him for who he really was.

Fact was, Jackson wasn't like Ace, who everybody knew played like he was just a good ol' boy, but who was smarter than most.

He wasn't like Kurt, either. Kurt had recently started his own landscaping business and was actually making a go of it. He, on the other hand, was only a highly skilled miner without a mine, reduced to serving drinks for minimum wage and tips.

And while he wasn't holed up like a hermit missing Beth, he wasn't exactly moving on either. Though his parents had recently been encouraging him to move on, he didn't see any need to do that. He'd loved Beth. Why would he want to move on from her?

"Jackson?"

He started. "Yeah?"

"For what it's worth, try not to overthink it, okay? It sounds like just talk, but I've learned that all things seem to happen the way they are supposed to."

"I'll keep that in mind. Now, can we talk about something else? Better yet, how about we play some pool?"

"I'm down for that. Always."

Jackson grinned as he followed his longtime buddy back inside and down the stairs.

Ace was a good friend and really had been at his side during some of the worst days of his life. Now it was time for Jackson to repay the favor. He vowed to be there for him and Meredith over the next couple of months. Planning for a baby and a marriage, all while managing a business and raising a fifteen-year-old, was a lot. Ace might end up needing his friendship just as much as Jackson had needed his.

CHAPTER 4

FROM LES LARKE'S
YOU, TOO, CAN HOST
A POKER TOURNEY:

*Music can help set the tone. Some hosts prefer an
upbeat, jazzy playlist. Others lean more toward
good old-fashioned rock and roll.*

Tuesday

"Dani, thank you so much for everything," Mrs. Burridge said as she handed Dani an envelope. "The house looks great. You're the best cleaning lady I've ever had."

Smiling, though she felt like an arrow had just pierced her side, Dani stuffed the envelope in her purse. "Thank you. That's nice of you to say." Inhaling, she tried to think positive thoughts and not let her doubts and fears get the best of her.

It wasn't that she was ashamed of being a cleaning lady. She wasn't. It was good, honest work, and she enjoyed helping other people.

She was also glad that Mrs. Burridge noticed how hard she worked. But what the lady didn't realize was that cleaning other people's homes was not her dream job. Not by a long shot. It was simply a means of getting where she needed to be in the future.

Walking to the door on four-inch heels, the lady said, "Now that the house is clean, we just have to hope and pray that the caterers come on time."

"Yes, ma'am."

Whether it was because she heard herself or the amusement in Dani's tone, Mrs. Burridge looked a little shame-faced. "I know in the grand scheme of things a dinner party doesn't matter all that much, but you wouldn't believe how awful my life is going to be if everything goes to hell in a handbasket. I'll never hear the end of it from my mother-in-law."

Stepping through the doorway, Dani smiled. "I've come to realize that if it matters to you, then it is important."

"Thank you, honey. You always know what to say. Have a good afternoon and tell that boy of yours hello for me."

"Yes, ma'am." After giving Mrs. B. another wave, Dani picked up her tote bag and plastic cubby of supplies and finally walked out to her car, a late model Chevy.

After she got in and lowered the windows to get a little air, she gave herself a little mental fist pump as she drove down the lengthy driveway at the edge of Indian Hill, the ritziest area of Cincinnati.

She'd done it. She'd cleaned two houses before two o'clock and she was only eight minutes from her apartment in Bridge-port. She was going to be able to be home when Jeremy got off the bus.

It had been doubtful there for a while. If Mrs. Burridge was everything fancy and elegant, her first house of the day was a far more modest one on the edge of Bridgeport. Though she cleaned two other houses in the neighborhood once a month, these owners paid her to come every week.

So the customer, money-wise, was pretty good.

But oh, she hated going over there. It was a sprawling older ranch with three kids, two cats, and way too much stuff that needed dusting and getting wiped down. The wife had a high-powered job in downtown Cincinnati, so her husband took care of things around the house. That didn't bother her.

What did was that he didn't take care of things all that well and depended on her to do everything when she got there. And that meant *everything*, even cleaning out the cats' litter box. She never knew what was going to greet her when she entered, though there was *one* constant: Reed Moore was always there. He always flirted. And he always made her feel like he was undressing her with his eyes.

Dani had been tempted to quit more than once. But then every second or third time she cleaned, Reed's wife, Ashley, would be there, too. Then, Reed would act so different that Dani wondered if she had been imagining things. Or she'd get another referral and pick up another client because of them. Dani was afraid if she dropped them, they might influence everyone else, too.

This morning had been particularly bad. Reed had followed her from room to room, leaning in the doorways and asking way too many personal questions. After the first hour, she'd gotten so flustered, she'd pointedly said she couldn't work while he was in the room.

He'd left, but he hadn't looked all that pleased about her bossing him around in his own house. Then, to make matters worse, she'd had to ask him for her check, and he'd made her wait almost ten minutes until he "had time" to get it.

The whole experience had given her the willies.

Luckily, though, Mrs. Burridge was one of her favorite clients. Though the society lady was a little snooty, she was very nice, paid on time, and always took time to ask how Dani was doing.

After parking her car in the reserved spot at the apartment complex, Dani realized she hadn't even opened her envelope. When Dani did, she closed her eyes and gave thanks. Mrs. Burridge had not only given her a sizable tip, she'd written a sweet thank-you note.

Sweet relief flooded her. She was going to be able to let Jeremy go to the batting cages with two of his buddies on Saturday after all.

Feeling like she'd just conquered the world single-handedly, she picked up her purse and tote bag and almost ran into Jackson getting his mail next to the entrance to their apartment building.

"Hey, Dani," he said, holding little Kate's hand with one hand and a pile of mail in his other.

"Hay is for horses," she teased with a wink at Kate.

As she'd hoped, Kate's eyes widened and she giggled. "You're funny, Miss Dani."

She gave them a little bow. "Thank you. It's an old joke but a good one."

"You're all smiles," Jackson murmured. "I guess you had a good day?"

"You know what? I did. It didn't start out that way, but it ended on a good note. That's something."

"Oh? What good happened?" They waited while she got her mail.

After tossing her two flyers and one bill into her canvas bag, she smiled at Jackson again. "My last client gave me a real nice tip. It was enough to be able to say yes to Jeremy and the batting cages."

Jackson held the door open of the main entrance to their building. "Batting cages, huh? That boy of yours is sure into baseball."

"He absolutely loves it."

"How long has he been playing baseball, anyway?"

"Since he was five." She couldn't contain the pride in her voice. Through all the moves and insecurity of Brian's jobs and then his death, she'd been able to provide at least one constant for their son.

"He must be pretty good."

Thinking about the mysteries of batting averages she shrugged. "I don't know how good Jeremy is, but he's always looked forward to swinging that bat. He usually hits it pretty far, too." Realizing she was bragging a bit much, she laughed. "Of course, this is his mom talking."

"Nothing wrong with being a proud mom. I bet your husband was real proud of him, too."

"Brian sure was." She stopped herself before she shared how Brian once spent so much money on a bat that they'd had to eat on the cheap for almost two weeks.

As they started up the stairs, he murmured, "What position does Jeremy play?"

"Sometimes catcher, sometimes shortstop." She shrugged. "He's super unpicky about what position he plays. The coach seems to be happy about that because he keeps moving him around during the game." Thinking about how his eyes lit up when he was on the field, she added, "He just likes to play."

"I know that feeling, but that's pretty special."

"What do you mean?"

"Only that I've never heard of a boy not caring about what position he's playing. I lived for playing first base."

They stopped outside his apartment door. "You played baseball, too?"

"Sure did. Until I graduated. Back when I was growing up, I didn't know a whole lot of boys who didn't drag out their glove come March. Now, I guess soccer and lacrosse are just as popular."

"I don't know about that. I'm kind of embarrassed to admit that I've never been all that interested in sports."

"Really? I can't imagine that."

She was pretty sure he was teasing, but just in case he wasn't, she said, "I was the girl taking dance and tumbling classes growing up. I know all about back handsprings and toe shoes, but not so much about soccer shoes."

His eyes lit up. "Those would be cleats, Dani."

"They wear cleats in soccer, too? Like in baseball?"

"Yeah, sweetheart. Like in baseball. And football, too."

She fumbled with getting her keys out of her purse. He'd called her sweetheart. Realizing that he probably hadn't even realized he called her an endearment, she shook it off. "Jackson, you better look out. Once I tell Jeremy you know what he's talking about when it comes to baseball, he's going to be pestering you with dozens of questions."

"I wouldn't mind if he did," he said as he unlocked his apartment door and Kate ran inside. "You tell him to knock on my door anytime with whatever he wants. I'll always be happy to talk to him."

While Dani wrapped her head around that, he leaned a shoulder against the open door. "I might know about playing ball, but I don't recall the batting cages wearing my parents out, though. Are they really that expensive here in Bridgeport?"

"No, but it's never just about the batting cages. Most of Jeremy's friends are on the team, so he always wants to go with them."

"That makes sense."

"It does to me, too. But that also means it's not just the cages that I have to pay for. It also means Jeremy needs money for Cokes and snacks. And since he's fourteen …"

"He's eating his fair share."

"He is … and then some," she said with a mock grimace. "Believe me, I've seen the cost of those cages skyrocket from ten to thirty dollars in a matter of minutes."

He whistled low. "I see what you mean." He smiled softly. "Sounds about how it is when I take Kate to the movies."

Pleased he understood, she nodded. "Exactly. No matter how much you try to convince yourself or your child that it's not necessary to eat at the theater, movies are never the same if you don't get a soda and have a tub of popcorn perched on your lap."

"I'm guilty of buying it all myself."

She smiled at him, pleased that she wasn't going to have to be embarrassed about her life on a constant budget. "Well, I better go on upstairs. I wanted to clean things up before Jeremy gets home. It's a rare day that I'm home before him. He's going to be surprised. And, hopefully, real pleased, too."

"You know, if you ever want me to watch out for him when you're not home, all you have to do is ask."

"That's kind of you, but he's fourteen. He doesn't need a babysitter."

"Yeah. He's fourteen. I don't know if you've heard, but sometimes they don't always make the best decisions."

"I'll keep that in mind," she said as Kate came back to the door.

"Daddy, you comin' in?"

"Yep. Now tell Miss Dani goodbye."

"Bye Miss Dani."

Dani leaned down so she could look in Kate's eyes. "I'll see you later, alligator."

"Crocodile!" Kate cried out before dissolving into giggles as her dad whisked her up in his arms and carried her inside.

The little girl's laughter echoed up the stairwell as Dani climbed the last flight to her apartment.

Kate was a happy little girl. Jackson really was a good father and a good man. She was thankful that they'd become friends. There weren't too many people in her life who she could be so honest with about the perils of single-parenthood or let her guard down about her financial problems. Even better, he never tried to have all the answers. He just simply let her vent.

As she let herself into the empty apartment, she decided to not only do a quick clean but make a batch of cookies, too. Jeremy loved oatmeal cookies, and Jackson and Kate liked anything sweet. She could bring them a couple dozen when she went downstairs to babysit later that night.

It was the least she could do for a friend.

CHAPTER 5

FROM LES LARKE'S
YOU, TOO, CAN HOST
A POKER TOURNEY:

If you want to go big, you might even want to
offer cigars after the game has ended. If you don't
mind the smell, it adds to the feeling of a special
night out.

Thursday

Jackson didn't mean to keep dwelling on his conversation with Ace, but every couple of hours, his buddy's comments would start to echo in his head again, reminding him that he had a lot to be proud of. Despite his worst fears, he wasn't washed up yet.

That conversation melded in his head with the most recent talk he'd had with Dani. Before he realized what he was doing, he'd find himself thinking about the things she'd said, some of the words and phrases standing out more than others. All of it reminded him that there might still be more to him than being Beth's husband the former crew leader of the Spartan Number Nine Mine.

Maybe there always had been.

Most days, Jackson's doubts would get the best of him, and he'd start believing he'd been blowing smoke, thinking that he could be something more. But then, just when he was on the verge of sinking back into the depression he'd battled a year ago, something would happen that would give him a string of hope.

Part of him resented his weaknesses. He didn't want to be the kind of man who dwelled on himself like there was nothing more important in the world. But he was starting to realize that, just like his former job, he didn't always have as much control over himself as he wanted to believe.

No, there was a stronger person in charge and He was stronger than Jackson could ever hope to be. What Jackson needed to do was worry less about trying to control everything and fall down on his knees in prayer every night.

All of these things were stuck on repeat in Jackson's head as he pulled bottles off the glass shelves and sprayed cleaner. Though Gen had looked at him like he had a screw loose the first time he had tackled those shelves, she'd said more than once that the Corner Bar seemed neater since she'd hired him on.

He had to think that was a good thing.

"Hey, Jackson, come help me with this door!" Gen called out around five that evening.

He strode over to the back-storage door and picked up the keg Gen was attempting to relocate. "Where do you want it, boss?"

"Let's put it in the bar and hook it up. After I talked to the distributor last week he brought over a keg of his new favorite lager." She grunted. "Of course, he didn't give me any notice, he just showed up."

"Sounds about right." After he hooked it up and poured a sample, he handed it to her to taste.

She pushed it back his way. "No, I've already tried it. What do you think?"

He tasted it, tried to look like he had an opinion worth noting, and shrugged. "It tastes all right to me."

She laughed. "You're the worst. You really don't care about beer, do you?"

"I like drinking it from time to time. And I like when other people want to drink it here and tip good when I serve it to them. That counts for something, don't you think?"

"Always."

Well at least he had that. When he turned around to rinse out the glass, Gen spoke again. "You might not be the most enthusiastic beer drinker on the payroll, but I'm starting to realize that doesn't matter much anyway."

There was something in her voice that gave him pause. "Wait. How come?"

"All these customers aren't flocking in to the bar to listen to your opinions about beer. They're here to eye those dimples of yours."

He felt himself turn beet red. "Come on, Gen."

Her eyes sparkled. "I'm serious! I watched what was going on the other night, and I promise you this: All the women coming in here sure aren't buying drinks from you because you're talking it up. They like looking at you. I even heard a couple of women who had to be in their fifties talking about how good you look in those Henleys you favor."

Comments like that from her used to make him a little wary, on the off-chance that she was hinting that there could be something more between them than he wanted. But now he knew that was just her way. Gen was as blunt as a worn-down pencil.

"I'll keep working out then. Glad these muscles are good for something useful." Instead of, say, *real* work in the middle of a mine shaft.

"Don't act so modest, buddy. I'm sure you've heard plenty of compliments about your looks before."

Like any of that mattered to him. "Didn't your momma ever tell you that beauty was only skin-deep?"

Just as she was about to answer, Gen stilled and cursed under her breath. "I cannot even believe this."

Concerned, Jackson turned to see what caught her attention. It was a guy who looked like he'd stepped right out of an old Marlboro Man ad, back when practically every other ad in every magazine was for cigarettes. "Something wrong, boss?" The man didn't look like he was there to make trouble, but one never knew.

"Nothing's wrong. I mean, nothing other than that guy over there is my freakin' ex."

Her voice sounded bitter. Maybe tinged with hurt. And that brought out all of his protective instincts. Staring at the guy, who was now looking at the two of them intently, Jackson felt his spine prickle. "He's your ex-husband?"

"Oh, hell no. I wasn't stupid enough to marry him." Her voice lowered as a new vulnerability seeped into it. "But I thought we would one day. I mean, we were serious."

There was a new note in her voice. Gen was usually direct and assertive. This wariness wasn't like her, and it immediately made him think of the worst. Turning to face the newcomer more directly, he felt his muscles stiffen. "Did he hurt you? Do you want him gone?"

Gen blinked in surprise. "No." She cleared her throat. "I mean, no, he never hurt me. He's … he wasn't like that. The two of us … Well, we just didn't work out."

"His name is Seth?"

"Yep," she murmured as they watched Seth the Old Flame slowly approach, his lanky body clad in worn jeans, broken-in Ariats, and a starched, white button-down shirt.

Jackson might not have been all country, but he'd worn

enough hats and boots to recognize that man's outfit for what it was. The guy had gotten kitted out to come calling on Gen.

Guys didn't break out the starched shirts without a good reason. This Seth character had come into the pub hoping to capture his old girlfriend's attention.

Which he certainly had. Course, it was in all the worst ways. Together, they watched Seth study Gen like she was the only person in the room.

"Hey, Gen," Seth said when he was a couple of feet away. "I was hoping to see you here."

Jackson waited for Gen to give him crap for entering her place uninvited, but she only said quietly, "It would be a surprise if I wasn't working, seeing as this is my bar."

He was still staring at her intently. "You got a few minutes to talk?"

"I don't think we have anything more to say to each other."

Seth's eyes flicked toward Jackson. "Is that right? You already got yourself somebody new?"

Already? Jackson inhaled. He sure as hell wasn't his boss' guy but he wasn't opposed to pretending they had something going on if Gen needed him to. The guy definitely needed to take a step back.

But Gen shook her head. "Get your head out of your ass. Jackson is my newest employee."

"He works for you?"

He definitely had enough of being talked about in front of his face. "Name's Jackson Koch. I'm her bartender." He held out a hand, wondering if the guy would take it or not.

"You're a bartender? Huh. I'm Seth Parks." After glancing at Gen again, he said, "I'm an old friend of Genevieve's."

Gen grunted. "You're something, all right."

Jackson figured he'd had enough of this reunion. Now that he was certain Gen wasn't in danger, he had a real need to give them some privacy. "Boss, how about I go in the back and do inventory for a few?"

After a beat, his boss nodded slowly. "That's a good idea. Thanks. I'll be fine here."

Jackson walked off, smiling to himself. By the looks of things, Gen and Seth might not have seen each other in a while but things between them definitely hadn't cooled completely. There were enough sparks between them to light up the Fourth of July. Neither of them seemed to be able to take their eyes off the other one.

Beth would have eaten this up. She always had loved a good romance. Though that memory did pinch his heart a little, he realized that all he felt was a lingering sense of emptiness. No longer the harsh feeling of grief.

And for once, instead of feeling guilty, he said a little prayer of thanks. It was nice not to be hurting for a change.

CHAPTER 6

FROM LES LARKE'S
YOU, TOO, CAN HOST
A POKER TOURNEY:

*If you aren't sure how many people to invite,
start with eight. There are usually eight spots on
a standard poker table. This will make everyone
feel like they're at a "real" game.*

Thursday

The moment Jackson closed the door leading to the storage room, everything between Gen and her old flame ratcheted up a couple of notches.

It seemed it didn't matter that they hadn't seen each other in almost two years, or that their last words to each other had been cruel. Or that she almost, *almost* never thought about him anymore.

From the moment their eyes met, she realized that whatever had been between them was still there. And it wasn't even lying there limply like old celery in need of the trash. No, it was alive and kicking.

Just like one of those cockroaches that didn't want to die.

While Seth continued to silently stare at her with his dark eyes, she did the same thing right back. Studying him. Looking for flaws. Then, after finding none, looking for everything she used to find so darn attractive.

Of which there was a lot.

She wasn't exactly proud about that, but who could blame her? She might not have ever wanted to see the guy again, but she wasn't *blind.*

Fact was, if those fifty-year-old women who'd been eyeing Jackson like he was a piece of Godiva chocolate were present, they would be practically panting at the sight of Seth. Shoot, they'd no doubt be staring at Seth Parks like he was the whole damn box of their favorite truffles.

Gen wouldn't have blamed them, either. Seth Parks, with his painted-on jeans, pressed shirts, permanent tan, and perfect jaw was simply too handsome for his own good.

He was also too cocky and full of himself. And way, way too familiar.

Continuing on her awful food analogies, she kinda figured he was staring at her like she was his favorite dessert and he'd been on the cabbage soup diet for two years.

He exhaled. Stepped forward. "I gotta say it, Gen. You look great. Happy."

The air she hadn't realized she'd been holding released from her lungs. "Thanks. You look the same as I remember." It was faint praise, bordering on surly. With another man, that wouldn't have been much of a compliment. With Seth, though? Well, nothing more needed to be said.

True appreciation lit his eyes as he laughed. "Some things never change, huh? Once again, I'd have to be starving to get a little sugar out of you."

That wasn't true. Back when she'd been dating him in

Lubbock, there'd been a time in their relationship when she'd lit up at the sight of him and hadn't cared who noticed. She'd used to pretty-up when he was going to take her out, sometimes even going so far as to put on a dress and heels that killed her feet but drew his eyes to her legs like a fly to honey.

He would never disappoint, either. He would always say she looked beautiful, pull her close, and ruin her carefully painted-on lipstick. And she, instead of giving him grief about it, would simply laugh and slap some more on, warning him that she would one day make him start paying for those expensive tubes of lip color.

But that was before everything between them had soured.

Before they'd shared one too many words and she'd taken off to Bridgeport. Before she'd made a mental promise to never, ever see him again.

Speaking of which …

"Care to tell me why you're here?" she asked at last. "The last time we talked, you told me that if I left, I'd be out of your life forever. That you'd never step one foot out of Texas."

One brown eyebrow arched. "You know you can't take anything I said that night seriously. We weren't talking as much as trading barbs."

He was right. Their relationship hadn't been calm, and it hadn't always been easy. Toward the end, all they'd seemed to do was yell or fume. "Even though you yelled it, I still heard the words loud and clear. Even whispered, the message would've been the same."

He nodded. "You're probably right."

No, she *knew* she was right. And because she found herself about to apologize, too, Gen hardened her heart and her voice. She needed to guard her heart, or it was going to get stomped on again. "You still haven't told me why you are here."

"Gen, can we settle down? You know I have a lot of regrets about the way I spoke to you."

She did too. But before she opened herself to him all over again she wanted to know where they stood. "So that's why you came up north to Ohio? So you could tell me that you regret the way we used to talk to each other. You could have written me a letter."

He folded his arms over his chest. "Like you would have opened up anything I mailed you."

He was right. She would have thrown anything he sent her away. Probably. "Why are you here? Because you have regrets?"

He looked down at his feet. "Not exactly."

Impatience and disappointment settled in her stomach. Souring it. She shouldn't have even crossed the bar to talk to him. "I don't have time for guessing games. I think you ought to head on out of here."

"Settle down, Genevieve. I aim to tell you, but now ain't the time. Not while you're working." He stepped closer, making her chin lift so she could peer into his eyes. "What about later tonight?"

She felt like rolling her eyes. He didn't have a clue about her current life. "I'll still be working, Seth. We won't start shutting down the place until well after midnight."

"You can't let that beefcake bartender of yours hold down the fort for a few?"

Seth's descriptor wasn't exactly wrong. Jackson did have that calendar-guy look to him. She hadn't been exaggerating when she'd told him that his swoon-worthy looks were bringing in women by the droves.

"It's Thursday night. I can't leave the bar on a Thursday night. It's too crowded."

Some of the heat she'd spied in his eyes cooled. "Of course you can't. You always put work first."

Not always. Once, she'd put *him* first.

But that knowledge stung. And, because she wasn't as good as she once was, she put in a little jab, too. "Seth, you don't get to come here unannounced and then give me crap for not dropping everything to see you."

He shifted his weight. "What if I told you that what I had to say was important? Real important. That I wouldn't have left the ranch and driven up here to Ohio otherwise?"

"When are you ever going to realize that running a bar is important to me too?" Boy, they'd had this same conversation back when she'd managed a burger joint and he'd wanted her to be free on Saturdays. "I can't just take off when it's sure to be filled to capacity. That isn't the way to treat my customers or the people I hired."

Dammit, this was her job and her reputation. Just because she wasn't a teacher or a nurse or an executive in some high-rise in Dallas didn't mean her goals didn't matter.

Something new flickered in his light-blue eyes. Maybe it was an acknowledgment that he wasn't being fair. Maybe it was the realization that whatever he'd come to tell her wasn't going to be as easy to tell her as he'd previously thought.

"So you're saying that if I want to see you, I'm out of luck."

No, that wasn't what she was saying at all. She'd told him that Thursday night was too busy for her to take off. But what he wasn't seeing—and maybe never had—was that she probably could get herself out of bed early enough to meet him for a late breakfast or lunch tomorrow. Or anytime on Sunday.

But, just like in the past, Seth Parks always only looked straight ahead. Never turned his head a couple of inches to the right or left, which would have allowed him to see that there was another path to take. It might be a little slower, maybe take a couple of minutes longer, or it might involve a couple of extra turns and a steep hill or two … but it would get him to that same exact spot.

"You heard what I said," she said at last.

He nodded. "All right then. I guess I'll see you around."

"Wait, around? You're not going back?"

"Not yet. I decided to hang out here for a couple of days."

"Just to talk?"

"No, just to get some answers."

"Seth—"

"I'll be seeing you, Genevieve." After nodding to her like she was an acquaintance he'd spied in aisle four of the Walmart, he turned and walked away.

Though she knew better, Gen stood and watched him, telling herself it was because she wanted to see if he would turn around. Not that she was checking out the way his backside looked in those Wranglers.

She'd almost fooled herself that she was being super sneaky, too … until she realized that he was watching her reflection in the window pane.

When he grinned, she turned around and braced her hands on the bar. What was she going to do?

"You doing okay, Boss?" Jackson asked he approached.

"No," she said.

"Anything I can do?"

"Oh, yeah. You can get me a drink."

Without a word, he pulled down the Maker's Mark, poured two fingers' worth in a shot glass, and plunked it down in front of her.

Then Jackson Koch proved he was more than just a pretty face. He didn't say a single word when she downed the whole thing in one painful swallow.

No, all he did was quietly pour her another one.

CHAPTER 7

FROM LES LARKE'S
YOU, TOO, CAN HOST
A POKER TOURNEY:

*It's the host's responsibility to plan the evening's
events. I suggest doing a mental walk-through of
how you'd like the evening to go. For example,
when will you serve drinks and snacks?*

Friday

"Mom, you never said what you thought," Jeremy said when they
were only about five minutes from home.

Dani tightened her hands on the steering wheel, though
she'd been waiting for her son to say something about Coach
Edwards' comment from the moment she'd heard it. She
supposed she should be thankful that Jeremy had waited so long
to bring up the subject in the first place.

But, even though he'd waited and she'd mentally been
preparing herself to hear the question, it still pinched. The
coach had recommended Jeremy not only to start on the
eighth-grade team, but to join a private baseball club, one of
the best in the area. "I don't think my opinion matters as much

as yours. What do you think about what Coach Edwards said?"

Jeremy gaped at her like she had a screw loose. "Coach thinks I can get on the Bats without a problem. He thinks I'm good enough to play first base and maybe even be a relief catcher for them." His voice quickened. "Mom, you know how much I love catching."

She smiled. "Oh, I know." Every time her boy crouched behind home plate, his whole demeanor changed. He went from being serious and quiet to completely engaged. It was like every bit of his body was vibrating, he was so excited to be in the thick of the game.

"So, what do you think I think?" He grinned again.

"Even though I know, I'd still like to hear the words."

He exhaled. "All right, fine. I want to try out for the Bridgeport Bats and get on that team. I think it's like the best news ever." After a pause, he said, "Coach Edwards doesn't just say things like that, Mom."

Stopping at the light, she studied him again. "Really?"

"Oh, yeah. If you suck, Coach says you suck. He doesn't mess around."

"Let's use some better language, please."

"Mom, it's not that bad."

"It's not that good."

"The guys say it all the time."

"Maybe not to their mothers."

"Mom, I'm fourteen …"

As they pulled into the parking lot, she glanced over at her boy, looking so earnest and grown-up all of a sudden. Honestly, it was like she'd given him twenty-five dollars and dropped him off at the batting cages three hours ago, and when she picked him up he'd turned into a young man. "Pick your battles, kid," she said, half talking to him … and herself. "Either we can

49

talk baseball and club teams, or we can talk about appropriate language to use with your mother."

"Fine. I'm sorry."

"Accepted. Now, you were saying about Coach Edwards being a straight shooter?"

He wrinkled his brow. "I was saying that he doesn't say stuff just to try to make you feel good."

"So if he says you have a chance to be a great player, it's true."

"Yeah. I mean, yes. But he didn't say I could be a great player, Mom. Only that I could probably do good playing first base or catcher."

Now, that was interesting—and surprising.

Because even though Coach Edwards hadn't told Jeremy that, he had told her that Jeremy had real talent. Then, he'd stopped and stared at her, awaiting the appropriate answer.

Unfortunately, Dani hadn't given him one. Instead, she'd simply stared right back, because she'd known she didn't have the right words to say.

The fact of the matter was that Jeremy couldn't play on that special club team. She didn't know a lot about baseball, but she knew enough about life to guess that everything about the organization was going to be expensive. They had three or four coaches. Private sessions at the cages. Even the uniforms looked expensive. All the boys who'd played on last year's team even had their names embroidered on the backs of their jerseys.

Those things alone were enough to make her bank account cringe.

But then there were all the practices. And the games! There was something like eighty-four of them.

Why did they even need all those games?

Then there was the traveling to those tournaments—some as far away as Florida. That meant she'd not only have to miss days of work, she'd also have to pay for multiple nights in motels and going out to eat the whole time. Being part of the Bats sounded like they'd be entering a baseball money pit with no end in sight.

But it also had made Jeremy look like he'd gotten season tickets to the Reds and Kings Island at the same time. He loved baseball. He loved being good at something. He loved having something to look forward to after so much in their lives had been so hard.

But, what she needed to do was tell him that it couldn't happen. It was going to be hard for him to hear, but that's how life was. Sometimes you just couldn't do what you wanted to do.

But just as she opened her mouth, she chickened out.

"I'm real proud of you, Jeremy. I agree, it's terrific that Coach Edwards signaled you and talked about that club team. You're right, it's really special."

"But?" His voice had a note of resignation in it that she knew his shoulders and expression would display, too. After all, hadn't they had lots of conversations like this over the years?

She sighed. "But I'm still going to have to think about this."

"I could do more chores around the house. I … I could even watch Kate sometimes for you."

"I appreciate it."

"But?"

"But, nothing." She sighed. "I'm not telling you *no*, son. I just need some time to think about it, okay?"

Little by little, all the enthusiasm that had shone in his eyes faded. "Yeah. All right." He unbuckled his seat belt. "Pop the trunk, would ya?"

She pushed the button on the dash. The trunk opened with a satisfying click, just as Jeremy closed his door and walked around to the back. She got out of the car a whole lot more slowly. Boy, she felt old all of a sudden. Old and tired. Why was life so hard?

As she watched Jeremy open the main door to their unit and close it firmly behind him, she reached in the back seat for her purse, then closed her door and simply stood next to the car. She loved being a mom, and she loved Jeremy more than anything in the world. But there were times when she would have paid money to take a day off from motherhood.

Just imagining that someone else would take over for one day—buying food, cooking it, driving Jeremy around, worrying about getting him everything he needed, doing all that laundry, even making him do his homework? That would feel like a vacation to Hawaii.

Shoot, while she was dreaming, she figured she might as well go big. Instead of frantically cleaning other people's homes, she could go for a walk, get a pedicure, buy a new outfit, and take a long bath. With bubbles. Maybe sip a glass of wine while she soaked? That would be incredible.

Maybe she'd even soak so long that her toes would—

"Hey, is everything okay?"

Startled out of her reverie, Dani blinked. It took her a minute to realize that Gen Schuler from the bar where Jackson worked was talking to her. "Sorry, I was just standing here daydreaming about having a Calgon day."

The other woman, with her long blond hair and athletic build, grinned. "I'm not sure what that is, but I think I need to hear more about it."

She laughed, feeling self-conscious. "I was just picturing a day off from my life. It involved a long walk, pedicure, shopping, and a long bubble bath, complete with a glass of wine. Oh, and a vanilla-scented candle!"

Gen's expression turned almost blissful. "Boy, all you're missing is chocolate."

"Ooh! Good point! Let me amend my fantasy. I'm now going

to also sit on my couch doing nothing but watching mindless TV and eating a giant slice of chocolate cake."

A look of longing drifted into Gen's eyes. "Now you're talking. When was the last time you had a day like that?"

"That's easy. Uh, never?"

Gen smiled as she shifted, making the five or six thin silver bangles on her right arm jangle. "I think I had a day like that about three years ago."

"How was it?"

"Since I still remember what it felt like to sit in a massage chair and watch someone else paint my toes, I'd say it was pretty freakin' good." She laughed as she looked down at her legs. She was wearing faded jeans and a pair of tan cowboy boots in need of a good shine. "So, does this mean you're planning a day like that soon? Because if you are, I'm in. I mean if you want company."

Thinking about the price of the Bats, and well, life, she shook her head. "Unfortunately, that's not going to happen any time in the near future."

"Damn. I was getting excited about having a decent pedicure too."

She laughed. "If I win the lottery, I'll give you a call."

"I'll look forward to it." After a pause, Gen said, "On a positive note, at least you've got a good man to spend your regular days with. Your Jeremy is as good as it gets."

She smiled. "I'm pretty partial to him, myself." Though she didn't really know Gen all that well, she couldn't resist sharing what was weighing on her mind. "I've not only been imagining taking a break from my life, I've been trying to figure out how to tell him something hard."

"What is it?"

"Nothing too serious in the grand scheme of things. It just has to do with baseball and fancy club teams with crazy price tags."

Gen nodded as she crossed her arms over her chest. "I'm one of four kids and three of us played sports. I was in select soccer and I still remember my mom's expression when she'd come home from the parent meeting with a stack of papers. It was shell-shocked."

"That's exactly how I'm feeling, and I haven't even gotten that paperwork yet."

"Somehow they all made it work. I played soccer and my brothers played basketball and baseball."

"What about the other one?"

"Brittany played the flute, which wasn't any cheaper, believe it or not. Flute lessons and marching camps and band competitions weren't cheap. Come to think of it, nothing about parenthood seems cheap."

"I guess they did it all, though?" Though Dani knew Gen was trying to make her feel better, somehow knowing that Gen's parents took care of the needs of four children didn't make her difficulties helping one any easier to bear.

"They had help, though. My grandparents helped a lot." Looking at Dani closely, she said, "Do you have any family who could give you a hand?"

"Not really. I could ask my parents but it's not worth it. They live in Indiana and are on a pretty tight budget. I can imagine exactly what they'd say if I asked for money. After they told me I was spoiling Jeremy, they'd bring up one of their favorite topics—how my husband should have had a better insurance policy. Then, they'd probably call Jeremy and tell him that he shouldn't expect so much and make him feel guilty for even asking."

"Ouch. That's terrible."

"It's how they are." Not really sure why she was sharing her whole life story with Gen in the parking lot, Dani continued. "I guess, to a point, they are right. But shouldn't we all expect more from time to time?"

Gen blinked, looking reflective. "Yeah. Absolutely. We're all worth it, I know we are."

"I like your way of thinking."

"I'm sorry about all this. It's tough when something that should be a good thing doesn't feel like it."

"Yeah, it is. But I'll be okay, and Jeremy will be, too. I better get on upstairs and make him some dinner. Jeremy's probably raiding the refrigerator as we speak."

"All right. But, hey, uh, Dani?"

"Hmm?"

"Wait a day on making a decision about baseball, okay?"

She felt her neck heat up. "I didn't share this with you as a weird way of asking for help. That was the last thing I wanted to do."

"I know you aren't asking. And no offense, but I'm not offering. But I do remember hearing about booster clubs helping out. Let me ask my parents what they know about this. And there's a couple of guys I know who I can ask, too."

No way did she want to be someone's new charity case. "That's kind of you, but—"

"Don't worry. I won't say your name. I'll just ask around. I'll get back to you in a day or two with some information. You can wait until then, right?"

Everything inside of her wanted to brush off the offer, but she was willing to swallow some pride if it meant being able to let Jeremy have this. "Okay, thanks."

"No probs."

Just as Gen was walking away, Dani called out, "Um, even though I can't really afford pedicures and shopping trips, I can definitely afford long walks. I can even bake a terrific chocolate cake. If you ever have time, let me know."

"Thanks. After the day I've had, I'd just about kill for that cake. Let's make a plan one Sunday and do that."

"Deal."

Hiking her purse on her shoulder, Dani headed up to the apartment, but to her surprise, her burdens felt lighter. She still didn't have a lot of hope but there was a sliver of it. And such a relief not to have to tell Jeremy *no* right that minute.

When she got inside, she heard Jeremy playing Xbox in his room. After thinking about laundry and her latest coursework that she could be doing, she turned on the oven and popped a frozen lasagna in for dinner, then opened up some cabinets and saw a couple of bars of baking chocolate, sugar, and a whole container of flour.

Maybe it was time to bake a cake. Even if it was so she could cut off a big slice and have Jackson deliver it to Gen when he went into work that night.

CHAPTER 8

FROM LES LARKE'S
YOU, TOO, CAN HOST A POKER TOURNEY:

The average poker night will last around three hours. Are you ready for that?

Friday

Jackson reckoned it had been a good night. Better than usual.

First, when Dani had arrived at his apartment at six, she'd handed him half a chocolate cake to bring to Gen. It had smelled so good, he probably would have begged Gen for a bite if she hadn't shared small slices with the rest of the staff before it got busy.

They'd all sat on the stools around the bar and eaten that cake in near reverent silence. It made him realize that he hadn't gotten just a good job in Bridgeport, he'd made some good friends here, too.

That warm feeling carried over into the rest of the night. The bar had been exactly how Jackson liked it—busy, but not filled to capacity. There was also a Reds game on, which meant that about half the customers were avidly watching the game.

Jackson was, too.

He'd started playing ball when he was four, and the love of the game had stuck. Right around eighth grade, he'd gotten a growth spurt and come into his own. He'd started pitching well enough to catch the attention of some of the high school coaches in the area. One of them had even come over to the house to see if Jackson would be interested in going to school in the next town over.

For a moment, his dad had even looked like he was going to think about it, but his mother had knocked that idea down flat. Children lived at home. End of story.

He'd ended up playing high school ball and trying not to dream about playing in college … or of skipping college altogether because he got drafted into the big leagues. Those things didn't happen to kids in Spartan. He'd been right, too.

Even Bobby Thomas, their star batter, hadn't gotten a ride to college or an invite to try out for a farm team.

All of that was why the game on TV was a good thing for him. He liked watching and rooting for those guys who were able to accomplish something that had only been a faint dream for him.

"We need another round on the porch, Jackson," Gen said.

"On it." Glancing out at the men sitting outside, he remembered that they'd ordered pitchers of the draft on tap. He filled two and brought them out.

When he got closer, he realized at least half of them were members of the Bridgeport Social Club, Kurt's poker group. "Brought y'all two pitchers," he said as he set the clear plastic pitchers down. "Anyone want a fresh glass?"

Three of the guys handed him their mugs. One of them was

peering at him closely. "Hey, you're part of Kurt Holland's crew from West Virginia, aren't you?"

"Yep. Moved here a couple of months back."

"Good to see you." He held out a hand and introduced himself. "Corbin Hayes."

"Good to see you again, too. Name's Jackson Koch."

"Ace calls you Cookie."

"Yep, among other things." Cookie had been his nickname when he'd been on the Spartan High School baseball team. After shaking the other guys' hands, he headed back inside for fresh glasses. "I'll be right back."

Just as he went inside, one of the Reds hit a double and brought in a runner. As he whistled with everyone else, Gen raised her eyebrows.

"I didn't know you were a Reds fan."

"Can't help but be," he said as he pulled four mugs out of the freezer. "These guys are awesome."

"You know baseball?"

"Yep. I played it growing up." Realizing she was looking at him intently, he said, "Why?"

"Nothing." She paused. "But maybe I should ask you something."

"Let me deliver these mugs first."

"Let Kimmy do it. Kim, run those out, would you?"

"Sure, boss."

When they were alone, Gen said, "I saw your friend Dani in the parking lot today."

"Dani, who babysits Kate?" he asked, just to make sure she wasn't talking about a man named Danny.

"The very one."

"Ah. Well, that's good." He looked at her blankly, trying to figure out what her point was. Though Beth had been a master

59

of making quick friends, that wasn't Gen's way. She didn't chat with friends of friends in the parking lot or try to make connections. From the time he'd started at the Corner Bar, she'd been all business and he'd been perfectly fine with that.

"Has she told you about her son?"

"Told me what?"

"About how he's really good at baseball and was asked to be on some fancy team," she said. "A club team."

"No. I mean, I knew he played baseball, but so do a lot of boys his age."

After she served a pair of college students a couple of shots after checking their IDs, she turned back to him impatiently, flipping her long blond hair over one shoulder. "You need to ask Dani about her kid and get more information."

"Because?"

"Because she babysits for you, Jack. And she's nice."

"I'll do that, and she is nice, but I'm not exactly following you. Why are you so interested in Jeremy's baseball career?"

"Because she needs someone to give a damn. So it might as well be me and you."

He already did give a damn. He was pretty sure Dani knew that, too. Though, she hadn't said a word to him about Jeremy and club teams. No, all they'd done was talk about that cake. "I'll talk to her about it soon."

"Good." She relaxed.

"Since we're talking, how are you? Have you recovered from Seth's visit?"

"No."

"Is he still around, or did he go back home?"

Looking weary, she shook her head. "He didn't say but I know he's still here. I think he plans to stay here for a while."

"Do you want to talk about it?"

Just like that, her usual hard demeanor returned. "There's nothing to say, Jackson. Plus, I don't want to start talking about my personal crap at work."

"Understood. I'll get back to work." Just as he turned around, she put a hand on his back.

"Wait." When he turned back to face her, she grimaced. "I'm sorry. I know I'm all over the place tonight."

"You were pretty good after that cake."

She smiled wryly. "Chocolate cake can usually solve just about any problem of mine … except Seth."

"He was that bad to you?"

"No. It is more like he and I have a long history, and it's pretty tough to admit to myself that I haven't dealt with it like I should have."

Thinking about how he'd lived in a fog for months after Beth died and he lost his job, Jackson reached out and clasped her hand. "That happens to all of us. When you're ready, let me know if I can help."

She squeezed his hand before dropping her own. "You know what? I think I need a break."

"Okay. Kimmy and I can handle things while you take a break."

"No, I mean, I've been thinking about going home for a couple of days. What would you think about being in charge on a Saturday night in a week or two?" She held up a hand. "And don't go telling me you don't know how to make a bunch of fancy cocktails. Both Kimmy and Melissa will be working, and they can make most anything."

"You sure you don't want either of them to be in charge?"

"Hell, no. Melissa just likes to come and leave and Kimmy? Well, that girl can't manage to get her laundry done. We can't put her in charge of a bar."

"So it will just be the three of us?"

"No. I'll make sure Trevor and Brad are on, too. I wouldn't leave you without a lot of help. So, what do you say? It shouldn't be too hard for you. I mean, you've managed people before in your old job."

He wanted to point out that he had managed men in a mine. But he didn't. She knew his limitations, and he knew the look she was wearing. She needed a break. "I'll give it my best shot."

"Thanks. I'll give you a bonus."

"There's no need." Now that he thought about it, Jackson knew he'd be fine being in charge. He didn't mind the responsibility. And, at the end of the day, he could always remind himself that he wasn't worrying about men getting hurt in a mine but just a lot of people getting a drink. If they messed up without Gen, then they messed up. "When you're ready, let me know and I'll fill in. The place will be here when you get back."

"Thanks. Appreciate it," she said as she walked over to a group of middle-aged women who'd just sat down.

* * *

Four hours later, when he finally got home, Jackson found Dani sitting at his kitchen table like usual. But this time, she wasn't wearing headphones and typing on her computer. Instead, she was looking out the window … and was only wearing a thin white tank top. Before he could stop himself, he was staring at her curves, gazing at the creamy expanse of skin across her chest and shoulders that was usually hidden from view. She sat up abruptly as he closed the door behind him.

"Hey," he said.

"Jackson!" Looking irritated at herself, she grabbed the sweatshirt she must have tossed on the table and awkwardly pulled it on. "Sorry about that. I got a little warm drinking hot tea."

"You don't need to apologize for being comfortable."

For a moment, she looked like she was going to comment on that, but she shook her head instead. "Let's try this again. How are you? Looks like you got home early tonight."

He glanced at his phone's screen. "Not really. It's a quarter to two."

"I guess time just went by fast."

"How was Kate?"

She smiled as she gathered her things together. "She was great. We played with noodles."

He just noticed that they'd done an art project. Looked like Kate and Dani had make a macaroni picture. "Thanks. That's real nice."

She laughed. "It's supposed to be a dinosaur. See the green?"

Before he thought about how she might take it, he grabbed her hand. "Looks like you got your fair share of being dyed, too." Flipping it over, he rubbed a finger along her smooth palm.

Goosebumps appeared on the inside of her arm and her lips parted. He stared at them. Noticed that they looked as soft and feminine as the rest of her.

And … there went his attention back to places where it shouldn't go. He dropped his fingers.

She used that hand to push a chunk of her hair away from her face. "Ahh, green food coloring works great, but it's a mess. Kate's not all stained though. I promise."

"My girl is wash and wear. She'll be fine." He followed Dani to the door, half listening as she chatted about the video they watched about a stegosaurus named Pete.

Dani looked so pleased with herself, he almost didn't mention his conversation with Gen. But then he remembered the expression on her face when he first walked inside. She really was upset about something.

"Hey, before you go, Gen told me that you talked to her about Jeremy's baseball?"

She froze. "I did, but it wasn't anything. We just both happened to be in the same parking lot."

"I heard he's thinking about playing for another team?"

"Yeah, but I'll figure it out. It's nothing for you to worry about."

"Are you sure? I played for years. I might have some ideas that could help."

If anything, that news only seemed to make her more upset. She picked up her backpack and slung it over one shoulder. "Thanks, but I'm not up for talking about it now. I'm really tired."

He reached out a hand and grabbed her backpack. "I'm walking you up to your apartment tonight. No arguments."

She smiled weakly. "Okay. No arguments tonight."

For some reason, her compliance didn't make him worry less about her. Holding her backpack, he led the way out of his apartment, up the flight of stairs, and down the short hallway to her door. "Key?"

Without a word, she handed it to him.

He unlocked her door, then reached for the light switch that was in the same place in both their units and flicked it on. A warm glow spread over her living room. He noticed everything was quiet. "Here you go. Thanks for watching Kate."

"You're welcome." She smiled up at him. "I'll see you later."

For a moment, he was tempted to kiss her cheek. Maybe wrap her in his arms and give her a long hug. Beth used to say one really good hug had a way of making everything better.

But she wasn't Beth, and he wasn't sure what Dani would say if he either hugged her tight or kissed her just once.

Suddenly feeling confused, he held up a hand. "Yeah. Good night, Dan."

Then he quietly walked back down to his own apartment, let himself back inside, and walked to Kate's room.

His little girl was sound asleep, mouth open, arms above her head, her sheet and blankets in a messy jumble around her hips.

Carefully, he straightened her sheets and smoothed her hair from her brow. He kissed her forehead, and then closed the door behind him as he left her room.

After showering, he crawled into his bed and attempted to relax. Tried not to remember when Beth used to greet him at their door with a dozen kisses and a home-cooked meal. Tried to forget the way she used to look sexy as hell dressed in one of his old high school T-shirts.

Or the way she used to take his hand after they put their baby to sleep and walk him into their bedroom right before she would slip into their bed and open her arms.

When he couldn't fight it anymore, he threw on a pair of sweats and walked out to the couch and turned on the TV. Mindless entertainment was always better than memories that burned.

CHAPTER 9

FROM LES LARKE'S
*YOU, TOO, CAN HOST
A POKER TOURNEY:*

*Try to prepare for something unexpected to
happen. For example, if you run out of drinks,
do you have a backup plan?*

Saturday

"I'm sorry Kate's already sound asleep," Jackson said to Dani the
next day as he carefully deposited his little girl on her queen-size
bed. "She's had a long day."

He'd called Dani earlier to offer to take Kate to her place.
Saying that she would be glad to have the chance to work at her
own place, she'd immediately agreed.

Dani placed a light blanket over Kate. "You had to work
earlier, didn't you?"

"I did. Gen wanted a couple of hours off, so I've been in
charge for the day."

"She told me the other day that she was hoping to take a few
hours off. How did that go?"

"Good enough. Saturdays involve a lot of deliveries, so I mainly just tried to keep track of everything."

"That sounds confusing."

"I'm finally getting the hang of it, so … so far, so good." Leaning down, he kissed his little girl's brow. "Missed my girl, though."

"Who watched Kate today?" Dani asked as she walked him to the living room.

Today Dani had on a pair of worn jeans, a Reds T-shirt, and bare feet. After noticing that she'd painted her toenails a pale pink, he pulled his head back to the conversation. "I got on the phone and asked my buddy Ace if they could watch her for a couple of hours today. Kate loves his son, Finn."

"Oh, I know. Even I've heard about Finn."

He laughed. "Usually, all Kate wants to do is be in the same room as the kid. But now there's something even better in that house."

"Even better than Finn? I can't even imagine."

Remembering his daughter's squeals, he grinned. "They have a brand-new puppy. An Australian shepherd. His name is Touchdown, and he's cute as all get out."

Dani's expression warmed. "Well, I was going to tell you I was sorry I couldn't watch her earlier today, but I take that back. I can't beat a puppy."

He chuckled. "I'm no competition for it either. Usually Kate gets a little clingy when I leave her with someone besides you but she barely waved goodbye to me. Then, when I went back, she was all smiles. Their neighbor girl had come over and was playing Candy Land with her."

"Sounds like she had a good day." Studying him carefully, her voice turned hesitant. "What about you? Did you get to relax at all?"

"I took three hours off and ate an early dinner over with Ace, Finn, and Kate. It was good. After I got her home, I gave her a bath. As soon as I got out of the shower and checked on her, she was passed out on the couch. She didn't even wake up when I carried her up here."

Dani smiled again. "I remember those days."

"How was your day?"

"Oh, it was fine. I made some cookies. They're chocolate chocolate chip." Turning around, she picked up a plate that was neatly wrapped in plastic wrap. "I thought you might want to take them into work."

He grinned at her. "I would say that you're thinking of me, but I think you might be baking for Gen, too."

"Maybe." She wrinkled her nose, as if a sudden thought had just occurred to her. "Uh-oh. Is that weird? I don't know her all that well."

"Not at all. She loved that cake. We all did. We'll like the cookies, too. Thanks."

"You're welcome. And, about Gen … well, when I talked to her out in the parking lot, we started talking about dream days. We both agreed that chocolate was an important component."

He was curious about what Dani's dream day might have involved, but something told him that now wasn't the best time to bring it up. Instead, he tried to look confused, though he wasn't. He'd been married to a girl who used to act like a Dove Bar was really special. "What is it with women and chocolate?"

Her eyes sparkled. "Since you are a man, I can only tell you that it's something you'll probably never understand."

Beth had said almost the same thing to him at least a dozen times. Just as he was about to turn around, he remembered the conversation they'd had about her tip. "Hey, I forgot to ask, how did the batting cages go?"

Everything about Dani's expression changed, kind of like the light in her eyes had just been turned out. "It went well. I mean it was fine."

"That's it? Did Jeremy have a good time?" He didn't want to prod too much, but he and Gen weren't going to know how to help her if she didn't want to confide in him.

Looking over at her son's closed door, she shrugged. "It was good enough, I think."

"Did something happen?" He hated playing this game with her, but he didn't think Dani would be very happy to find out that he and Gen had been talking about her. "Did he get in a fight with the other boys or something?"

"A fight? Oh, no, nothing like that." Steeling her shoulders, she kind of smiled. "It was … nothing that you need to worry about."

"Are you sure? I mean, I think we've moved beyond just a work relationship, don't you?"

"We have, Jackson. And … and, well, I thank you for caring, but this isn't anything I want to discuss right now."

"You sure?"

"Positive." Pasting a plastic smile on her face, she said, "Now get on out of here before you're late."

He was in no hurry to get out of there now, but she was right. He had to work—and this was her business, not his. The Lord knew that there were plenty of subjects he didn't willingly share with many people.

Holding up the plate, he smiled. "I'll put the cookies in our break room. Thanks again."

"It was nothing. Have a good night."

After another long look at Dani, wishing that he could solve her problems for her, he walked down the stairs, stopping to grab his backpack, which he'd left outside her door when he'd carried Kate inside.

Less than ten minutes later, he was walking through the back door of the Corner Bar.

Chad, one of the bar's part-time servers, was in the break room checking his phone. "Hey, Jack." Just as he was about to turn back to his phone, he eyed the plate of cookies. "You brought in more food?"

"Yeah. My babysitter and Gen are friends. She made the cookies for her. Actually, for all of us."

Grinning, Chad pulled one off the plate and put half of it in his mouth. "Oh my gosh, this is good. Tell her thanks, would you? It hits the spot."

"I'll pass that on to Dani." He'd never been all that into sweets, but he was starting to think Dani might be slowly changing his mind about that. "I'm gonna set this plate on Gen's desk then head out," he said after clocking in. "Anything new around here?"

"Beyond some cowboy sitting at the bar and watching Gen like she was his lifeline? Nope."

"He's back?"

"Wait, he was here earlier?"

Irritated now, he put the cookies on her desk, grabbed a clean apron, and walked out into the bar, which was already half-full. Since it wasn't even six yet, he figured it was going to be a long night.

Gen was working the counter the way she always did, methodically pouring drinks while chatting with one or two customers at the same time. However, it was apparent after a minute of watching that something was seriously off with her. Her smile was a little too bright. Her interest in the customers' stories a little too forced. She wasn't near as relaxed as she appeared to be.

He had a pretty good idea why. But just to make sure, Jackson took stock around the room, looking for the person who she was avoiding.

And sure enough, there sat Seth in one of the chairs at the far end of the bar. Dressed in a ball cap and a different shirt, everything else about him looked the same ... especially the intense look he was sending Gen's way.

Jackson knew there were two things he could do. He could remind himself that he had his own problems, all of which were bad enough to keep his focus on himself and not on his boss and her old flame or whatever he was.

Or, he could remind himself that Gen had given him a job bartending when the only experience he'd had in bars was sitting at one and having a beer every now and then.

Hoping he wasn't just about to get himself into the middle of some lovers' squabble where he ended up being the loser because he couldn't mind his own business, he walked to Seth's side.

"Anything I can help you with?"

Like he was pulling himself away from her, Seth slowly refocused his attention on him. "Yeah. You can leave me alone."

Jackson wasn't a fighter. Never had been. But there was a part of him that almost welcomed the excuse to lay one on the guy hard enough to land him on the floor. "Excuse me?"

"I don't need to repeat myself," he muttered with a thick drawl. "You heard me." Seth picked up his beer and took a slow sip, all the while turning his attention back to Gen.

Who, Jackson knew, was now acutely aware of what was going on between the two men.

But because she didn't call him over, Jackson continued, a sixth sense telling him that he needed to tread carefully, because it was about to become apparent that he wasn't going to deck the guy for his boss' sake but for his own. "I don't want any trouble and I know Gen doesn't either."

"I'm not making trouble."

"I don't know what happened between the two of y'all but it's obvious that you being here isn't making things better."

Seth turned his way again. This time, even in the dim light, Jackson could see that his dark eyes were filled with irritation. "You're right. You have no idea what happened. No idea at all. So you'd do good to stay out of it." He looked over Jackson like he was hardly worth his time. "What's your story, anyway? Pretty boy like you could probably have any woman you want. Why are you after Gen?"

At another time and in another place, Jackson probably would have slugged him for calling him that. But losing Beth had reminded him that not every slight was worth making an issue out of it. "I'm not after any woman. Just trying to help both of you out."

"What? You into men?"

Jackson normally wouldn't have cared if the guy thought he was or not. He was a big believer in giving everyone their privacy. In his world, all that mattered was if a man took care of himself, looked after the people he cared about, and paid his own way.

But, there was something about the pain in the man's voice that told him that Seth Parks wasn't a complete jerk.

No, he was hurting real bad.

"If I was into men, it wouldn't be any of your business. But I'm definitely not into Gen."

"Because she's your boss?"

"No. Because I was into my wife."

Seth's light-blue eyes blinked. "Was? What happened? She left you?"

Jackson silently counted to five while a fresh wave of pain sliced threw him. "Yeah. She died."

Seth flinched. And with that flinch, his whole body looked like it deflated. "Damn. I'm sorry."

Jackson shrugged. Almost acting like it didn't matter when there was a time it had been all that mattered. "Beth was a good woman and gave me a little girl. Right now I don't need another woman to look after."

"You have a daughter?"

"Sure do. Her name's Kate."

"How old?"

"She's almost four." Smiling softly, he said, "She's everything to me."

"That's good. Kids are good."

There was that note of pain again. "Look, I don't want to tell you what to do or cause a scene. I'm just trying to let you know that whatever problem you and my boss have probably isn't going to be solved in this bar tonight. Most nights we're all too busy to go to the bathroom, let alone talk about anything of worth."

"I hear what you're saying, but I don't have much choice. Gen didn't want to talk to me when I first came by and didn't want to call me either. So, I'm going to force it now. 'Cause, it's going to be discussed. Because a man doesn't discover that his ex-girlfriend tried to ruin his life and never talk about it."

While Jackson stood there gaping, feeling like all the air had just been knocked out of him, Gen walked to the end of the bar where Seth sat and leaned over and slapped him hard enough to break up every conversation in the bar.

Silence rang loud and clear as she leaned even closer, tears running down her face. "You bastard," she hissed.

As Jackson took a step back, he realized he hadn't been wrong. It had been a real bad idea to get in the middle of their argument. He should have ignored the guy and focused on the other thirty customers in the bar. He stepped back, walking away from the pair. They obviously needed their privacy.

Beth would have looked at him and shaken her head. Right before she would have said that she'd told him so.

CHAPTER 10

FROM LES LARKE'S
YOU, TOO, CAN HOST
A POKER TOURNEY:

*After sending out your invitations,
communication is key. Plan to either email or
text your guests to follow up. Some people need
more than one reminder.*

Saturday Night

She'd told him to go away. He hadn't.

Seth gave Gen some time to cool off. Two days. That was a lot, considering how long he'd already waited to get answers.

Though she was probably going to tell him that she'd rather see him when hell froze over, he wasn't of the mind to wait any longer. He needed to see her, tell her his piece, and then get out of Bridgeport, Ohio, before he forgot how badly she'd done him wrong.

Fact was, she'd hurt him something fierce. He wanted to hate her. But he couldn't take his eyes off Genevieve Schuler.

Eighteen months later, she looked exactly the same. Beautiful. Her long blond hair still tied back in a ponytail. She was again wearing old jeans, worn boots, and a faded band T-shirt that fit like a glove. Still wearing about a pound of silver on her wrists, those thin bangles drawing his attention every time she moved a hand.

Still so hard, so tough. So afraid to let any vulnerability show. Most people probably didn't know why she was the way she was.

Unfortunately, he knew all too well.

Seth was vaguely aware of the bartender eyeing him and Gen with concern. A number of the staff and customers were staring, too. Hell, if someone passed out popcorn, they'd probably even stop pretending they were doing anything but watching Gen and Seth's pain come to surface.

But he couldn't see anything but the way three tears traipsed down Genevieve's cheekbones. If he hadn't recently cried for what she'd taken from him, he might even feel real bad about that.

"You need to leave," she said.

"No, I need to talk you," he countered. "I told you that yesterday, and I'm telling you again." Gesturing his head in the direction where the bartender had been, he said, "I suggest you tell your staff that you're taking the rest of evening off for personal reasons."

"You suggest? Who do you think you are?"

"Don't make me answer that."

Gen looked so angry, her breath was coming in raspy pants.

He'd seen that before. At one time, he would have done just about anything to avoid seeing her get so riled up.

But things were different now.

"I'm not backing off, Gen. I tried to speak to you earlier. I tried to meet with you someplace else, but you didn't want any of that."

"I own a bar and it's the weekend. I don't have time for this."

They could play these games all night. Maybe they had before?

Everything between them had gotten so muddled, he didn't know anymore.

All he did know for sure was that he wasn't going to be able to sleep, eat, or even leave Bridgeport until he said what he'd come to say. And when he knew for sure that she'd actually listened.

He tried again. This time softening his voice, hoping she heard something in his tone that would encourage her to let her guard down, even for a little bit. "I know you don't want to talk to me."

She raised one shoulder. "Really? Was I that obvious?"

Damn, but she could bring a grown man to his knees. "I get it. You never want to see me again. I promise, as soon as we get this conversation over with, I'll go away and leave you alone."

"Will you promise that I'll never have to see you again?"

"If that's what you want." He gritted his teeth before continuing on. "This is important, Genevieve. I wouldn't be here if it wasn't. You know I wouldn't."

She stared long and hard at him, her brown eyes flickering over his face. Then, at last, she nodded. "Let's go to my office."

He would've rather gone somewhere more neutral, but he didn't argue. "Lead the way."

"Let me go tell Jackson that I need a few."

He nodded, but she didn't see his agreement; she'd already turned to the bartender. The guy had been serving beer and mixed drinks the whole time they'd been standing there. It was obvious that he'd been hovering as much as he dared, just in case Gen needed him. The guy was good-looking, and from the way his expression softened when she leaned close to chat, he was certain that the guy hadn't been telling the whole truth. Jackson might be missing his wife, but there was something between him and Gen.

After Gen exchanged a couple more words with Jackson and touched base with two of the servers, she returned to Seth's side.

"Come on. Let's get this over with," she muttered as she turned down the hall.

She didn't even look back. She was expecting him to follow.

Usually, that would have grated on him. Now? He was just glad they were finally going to be able to do what he'd come there for. Within fifteen minutes, the conversation he'd been dreading would be over, and he could head back home to Texas.

* * *

The minute they walked into her office, Gen closed the door. It was a miracle she hadn't slammed it—she was so mad she could hardly think straight.

Embarrassed, too.

She hadn't liked the way Jackson had looked at her, like he was concerned that she was making a bad choice. Didn't like how more than one of her customers had watched Seth and their little tête-à-tête like it was the latest soap opera come to life.

She liked her private life private. Seth showing up was messing up two years of hard work and professionalism. And because Bridgeport was so small—and half the men and women in her bar had nothing better to do—she knew they'd be bringing up this scene for years to come. Damn it.

Folding her arms over her chest, she glared. "You have five minutes, so you better start talking."

A muscle in his jaw jumped. "Don't talk to me like that. You know I wouldn't be here if it wasn't important."

But that was the problem. She had no idea what his issue could possibly be. All of a sudden, a dozen bad scenarios filled her brain. Was he sick? Was his momma sick? Had one of their old friends gotten in an accident or something? "Seth, what do you want?"

He closed his eyes, like he was struggling for patience as much as she was. And maybe he was.

"Two days ago I ran into Valerie Gutierrez outside the post office."

"Valerie?" Valerie had been one of her old neighbors. She'd been friendly. Gen had known her well enough to chat for a spell at the restaurant or to talk in the front lawn when they got their mail.

Not well enough for Seth to make a trek up from Lubbock to relay news about her.

"Yeah. Valerie." For some reason, he punctuated those words with a meaningful look. Like she should have been able to read his mind.

She absolutely could not. Impatient now, she folded her arms across her chest. "Well, what did she have to say?"

"She wanted to know how I was doing."

"Okay." When he didn't say anything, she said, "Seth, I'm still completely in the dark here. What is your point?"

"Genevieve, she was worried about how I was doing because of what happened with the baby."

"Baby?" The word hit her hard in the center of her chest, reminding her of everything she'd thought she once had and how empty she'd become when it was lost.

But what she didn't know was what it had to do with him and Valerie.

Right as she was about to throw up her hands and tell him to stop speaking in riddles she caught sight of his expression. He looked crushed.

Torn-up-aluminum-foil crushed. Devastated.

"Seth, I'm not trying to be mean, but I'm not following you."

His eyes widened before he hid his reaction. "I can't believe you're going to make me say this."

"Just say it!"

"Valerie told me about your abortion. About how you aborted our baby."

"What?" She shook her head as she tried to gather her breath. "No."

"Gen. She works at the doctor's office where you went."

"I don't know what she does there, but she's not a doctor or a nurse, Seth."

"She's one of the receptionists."

"Well, whatever she is, she's also wrong."

His eyes were piercing. "Are you saying that you were never pregnant with my baby? A baby you didn't feel the need to tell me about? That you decided to get rid of that baby before telling me about it?"

Pain reverberated through her. Made her reach out for the plain wooden chair that was pressed against the wall of the cramped room. "I was pregnant. But … but I had a miscarriage. I lost our baby almost right away. At eight weeks."

His whole face went slack. "You didn't have an abortion."

Still stunned by his accusation, she shook her head. "No," she murmured, half to herself. Looking up, she met his eyes. "No, Seth."

Seth made a choking noise.

Gazing into his eyes, she saw the same pain reflected there that had been in her heart. Though it hurt like hell, she firmed her tone. Spoke louder. "I wouldn't do that, Seth. And I didn't."

"Genevieve, I didn't even know you were pregnant."

Oh, it was so hard to hear him call her that. "We'd broken up."

"That doesn't matter. You should—"

No way was he going to Monday-morning quarterback her. "No, you listen to me. You may not remember how things were between us, but we were like fire and ice. Like oil and water."

He grunted. "More like kerosene and a match."

"Exactly. Things between us would simply combust. We argued and fought and would break up for a couple of days …"

"Then we'd hook up again and be together for a while."

"And then we'd break up again after saying a lot of things we couldn't take back." Before he could counter her statement, she said, "Do you remember our last fight?"

Slowly, he nodded. "It was bad, though I don't even remember what it was about."

"That night—just before I ran out of your place—we both swore that we were over. For once and for all."

He shoved his hands in the front pockets of his jeans. "Is that when you found out?"

She nodded. "I started feeling bad a couple of days after that fight. A little nauseous, a little off. At first, I thought I had the flu. But it lingered. Then, one night, it all clicked, and I got myself to the store and bought a test."

"You should have told me."

"I was going to, and I would've, Seth." Pushing back all the doubts, all the hurts, she cleared her throat. "You probably don't remember, but you were out of town. In Kimball or Tyler, maybe? One of your buddies was having a bachelor party."

He blinked. "I was at Lake Cumberland. I remember." After another pause, he said, "And then I had to go to Nashville for work."

"We'd gotten in that argument, and it was only two weeks later. There was no way I was going to call you and tell you the news over the phone. Can you even imagine?"

He looked down at his polished boots. "Hell, Gen, I might not have even picked up. I was so stupid then, always flying off the handle."

She was tempted to point out that their current conversation wasn't showing that he'd changed all that much.

Still looking at him intently, she said, "I figured when you got back I'd give you a call. I needed a couple of days to get my head around the news. I reckoned by the time you got back I'd be calmer. Then, it wouldn't be so difficult to tell you the news."

"What happened?"

"The baby didn't make it that long." Each word felt like a shard of glass being pulled out of her, leaving her cut and hurting.

But though even thinking about that time brought so much pain, she forced herself to continue. If nothing else, Seth needed to know the truth, and she needed to be the one to tell him.

Heck, maybe even a part of her needed him to see her pain. "I realized I was pregnant on a Thursday. On Saturday morning, I started bleeding. Scared, I drove myself to the emergency room. When they checked me out, the doctor said I'd miscarried." She drew a breath, realizing that she would have been proud of herself for sharing the story so succinctly—if every word hadn't felt like another bullet hole in her heart.

"You had to drive yourself to the hospital?"

Seth's voice was soft, reminding her that even though they'd fought like cats and dogs, he'd always hated that she hadn't had a decent family to have her back.

"There wasn't anyone else. You know that."

He closed his eyes. "I'm so sorry."

"Me, too. And … well, I'm sorry I lost our baby."

He reached out and gripped her hand. He held her firmly, just like he used to. "It wasn't your fault."

She nodded. Forced herself to speak about it some more. "I know that now. It was hard and a shock … but my body knew that something was wrong. There wasn't anything I could have done." Her voice drifted off as she pulled away from him and sat down. She hated to remember the conversation even now. The doctor had been sympathetic but almost clinical in her description.

A couple of hours later, she'd gone back to her car and driven home, feeling numb and alone. So very alone.

"I still wish you would have called me. No matter what had happened between us, I would've dropped everything and been there."

Maybe the man he was now would have. But the person he was back then? She just wasn't so sure. But even if she had called him, he wouldn't have been able to be there.

And, well, she just wasn't sure that him knowing would have made things easier. Things between them had been so toxic.

She shrugged. "Seth, tell you what? We weren't in a good place. And when we did cross paths almost a month later, it was pretty obvious that it was just as painful for you as it was for me. We didn't have anything left."

He walked closer. Then, to her surprise, he crouched down, placing himself eye level with her. "I'm sorry."

Those two words meant more than he would ever know. This whole time, it had been her secret. She hadn't told anyone. Not her girlfriends, not her family. It hadn't felt right to tell anyone about the miscarriage before him and she hadn't been able to bring herself to tell him.

After a few months passed, she even almost convinced herself that her pain had been her overreacting. "Why would Valerie go and tell you I had an abortion? Why would she be talking about me in the first place? This was almost two years ago."

"I don't know, but I intend to find out." His voice hardened. "Besides her being flat-out wrong, she shouldn't have been sharing patient information. I'm going to speak to the administrator over there."

"I hope you do. I hate the thought of her talking about all the patients like that."

"Me, too. I'll get some answers."

"If you learn something, let me know, okay? I promise, Seth, I never told anyone."

"As soon as I discover why she did what she did, I'll tell you. I'm sorry, Gen."

She was, too.

Suddenly, she was so tired. She felt weepy, too. The last thing she wanted to do was go back to work. Rubbing her temples, she tried to tell herself that she could worry about this conversation later.

But she knew that was a lie.

"I'm going to go home," she said.

He nodded. "Want me to drive you?"

"Thanks, but I've got it. I hate leaving Jackson in the lurch, but I just can't ..."

"I'll tell him you had to leave. And then I'll offer to work behind the bar if he needs help."

"What?"

"Hand me your keys. I'll stay here and lock up, then meet you here in the morning or you can call me, and I'll bring the keys to your house."

"Seth, you don't need to do that."

"You know what? I think I really do." Dragging a hand through his dark-brown hair, he continued. "My only other option is to go sit in a hotel room and I can't do that. Even if you don't know me anymore, I think you know that I can work a bar as well as anyone."

She didn't know why she didn't even consider arguing, but she just got to her feet, rooted through her desk drawer, and pulled out a thick ring of keys. "I would stand here and tell you what's what, but I don't think I can even do that right now."

"I'll figure it out. Your employees will help me, too. Go on, Gen." His voice was hoarse. In that moment she realized that while they may never find love again, he now had a better idea about the type of person she was.

The type of woman she'd always been.

She looked at him. Almost yearning to beg him to see that she was different now, too. But she couldn't even do that.

Instead, she opened another drawer, pulled out her purse, pulled her car keys out of that, and walked to her door. "Thanks," she said simply.

Pain flickered in his eyes. "Don't thank me for this, Gen. Just go on home and rest, okay?"

She smiled tightly before walking outside. It was the first night in memory that she was going home before eight o'clock. For once, she didn't even care.

CHAPTER 11

FROM LES LARKE'S
YOU, TOO, CAN HOST
A POKER TOURNEY:

*In order to host a successful tournament, it helps
to know the game. If you aren't sure of your poker
skills, I suggest you read one of my other books.
Or even watch a few videos.*

Saturday

When Seth returned to the bar with a weary look on his face, Jackson feared something bad had happened between him and Gen.

When he realized Gen wasn't following, he knew it.

"Where's Gen?" he asked, hoping he sounded more relaxed than he felt. "Is she on her way out?"

"Ah, no. She had to go home," Seth replied, each word sounding like it was being torn from him. "I'm going to help out."

She'd left? The woman was a workaholic and loved this bar. She never just took off. "What happened?" he asked as he stepped forward into the guy's space.

But instead of looking angry, Seth's expression turned even more devastated. "I can't talk about it."

He realized then that Seth hadn't hurt her. No, he was hurting just as much as Gen had to be. "Is she okay?"

Seth sighed. For a moment Jackson thought he wasn't going to answer. Then he shrugged. "Yeah. I mean, I don't know. I think so." Looking around the bar like he'd never seen one before, he muttered, "Where do you want me?"

On another night, Jackson would've told Seth to just head on home. But the place was packed. He needed to start serving up drinks and helping out Kimmy and Brad before they up and quit. He pointed to the gate at the back of the bar. "Come on back. Want to tend the tap?"

"Yeah, that's fine. But I can do more than pour beer."

"Good to know. For now, pour beer and wine and try to keep up with the tabs. Get Kimmy and Brad to help you."

"Got it."

Though his mind was still on Gen, Jackson forced himself to remember that she'd hired him to tend her bar, not worry about her personal problems. Pulling himself together, he smiled at the trio of women who'd been waiting impatiently. "Sorry, ladies, what can I get you?"

"Two glasses of merlot and one Truth on tap."

Jackson looked at Seth. "You get that?"

"I think so. Repeat it though."

He barely refrained from clenching his teeth. "Two glasses of the house merlot. Pour one draft." He gestured to the bottles behind the bar in the hopes that would be enough.

Luckily Seth nodded and got his head in the game. Turning back to the women he said, "New guy will have y'all taken care of in just a minute."

The brunette with the credit card smiled. "Thanks."

"Anytime, darlin'," Seth drawled as he glanced at the next person in line. "What will you have?"

"Bourbon on ice. Woodford Reserve."

"Gotcha." Glancing Jackson's way, he muttered, "Settle down. I've got this."

It seemed he did. Nodding in his direction, Jackson turned to the next customer.

For the next half hour, it continued. He took orders, grinned at the ladies, and talked sports and weather with the men. When he realized Seth was doing much the same thing and didn't look frazzled, he began to relax. It seemed the guy knew his way around a bar after all.

When he finally took a break, Jackson looked over at Kimmy, who had just come with an order and was waiting for Seth to fill it.

Just as Jackson was about to offer to fill it, he saw that Seth was still doing just fine. He worked with ease, no longer hesitating as he poured drafts, pulled out beer bottles from the cooler, and searched for wine. He was talking to Kimmy and grinning at one of the customers chatting with him over the counter.

Jackson breathed another sigh of relief. They were going to get through the night after all.

Another hour passed, then two.

Finally, around a quarter after twelve, things began to slow down. Kimmy finally took her break. Melissa had shown up around eight and had taken over the outside patio. Brad had just come through, checking stock and ice. Jackson washed some glasses as he watched Seth finish filling a couple's order.

When the couple turned away, he said, "Thanks for filling in. You're doing a great job."

Seth laughed as he picked up two empty bottles and tossed them in the recycle bin. "It's been crazy. Is it always like this?"

"On a Saturday night? Pretty much."

"I don't know how Gen does it."

"If you saw her in action you wouldn't wonder. She treats everything in here like it matters. Plus, she's been tending bar for most of her life." Realizing he sounded condescending, he added, "Course, I guess you know that."

"I knew she knew her way around a bar, but I didn't realize she did *this* every night. She managed a burger place back in Lubbock. Things moved slower there."

"Well, this is how it usually is."

"So it's crazy busy."

"Yep."

"Damn. No wonder she said she's always exhausted."

For some reason, Seth's appreciation of Gen's skills made him thaw a little toward the guy. "I thought the same thing when I first started working."

"You struggled a bit?"

"No. I struggled a *lot*. Serving bar is a whole lot harder than I thought." Shaking his head at the memory, Jackson said, "The first night I knocked over a tray of wine glasses and got every other order wrong. I thought she was going to fire me two hours in."

Seth grinned. "I guess you got better?"

Jackson shrugged. "I'm almost adequate now," he said before making another round of drinks for two couples who were sitting at the far end of the bar. "It turns out that I just had to take the time to learn a new skill."

Thinking about what the guy said, and how his voice sounded like he was both frustrated by his problems and had also come to terms with it, Seth was reminded again that he wasn't the only person in the crowded bar harboring secrets.

Soon Brad went on break and Kimmy returned. During the next hour, Kimmy started chatting more with the customers and running back and forth less. Glancing at the clock, Jackson saw it was already past one.

88

"When will you shut it down?"

"Gen usually starts last call around one-thirty or one unless it's a special occasion." After seeing another group of people exit, he made a decision. "I'm thinking we might as well do last call in fifteen or twenty minutes."

"Sounds good."

"While we've got a lull, do me a favor and work on the glasses." They had a dishwasher in the back, too, but it saved time and energy to wash as much glassware at the bar sink as possible.

To his surprise, Seth pulled out the dish soap and started washing and rinsing glasses like he'd spent the day before doing the same damn thing.

Jackson reminded himself that he shouldn't have expected any less. Not everyone looked like their history—and he sure as hell knew that not everyone got away with doing the job they'd planned on doing.

After filling one of the waitress' orders—three drafts and a Bacardi and Coke—Jackson picked up a cloth and started drying. It didn't take long to realize that one of them wasn't near as quick as the other at maneuvering glassware.

"Gen told me you haven't been working here long."

"Yeah. Just a couple of months." Figuring that he might as well share a little more, he added, "I'm new in town."

"Yeah?"

Jackson nodded. "Moved to Bridgeport from a small town in West Virginia."

"What do you think of Bridgeport?"

"It's better than I thought it would be."

Seth smiled. "If you didn't think it was gonna be good, why'd you move?"

He waited, hating to share too much of his backstory. Not

because he didn't like talking about Beth, but it always seemed to take people off guard. "After my wife died, I lost my job."

Seth turned to him and examined him more closely.

"Damn. That's rough. I'm sorry."

"Thanks."

Seth rubbed the back of his neck with his hand. "Sorry if I pried. I seem to be having a problem with assuming no one else has ever had to deal with something difficult."

"No need to apologize. If I didn't want to say anything, I wouldn't. But I started realizing a couple of months ago that holding everything in wasn't exactly doing me any favors."

Seth looked at him again for a long moment. Then, like the sight of an eagle flying overhead out of nowhere, he smiled.

A full-on grin.

"What did I say?"

"Oh, it ain't you. It's more like what you just said hit home. I came here to hash out some things with Gen. You might have noticed that I was plenty ticked off with her?"

Because it seemed the guy needed an answer, Jackson nodded as he picked up another wine glass and ran a towel along its inside.

Seeming gratified that Jackson had even given him that, Seth said, "Tonight I realized that we should've brought out everything in the open a while back. Like maybe eighteen months ago."

"Letting things stew has never worked out well for me."

"Not for me, either. I've been stupid, and what's even worse is that I knew better, too. And if I would have listened to myself and actually tried to think of her needs instead of mine, I could have saved myself a lot of trouble." Mumbling to himself, he said, "Would've made things a whole lot easier for Gen, too."

There was obviously a whole lot more going on than he'd first imagined. "Do you think y'all are going to be okay?"

"No."

Jackson raised his eyebrows. "That's a pretty definite answer for a guy who came out here to try to fix things up."

"Yeah, it is." Everything in his expression shut down. "Actually, there isn't a 'y'all' anymore for the two of us. Just a lot of *what-could-have-beens*. I made a lot of mistakes that I don't know if I'll ever be able to repair."

The guy sounded low enough to be the subject of a country and western song. To his surprise, Jackson found himself wanting to help in some way. "So, what are you going to do now? Just up and leave?"

Seth stiffened. "I was, but I decided to stay a while longer."

"Why? Do you even have a plan about how you're going to fix things?" Jackson figured the question was fair game since he'd already told him plenty about his history.

"I don't know. I hadn't planned on it, but now I think I need to try to fix some things. I can't turn my back on her and pretend that I didn't just cause her a lot of heartache." Turning back to the suds in the sink, he mumbled, "If that's even possible."

Jackson was prevented from offering any more bright words of advice because both Kimmy and a string of college-age guys approached the bar at the same time.

Fifteen minutes later he announced last call. From then until close, Jackson concentrated on filling those last orders and cleaning up for the night.

After they closed, the five of them swept and mopped, took out trash, and tallied the receipts. After writing down everything as clear as possible for Gen, Jackson counted out the tips.

After Brad walked Melissa and Kimmy out, Jackson passed Seth his envelope of tips. "Here you go."

"No thanks."

"Take it. You earned it."

He shook his head again. "No way. I'm not taking money from Genevieve."

"All right. I'll put it in the safe. Thanks again. You might as well head on home and get some sleep."

But instead of rushing out, Seth stayed in the middle of the empty bar. Looking lost. "Yeah. I guess I better go."

"Hey, Seth?"

"Yeah?"

"It might not mean anything, but … take it from someone who knows. It's not too late to fix whatever's wrong between you two."

The guy pivoted on a boot to stare at him. "You think?"

"No, *I know.* If you're both alive, there's still time."

Looking pained, Seth nodded before he walked out.

After Jackson watched him get in his truck, he locked the door again, then turned off the lights. Took the night's receipts and cash and locked it in the safe in Gen's office.

He went into the bathroom and washed his face and hands and changed his shirt.

Just like he always did.

And then he set the burglar alarm and walked out into the night. There was a slight chill in the air and for once, the sky was clear. He looked up and stared at the thousands of stars twinkling back at him.

For a second, he allowed himself to think of Beth and the life he used to have.

Then he breathed deep and started walking. Realizing that he had a new life now. One that might just be all right after all.

CHAPTER 12

FROM LES LARKE'S
YOU, TOO, CAN HOST
A POKER TOURNEY:

*Though books and videos are helpful, I can
promise that nothing beats experience. Even
when you lose, you can still learn something.*

Sunday Morning

The knock came again on her front door, not ten seconds after it had come the first time. The voice came through loud and clear, too.

"Genevieve, open up."

"I don't take orders from you, Seth." And, yes, she was standing on the other side of the door yelling at him.

"Don't be like that. You know I'm not ordering you to do anything. I just want to talk."

"It doesn't feel that way. You're sounding really bossy." He was also sounding a little desperate. Kind of the way *she* was feeling.

"Calling me bossy instead of a son of a bitch is good, darling," he drawled. "I call that progress."

Only he could make her so mad and so … so turned on. It was that drawl's fault.

"Please, baby?"

She was melting. She really was. But she needed to be tougher if she was ever going to protect herself. "Don't call me baby."

"All right. Can I call you darlin' instead?"

She stared at the wood, slightly flummoxed. How that man could tease her after last night's conversation was beyond her.

But maybe that's why she used to love him. Picturing how he must look, she could practically see him smiling at the door. She was kind of afraid she would start smiling, too. She was tempted.

But if they got face-to-face, she would lose her gumption. She was sure of it. Taking a deep breath, she forced herself to say the right words, even though they tasted like cheap gin in her mouth. "I think you need to leave."

"I'm not going to." Before she could respond, he continued in a much softer voice. "Gen, I know you're upset with me. I know we have history. I know you're hurting. But all that means is that you need to give me a chance."

"It doesn't. It means that we need to give each other a break."

"People are passing by. I see them staring, too. They're wondering what the hell I'm doing out here. You're gonna cause talk, you know."

It was unbelievable how he so neatly transferred the blame to her shoulders instead of his. "Let them talk. And if they do, I'll just go ahead and tell them to—" She cut herself off before she really went down the deep end. Because what was between them had nothing to do with neighbors talking. She knew that, and he did, too.

Standing there, staring at her front door, Gen wondered if she was ever going to do what she really wanted. Was she ever going to finally stop the noise that was in her head and listen to her heart?

And for that matter, was that what her heart was hoping for? To have to avoid Seth Parks for the rest of her life?

No. She didn't know a lot, but she'd learned over the last two years that life was too hard to *not* give people second chances. Maybe she needed to heed that lesson and for once actually do the right thing. She needed to stop running, stop avoiding what was hard and face it.

She needed to face Seth. After taking a breath, she called out, "You know what? Fine. I'm going to let you in, but you're only staying ten minutes."

"Okay. Let me in, Gen."

She unlocked the deadbolt and turned the handle. And there he was. Six feet, two inches of muscles, brawn, dark looks, and almost-perfection. He was wearing an old light gray T-shirt that most would probably find too tight.

She did not.

His old jeans were so faded they were almost white where the fabric fit him snugly. Some might find them out of style.

She did not.

His hair was a little too long, curling at the ends. He needed to shave, like yesterday. His lips looked slightly chapped. He was a mess.

She happened to think he was also gorgeous.

Which meant that he was also dangerous for her to be around.

And it was only almost-perfection because there was no way she was going to allow herself to think about him in any other way but flawed. Imagining him as perfect had only given her hours of hurt.

He walked through the door and simply stared at her. "Okay? Are we okay?"

She nodded. "Yeah. I think so."

"Good."

She turned on her barefoot heel and led the way to her small sitting room and sat down. Then, on purpose, didn't say a single word, because she didn't know what to say.

Seth sat down across from her, leaned his elbows on his knees, and studied her for a long moment.

"Girl, you love hard."

Out of all the things he could have thought to say to her, that was what he chose to say? "What?"

"You love hard. Never halfway. Of course you were going to mourn for our baby."

He went there? Without waiting even a couple of seconds to warm up to the topic? "Stop." She jumped to her feet.

"I'm not going to stop. We need to talk about this."

"No, we don't."

"Okay. How about this? I need to talk about it. I'm going crazy, thinking about you handling all of this alone while I was just out doing my thing." His voice thickened, like each word was made of glass and they were hurting him to speak. "The guilt is killing me."

"You don't have anything to feel guilty about."

"I should have been there by your side."

She couldn't think about it. Couldn't think about how it might have felt to not be alone. To have had someone else to lean on. "You didn't know. You can't fault yourself for that."

"What happened? Would you at least share what happened with me?"

"I already told you. We had sex. I got pregnant."

"I know I was out of town, but I sure wish you would've called me."

"At first, I really couldn't believe it. I think I took seven pregnancy tests."

"I would've done the same thing." The corners of his eyes crinkled. "I mean, I would've been in shock."

Seeing that smile, her body eased some. That was something they'd always had in common. They liked to be in charge. Liked to plan. Didn't like to ever be unprepared. She realized then that an unplanned pregnancy would have set him off just as much as it had her. Not because he would've blamed her … but because it had happened out of his control.

"When I got in to see the doctor, she confirmed I was probably eight weeks pregnant." She scanned his face. "Not very far along at all. I went home with about a dozen little brochures and a prescription for prenatal vitamins. I couldn't believe it."

"So?"

"So, I knew I had to tell you, but I wanted to be ready when I told you. Because I knew you were going to have questions. I knew you were going to want to make plans right away, and I wasn't ready for that."

"I would like to think I wouldn't have been such a jerk and pushed you, but I might have."

Worrying about his reaction and what he would want to do with their relationship had scared her. "I decided to give myself a week. I was going to read the pamphlets, start taking those vitamins, and drink more milk. I had a plan."

"And you don't even like milk."

She chuckled. "My first gallon of milk was chocolate." It was almost kind of nice sharing this part of the story with him. The rest of it was so hard, she hadn't let herself remember how she'd felt the first time she went to Kroger with a baby in mind.

"Like for kids."

"Yeah." She sighed. "Then, like I told you, I started having cramps in the middle of the night. That's when I realized I was bleeding."

"What did you do?"

"I drove myself to the hospital."

He closed his eyes. "I still hate that you were alone."

It had been rough. She'd been hurting and bleeding and scared to death. "When the emergency room doctor examined me, he said that I had lost the baby. That I'd had a miscarriage." Afraid to look at him, she gazed at her hands, which were tightly clenched on her lap. "They kept me overnight. Well, until around four o'clock the next afternoon to make sure I was okay. And then I went home."

She'd gone home, taken one look at that chocolate milk in the refrigerator and the vitamins on the kitchen counter and dissolved into tears. Cried all night.

"Genevieve."

She lifted her chin. Forced herself to meet his eyes. "What?"

He didn't look mad. His expression looked carefully blank. "I wish you would've called then."

"I couldn't." How could she have looked into his eyes and absorbed his disappointment?

"I'll rephrase. Why didn't you trust me enough to know I wouldn't hurt you?"

"Because then I would have had to look into your eyes and tell you that I wasn't good enough. That there was something wrong with me." Her voice cracked, revealing that she wasn't even close to being okay, or feeling good enough, or being anything that she would have hoped to be with him.

But then it didn't matter anymore, because he was on his feet and pulling her into his arms.

"Seth—"

"Shh. I know. You hate me. I should have known better. You're right." He was saying everything she'd thought about him. Making her realize that she'd been hurting so much that she hadn't had the energy to think about anyone else.

It made her feel a little cold. Like she could have done something different. Been different. Been better.

But he still pulled her closer.

Maybe in another time, on another day, she would have stiffened in his arms or even pushed him away. Instead, she relaxed against him. Wrapped her arms around his waist and held on tight. "I'm sorry," she whispered.

"There ain't nothing to be sorry for."

"I made a lot of mistakes." She'd had secrets. She'd been angry with him. Really angry.

Actually, she'd done so much wrong.

"I made mistakes, too. The biggest one was letting you get away. I should have held on to you. Been braver. Been better. Told you that I loved you no matter what."

"You loved me?"

"I did."

"Even though we weren't good for each other, I loved you, too."

"Gen, last night, after I got home from the bar, I thought about us. Thought about how I needed to see you even when I was so upset." His voice thickened. "That's when I realized something."

"What?"

"That my feelings for you never left. I grew up and got smarter, but I couldn't forget how things were between us."

She hadn't been able to forget either.

The two of them had been good sometimes, too. She'd spent so much of her life alone. She'd learned the hard way not to depend on other people, not to let her guard down ... and then she'd met Seth.

"What are you saying, Seth?"

"That I'm pretty sure I still love you."

Oh, those words. They still made her get choked up. "Seth—"

"I know you're confused and probably angry and who knows what else. But I'm determined to win you back, Gen."

Gen gaped at him. Realized that maybe, just maybe, he wasn't the only one who still had feelings.

For a split second, she even thought about stepping away. Shielding herself from further pain. But then what would she do?

There was only so much pain and heartache one woman could bear.

"Just because you think you still love me … it doesn't mean that we're okay."

"I'm still going to stick around."

"We might still argue."

He smiled down at her. "At least we'll be together," he murmured.

"Seth …"

But she couldn't say another word because he kissed her … hard. Kissed her like he was afraid to let her go.

Before she knew what she was doing, she let her arms drift up and hold him tight. Kissed him back.

Because right then, right there? Being in his arms and kissing him back was enough.

CHAPTER 13

FROM LES LARKE'S
YOU, TOO, CAN HOST
A POKER TOURNEY:

*Even if you aren't 100 percent sure how to play
poker, it's best to appear confident. As host, you
set the mood and influence the actions of the
other players. If you play too tentatively, everyone
around you will, too.*

Two Weeks Later

Dani had given in to Jeremy's baseball dreams. Maybe she was
fooling herself, or just too weak to face reality, but she'd told
Jeremy that he could try out for the Bridgeport Bats.

He'd been elated and extremely thankful. She'd been so happy
to see a glimmer of his old self, Dani had laughed when he'd
volunteered to start doing all the dishes and her laundry, too.

"All you need to do is try your best," she'd said. That was
the truth, too. All she needed was for him to be happy again. As
she'd expected, he'd been drafted quickly and was now part of two
teams. His middle school team and the intensive club team.

Then, practically the next night, reality had set in.

Already she was kicking herself for being so stupid and not

actually thinking things through. The Bats organization wasn't just a lot more work for Jeremy, his being on the roster meant *a whole lot* more work, money, and time from her.

Baseball had suddenly become the bane of her existence. Oh, not watching Jeremy play—that was often the highlight of her day.

It was everything else that came with it. The practices that ran late. The practice uniforms that always needed washing, the other parents, who were very nice, but seemingly oblivious about how much "just" a hundred dollars meant to a single working mom.

Because the practices had started running later and Jackson had to work, and Kate had become one of her primary sources of income, Dani had also started to simply take Kate with her to the practice field.

That meant she got the three-year-old a little bit earlier most days and was dragging around a tote bag of activities for the little girl to play with during the practices. She'd also had to have a bigger variety of snacks for both her fourteen-year-old and a tiny girl.

During the practices, Kate was a good girl. She seemed to love being outside and playing so much. But all that time playing outside meant she got dirty. So that meant more laundry, since she wasn't going to make Jackson deal with extra dirty little girl outfits because of her schedule.

All of this extra time and energy was taking a toll on her school work. She was simply too exhausted by the time Jeremy was asleep to do much besides put clothes into the dryer and open a textbook. But the last two evenings, she'd fallen asleep at Jackson's kitchen table.

Just like she'd done that night.

Jackson letting himself in had woken her up with a start. When she'd heard the door click, she'd cried out and almost knocked over a chair when she'd stumbled to her feet.

Then, seeing him standing in front of her, looking concerned and uneasy, she felt like crying. "I'm so sorry," she blurted.

Instead of glaring at her, Jackson motioned her to sit back down, then pulled out the chair across from her. "Sorry for what?" he drawled. "Falling asleep again?"

Again. Boy, could she feel any worse? "I'm so sorry, I know you pay me to watch your daughter. Not fall asleep while she's under my care."

"Um, Dani, believe it or not, I sleep at night, too." He narrowed his eyes. "Did you really think I would get upset if you fell asleep?"

Now she was making him sound like some kind of ogre. "No. I mean, of course not. I like staying awake for you, though." She waved a distracted hand over her books. "Plus, I've got all this schoolwork. I need to get it done or I'll have to take an incomplete for the class. I don't know what's going on with me."

"I do," he said gently. "You're exhausted."

"I guess I am." She was on the verge of apologizing again but stopped herself. Honestly, there was nothing else she could say.

Pure compassion filled his gaze. "I feel bad about making you take my daughter all afternoon and evening. How about I ask around and see if someone else can watch Kate from time to time? My buddy Kurt's fiancée is a high school teacher. She might know of a teenage girl to look after her a few nights a month."

"No!" Realizing she'd practically yelled that, she rushed to soften her response. "I mean, it's okay, Jackson. I'm just getting my bearings." Because he was still looking at her intently, she said, "I wasn't expecting Jeremy's schedule to be so crazy. Um, as soon as I get used to it, things will get easier."

"Maybe I can help. What's kicking your butt?"

The honest, blunt question made her laugh—and maybe

made her be a little more honest than she intended. "The pressure of Jeremy being part of the Bridgeport Bats."

"What's been going on?"

"Nothing that I shouldn't have expected," she said with a wry twist of her lips. "Extra practices that never seem to end on time, the long games, eating on the go, tons of laundry, and an amazing amount of money that's needed for everything from practice bags to batting cage times."

"That's a lot."

Feeling weak, she nodded. "That's not even counting his regular team or school."

"Or your job cleaning houses."

Yep, that too. "I'll figure it out."

"Dani, you should have told me about just how much you've been doing."

"Why? It's my problem, not yours."

"You help me with Kate, honey. I can help you with Jeremy, too."

No, he *paid* her to help with Kate. And she needed every penny of that. If he started doing her favors, she'd feel obligated to do the same for him.

Standing up, she stretched her arms. "Thanks, but I've got it."

Getting to his feet as well, he placed a hand on her arm. "Dani, let me help." Searching her face, he said, "Do you need to borrow some money for all those fees?"

"Of course not."

His mouth thinned into a line. "I hate to think of you working yourself to the bone like this. Have you talked to the coach?"

"About what?"

"About getting financial assistance. There's always funds available for kids who need a little bit of financial help."

She gaped at him. "Really?"

"Yeah. Really. We had kids on our teams back in West Virginia that needed a helping hand from time to time. No one thought anything about it."

Dani didn't think this Bridgeport team had the same kind of setup. But how could she tell Jackson that? He really was trying so hard to help.

Pinning a smile on her face, she said, "Thanks for letting me know. I'll, um, ask Coach Edwards if there's a fund for people like me." Boy, even saying the words felt like she was swallowing Ajax.

"There's no shame in being a widow on a budget, Dani," he said softly.

She supposed not, but as far as she was concerned, she felt like she was raising her boy to always be aware of how much she couldn't do for him.

Making up her mind, Dani nodded. "Thanks for the idea. I'll give the coach a call tomorrow." Or she'd email him. That might be easier.

Of course, she was still going to have to figure out how to get Jeremy to all of his practices. But that was a problem for another day, right?

He looked at her curiously. "How come you don't look any happier?"

"I am."

"But?"

Pride meant that she didn't want to tell him the rest of her troubles. But the late night and his kindness loosened her tongue. "Jackson, there's a ton of practices. The other mothers carpool, but with my schedule, that's kind of hard to do."

"So you need help driving him."

"I do. I mean no, I don't." Feeling rattled, she blurted, "I can handle it."

"I'll help. I *want* to help."

"Jackson, that's kind of you, but you pay me to watch your little girl, remember? I know how much you work."

"I'll figure something out. I'll ask Ace and Kurt if they have any ideas." Looking at her intently, he said, "The important thing is that you remember that you aren't alone. You might not have a mess of family around, but you have friends. Lots of friends."

She chuckled. "You're making it sound so easy."

"That's 'cause it is." He paused, then said, "You could also tell Jeremy that you aren't sure if he can continue."

Even thinking about saying such a thing made tears form in her eyes. "I can't do that. He needs this, Jackson."

"He needs you. I promise, it's okay if you tell him that he can't always get everything he wants."

"He already knows that." Her boy had a childhood filled with frequent moves and ended with his father dying. There was no way she was going to let Jeremy deal with one more disappointment if she could help it.

"He loves baseball that much?"

She nodded. "He's also that good."

"Then that is what matters." Reaching out, he took hold of one of her hands in between both of his own. "You're right. Everyone needs a dream to reach for, don't you think?"

Before she even realized she was doing it, Dani shook her head.

Smiling softly, Jackson stepped closer and gently kissed her on the lips. After staring at her for a moment longer, he smiled. "Let's get you out of here."

Feeling stunned by both the kiss and how she felt about it, Dani quickly gathered her things and shoved them in her canvas tote bag. "Good night."

"I'll walk you up."

When he held out his hand, she handed over the tote and then quietly walked by his side out his door and up the stairs. After she unlocked her door, he stepped in and turned on her light.

And then kissed her again before pulling her into a warm hug. Before Dani realized she was doing it, she rested her head against his chest and wrapped her arms around his middle.

"It'll be okay, Dani," he murmured against her hair. "I promise."

She didn't know how it could be, or how Jackson could make such a promise.

But right then, standing in his arms, she almost believed he was right.

When he pulled away, she pressed a hand to his chest. Finally looked up into his eyes. "Jackson?" They'd kissed several times now. Didn't that mean something? Did they need to talk about what had just happened?

He ran a hand down her back. "Don't worry anymore. Not tonight. 'Kay?"

Out of words, she simply nodded.

Looking pleased, he smiled. "Night, Dani. Get some sleep, sweetheart," he said as he turned and walked back down the stairs.

"Night," she murmured. Trying to recall the last time anyone had listened to her complain but didn't offer judgments. Or, the last time anyone had kissed her, held her, or called her sweetheart.

When was the last time Brian had done those things? Maybe before their last move? Before he got his new job?

She couldn't remember.

No, the only thing that seemed to come to mind was the knowledge that it had been far too long.

CHAPTER 14

FROM LES LARKE'S
*YOU, TOO, CAN HOST
A POKER TOURNEY:*

*Determine ahead of time the desired intensity
of your poker group. Some guys are real sticklers
for doing everything by the rules, which can get
tense. It's up to you to set the tone.*

Sunday

It was nice to think about someone else. As Jackson drove up
Highway 48, curving around a grouping of five clapboard houses
that had recently been remodeled, it occurred to him that he'd
been solely focused on himself of late. Maybe for too long.

Though he knew he should give himself a break—after all,
losing one's wife and job in the space of eight months was a lot
for even the strongest person to handle—he was starting to think
that he'd fostered that self-pity a bit too long. Like two years too
long. Dwelling on his hardships hadn't done either himself or
Kate much good.

Accepting all of his friends' help and sympathy hadn't
helped him in the long run, either. He'd stopped wondering

what problems they might have been dealing with. Almost as if no one could have a problem if they weren't dealing with a spouse's death.

But whatever the reason, it was only after meeting Dani that he'd realized just how much he'd been living in his own particular circle of hell. Worse, he'd almost been feeling justified about being there.

Usually, all this reflection would make him wonder what advice Beth would have given him. But he didn't need to look that far. No, he realized that both of his parents had been hinting quite a bit that it was time to get over himself. Yes, he'd had some traumas. But he wasn't alone in missing either Beth or his job.

"Daddy, we gonna see Finn today?" Kate called out from the back seat, bringing him back to the present.

He glanced back at her in the rearview mirror. "I don't think so, baby. We're going over to see Kurt and Sam and Emily."

"Daddy, you can't call me baby anymore."

Boy, his girl always had something on her mind. "Why ever not?"

"'Cause Miss Dani says I'm a big girl now."

"She did, did she?"

"Uh-huh, 'cause I don't have any more accidents and I'm going to be in preschool before I know it."

He couldn't help it, he burst out laughing. "You're right, sweetheart. You are a big girl now." And Lord help him if he ever had to go through the perils of little girl potty training on his own again. Sweet Kate had taken a small eternity to get the hang of it after the move, and every setback had involved lots of emergency baths, showers, and loads of laundry.

As for preschool? He could hardly believe it was looming.

"Sweetheart?"

"I'm not a sweetheart neither."

109

He chuckled. "You don't like that name either?"

"Nope. My name is Kate, Daddy. Kathryn Elizabeth."

"It sure is." Boy, if she was this bossy now, what was she going to be like when she was fourteen?

Luckily, he wasn't going to have to worry about that for a while. "We're here," he said as he pulled into Kurt's driveway.

"Yay!"

"If I'm not mistaken, your buddy Finn is, too."

She craned her neck to look out the window. "Really?"

"Yep."

"Hurry, Daddy."

After grabbing his cell phone, he reached in and released the straps of her car seat. Just as she was about to scramble out, he leaned close. "Hold on, Kate."

She stilled. "Yes?"

"Don't forget to be a good girl now, you hear?"

"Yes, Daddy."

Swinging her to the ground, he reached for her hand. "Come on, let's see where everyone is."

Pointing to where Kurt, Emily, Ace, and Troy were standing on Kurt's front porch, she called out, "There they are!"

"There's my girl," Kurt called out. "Looking so pretty today, too."

Kate giggled. "Hi, Mr. Kurt!" As soon as Jackson released her hand, she charged forward, hugging Kurt's knee before he could kneel down to give her a proper hug.

After she left Kurt's side and said hello to Emily and Troy, she hurried over to see Sam and Finn.

Kurt straightened and shook Jackson's hand. "Good to see you, buddy. Glad you stopped by. Em and I were just talking about going downtown tonight. Want to join us?"

"Downtown Cincinnati? Where, Over the Rhine?"

Emily chuckled. "You know I'll never get Kurt that far. We're just going to downtown Bridgeport."

"What do you say?" Kurt asked. "Kate's welcome, of course."

"Or, do you have to work?" Troy asked.

"No, I don't have to work tonight. Let me think about it, though. I've been putting in a lot of hours. I was thinking about staying home with Kate."

"All right."

After double-checking that the teenagers were all right with Kate tagging along after them, Jackson took a seat next to Ace and Troy. "What have y'all been up to today?"

"Making a picnic table," Troy said.

"What?"

Kurt groaned. After looking like he was making sure the space was clear, he lowered his voice. "Em started telling me how she'd always wanted a picnic table. She was gonna go to Home Depot and take one of those classes."

"She and Campbell were going to construct it together," Troy said.

"So, how did it go from that to y'all building it together?"

"I'm not gonna sit around and watch my fiancée build a table," Kurt muttered.

Jackson laughed.

"What's so funny?" Troy asked.

"Only that you just bought yourself a world of hurt. You took their project away. She pissed?"

"No." Looking out for Emily again, Kurt mumbled. "Maybe a little."

"Maybe a lot," Ace said, grinning. "She's covering it up real good for you, but before y'all got here, she and Campbell were having a minor meltdown about how we took their project away and weren't even doing a very good job of it."

"Guess we arrived at the perfect time."

Kurt fished out another bottle of water and drank half of it. "I'm hoping Emily will cool down presently. What do you think my chances are of that happening?"

Jackson wobbled a hand. "Fair to middling."

Kurt grunted. "Did you come over here to offer relationship advice or help build?"

"I'll be pleased to do both, but I actually came to ask you a favor." Looking at all three of them, he added, "Come to think of it, I could use some help from all of you."

"Name it," Troy said immediately.

Ace's expression turned worried. "What's going on? Do you need a loan or something?"

"No, this time, the favor isn't for me. It's for Dani, the gal who watches Kate."

Ace's expression sharpened. "I know who Dani is. Doesn't she live in your apartment complex, too?"

"Yeah. I mean, she lives in the apartment above me." Thinking it would be best to simply dive on in, he continued, "See, here's the thing. She also lost her spouse. Plus she has a fourteen-year-old, so she's a single mom."

"Man, that's hard," Troy said.

Jackson nodded. "I know it's been real hard. Especially because her man didn't have any life insurance to speak of. He left her without a cushion."

Ace leaned forward, resting his elbows on his knees. "So, money's tight."

"Really tight. Dani cleans houses during the day, runs Jeremy around after school, then watches Kate for me in the evenings." Thinking of how that woman never did anything just for fun, he added, "She's also been taking come college courses online. She works on those late at night."

"So she never sleeps," Kurt said.

"Not much. Not enough." Looking at the three other men, seeing the sympathy in their eyes, Jackson felt himself relax slightly.

Not because they understood what he was getting at, but because he knew they understood people like Dani. All of them had grown up without a lot of money. Their fathers worked long shifts in the mine and their mothers did odd jobs in order to pay for extras.

Each of them had grown up being expected to do chores, take care of younger siblings, and take care of themselves. No one was sitting at home, waiting for them to get off the school bus. Instead, they'd let themselves inside.

"What does she need, Cookie?" Troy asked.

"Oh, sorry. Her boy Jeremy is a good enough baseball player to join the Bridgeport Bats. It's a club team."

Their expressions cleared.

"Let me guess," Troy said, "playing for the Bats costs an arm and a leg."

"At least," Jackson muttered.

"She also didn't think about saying no," Ace murmured.

"And she's having trouble paying for it," Kurt said.

"Yes, to all of what y'all just said." Jackson sighed. "Jeremy's a good kid. I've already gotten the impression that he's gotten used to not asking for anything, especially if it means that his mother's going to have to do without."

"But he's a kid who's already lost his father," Kurt said.

"And his mom's sweet enough to run herself ragged trying to let him be on the team. I'm worried about her. The coach is holding practices three times a week, plus there's an expectation for the kid to go to the batting cages weekly, too."

"Which ain't cheap," Ace said. He rubbed a hand along the

scruff on his cheeks. "Lord knows I've had to figure out how to get Finn to special coaching sessions over the years. It all helps, but that help always costs something."

Jackson nodded. "Exactly."

"Has she talked to the coach?" Ace asked. "If Dani tells him how things are, he might cut some money off of her dues."

Troy nodded. "If he's that good, they'll call it scholarship money."

"She said she would, and I'm sure the coach will help as much as he can. But we all know that there are other expenses, too. Like I said, she's got some pride involved. I know Jeremy already feels different from the other boys, seeing as how he's the only one who doesn't have a dad."

"I can understand that," Ace murmured.

"I told Dani that I'd help run Jeremy places, but she didn't seem real excited to take me up on that. And, to be honest, I don't have that much extra time in the evenings. That's when she needs help the most."

Now that he'd put it all on the table, Jackson turned to Kurt. "I thought maybe Sam might need to do some community hours or something. Maybe he could help with one of the weekly practices? Or I could pay him."

Kurt shook his head. "You don't need to pay him. I'm sure Sam will help, but I don't know how often he'd be able to. He's working a lot of hours to have spending money for college. Plus, he's got Kayla."

Troy leaned forward, resting his elbows on his knees. "Oh, hell. We can all step up. I can't think of the number of times my momma had to call around to get me picked up from one practice or another. I'll be happy to run the kid around from time to time."

Kurt nodded. "And we can all chip in to pay for his fees and uniforms, too."

Jackson nodded his thanks. "I appreciate it, especially seeing as how y'all wouldn't know her or her boy if they knocked on your door."

"It's nothing," Ace said gruffly. "Don't think anything of it. It's good to hear about a woman sacrificing so much for her kid. Not every mother does."

Jackson knew Ace was referring to his boy Finn's mother, whose priorities weren't always her boy. Her neglect was one of the reasons Ace had moved Finn to Bridgeport. "Again, thank you. But if it was just a matter of paying for things, I would have done it. I don't have a lot of extra, but I could help Dani and Jeremy out without hurting. But she isn't one to accept charity."

Troy waved a hand. "I'll talk to her." Brightening, he said, "I'll say that my company wants to help sponsor the team."

Thinking about Dani, about how private she was, Jackson knew if Troy showed up and started steamrolling her, she would get pretty flustered. "I was thinking maybe the Social Club could do something."

Kurt's expression sharpened. "Like how? Ask for a donation next time we play?"

"Maybe make a percentage of the pot go toward an anonymous family in need?"

"Do you think she would accept some financial help that way?"

"I think so," Jackson said slowly. "Especially if I told her that the Social Club does things like this from time to time."

"Except that we don't," Ace murmured.

"But we could, right?" Troy asked as he sat up a little straighter. "Maybe we should." Glancing at Kurt, he continued. "Maybe we should think about doing something more. Hell, how about this? Twice a year we could hold an extra tournament and give the winnings to a local family needing an extra hand."

"That sounds good, but what do you think all the other guys would say?" Ace asked. "Some of them only come for the chance to make a few bucks."

"But a whole lot more guys show up because it's an easy night out with the guys," Troy pointed out. "They'll put forty or fifty bucks in the pot just for that. I'm sure of it."

Jackson liked the idea, but he didn't want to push something on an old friend who'd been nothing but nice to him. "What do you think, Kurt? Do you want to think about this? You can let me know in a day or two."

"I don't need any time, Cookie. If the BSC has a way to help a kid play ball, then I want to help."

Jackson was starting to feel optimistic but wanted to be sure. "Really? You don't think you're gonna get crap for it from the rest of the guys?"

"I don't really care. I started this social club. I think that means I have some say in how it's run." Kurt smiled. "As far as I'm concerned, we can do anything we want, 'cause it all takes place in my garage."

"Thanks a lot. I knew I could count on y'all." Already he was thinking of a way he could tell her. "As soon as I talk things through with Dani, I'll let you know."

Troy rolled his eyes. "No way. You'll wait too long and that kid and his mom have dues to pay right now. Call her up."

"It ain't that easy."

"Sure it is," Troy said. "We're all friends."

"Bring her on over for a barbecue soon," Kurt said before Jackson could get in another word. "And before you start saying that she could be uncomfortable, we'll ask the girls to come over too. They'll be happy to do that."

"Finn and his girlfriend Allison will be here. That should take care of Kate."

"Ask her soon, Cookie," Kurt said. "The only way we can get this rolling is by getting her okay."

"I hear you," Jackson said. Now all he had to do was find a time that she could come over to Kurt's to talk.

He hoped he didn't mess this up.

CHAPTER 15

FROM LES LARKE'S
YOU, TOO, CAN HOST
A POKER TOURNEY:

*Be sure to have a tasty array of snacks for everyone
to munch on. Popular choices are vegetable sticks,
minisandwiches, and tortilla chips.*

Tuesday

"Dani, I'm getting the feeling that you've been avoiding me,"
Reed Moore said as he entered his living room.

Dani gritted her teeth as he stepped on his pure white carpet
with his shoes. Why people bought carpet like this and then never
treated it well was a mystery.

Almost as much as why a rich man like him would be creeping
on a thirty-three-year-old cleaning woman in old shorts and a
T-shirt. "I'm not avoiding anything," she said as she continued to
wipe the chrome shelves that lined an entire wall. "Just trying to
get my work done, sir."

He smirked. "We already talked about you calling me that.
Call me Reed."

Oh, she really did not want to. Keeping her eyes firmly on her work, she murmured, "It's better if we keep things professional, Mr. Moore."

"Better how?" He stepped closer, causing her instincts to send out alarm signals. "You clean my house. That's personal. I think that means we know each other pretty well."

No, that meant she knew he never vacuumed and had a big collection of dirty magazines. Looking at him at last, she said, "Mr. Moore, I'm sorry but I can't talk right now. I've got to get this room done. I'm on a pretty tight schedule today." Pulling out her dust rag, she walked to the other side of the couch. She needed to keep as much space in between the two of them as possible.

"For what?" He looked at his designer watch. "It's only a quarter to eleven. I know your kid doesn't get home for hours."

She hated that he knew that she had a child. Hated that he even knew that much of her schedule. Reminding herself that she had groceries to buy and bills to pay, she started wiping down the shelves faster. "I have another house to clean."

"I'll pay you for the time you missed." When she turned back at him in shock, he grinned. "You can hang out here all afternoon. You'll never miss the money."

It felt like her ears were bleeding, she was so offended. But maybe she'd misunderstood? "What are you suggesting that we do all afternoon?"

"Come on, we're both adults." His voice was impatient now. Harder.

She was beginning to go from irritated to scared. "I think I'd better leave."

Just as she turned to walk out of the room, he grabbed her arm. "Dani, if you walk out of this room right now, you're going to really regret it."

"If I stay here another second I'm going to regret it even

more." She yanked on her arm. He was gripping it really tight now. "I suggest you take your hand off of me. Now."

After another small tug, he dropped his hand, looking like she was tainted. "Go on then. Hurry out, but don't expect to be paid."

Dani bit her tongue before she did something stupid and told him exactly what she felt about men like him. Dropping the rag she'd been using on the floor, she walked to the door.

She slipped on her old Keds, picked up her basket of cleaning supplies and purse, and rushed out the door. Her heart was racing as she walked, each word and action of Reed Moore repeating in her brain. She'd always felt he was slightly slimy, but his actions and words today had taken his behavior to a whole new level. He'd actually grabbed her! For a moment there, she'd been afraid he wasn't going to let her go.

The moment she got into her car, she'd locked the doors, half afraid that he was going to come after her. Unable to help herself, she looked back at the house.

But the front door was still firmly shut, and all of the windows looked dark. He was nowhere to be seen. With shaking hands, she directed her car down his driveway. Thank goodness she was never going to have to see him again.

Just as she was about to head over to Mrs. Burridge's house, she glanced at the clock and realized she was way too early. Mrs. B. wasn't always home when she cleaned, but she'd told Dani more than once that she liked to completely prepare the house before she arrived. That meant she had almost two hours to kill.

Most days she would've just gone home and used the time to work on supper or to clean her own place. But there was no way that she could handle that—she was too rattled. She was also on the verge of tears.

Deciding that she needed to take a break, she headed down to

Bridgeport's Main Street. She was going out to lunch.

As she drove into downtown Bridgeport, on the way to a fast-food place, she spied a taco truck near the bike path. Deciding that option sounded a whole lot better than a burger, she parked on the side and then joined the crowd in line.

"Dani?"

She turned to see Jackson, Kate, and another man had just walked up behind her. It took a minute, but she smiled brightly. "Hi, guys. This is a nice surprise."

"Hi, Miss Dani!"

Reaching down, she gave Kate a quick hug. "Hi, good to see you, Kate." She could practically feel Jackson's gaze sweep over her ... and suddenly realized that she wasn't exactly dressed for being seen in public. "Don't look at me," she teased. "I look a fright. I'm in the middle of my workday."

Obviously thinking they were playing a new game, Kate closed her eyes as she started bobbing on the balls of her feet. "Where should I look now?"

Jackson put a hand on his little girl's shoulder. "That's just an expression and you can look anywhere you like." Turning back to her, he said, "And don't be silly, Dan. You look fine."

Protesting again would just make her seem vain. "I was going to run through the drive-through, but this sounded too good."

"We thought so, too. By the way, this is Troy. He's one of my friends from Spartan."

"Hi, Dani," he said, holding out his hand. "I've heard a lot of good things about you, both from Kate and Jackson."

"It's nice to meet you. And it's good to hear I'm getting positive reports about my babysitting."

Troy smiled. "Not just about your babysitting."

Smiling back at him, Dani blushed. Troy looked like he should be in a Hollywood movie or something, he was so good-looking. He was easily almost as handsome as Jackson. "What are you guys up to today?"

"Since I'm not working tonight, Kate and I are making a day of it. We went to the park this morning."

She was prevented from replying when the people in front of her moved away and it was time to order. After ordering two fish tacos and an iced tea, she got out her wallet.

"We've got this, Dani," Jackson said.

"Are you sure?"

"It's seven dollars. I'm sure."

"Thanks."

After they ordered and their numbers were called up, Troy said, "Come sit down and join us."

"Are you sure? I don't want to impose."

"We're positive," Jackson said easily, giving her another long look.

She walked by their side to a picnic table a little down the way. After they all sat down, and Jackson placed Kate's quesadilla in front of her, they started eating.

And boy, was it good! Especially after the morning she'd had. She really did need to remember the benefits of treating herself every now and then.

"So, I don't usually see you in town during the day. Did one of your houses get canceled?"

"No. I left one of them early and had almost two hours to kill before I went to another house."

Just as Jackson was about to nod, his eyes narrowed. "Wait a minute. Something doesn't sound right in your voice. Did something happen?"

Though she meant to shrug off his concern, his kindness triggered all the emotion and fear she'd been feeling just a short hour ago. "I had kind of a strange situation this morning. I had to get out of there." Her eyes widened. Shoot! She sounded like she was on the verge of crying.

"What happened?" Troy asked.

After peeking at Kate, who was playing with Jackson's phone and eating her lunch, she said, "My morning house belongs to a married couple, but the wife is the one who works full time. The husband is the one who takes care of the house."

Jackson nodded. "Okay ... and you have a problem with that?"

"With the man staying home? No! Of course not. It's um, this man in particular." She picked up a chip and dipped it into the fresh salsa that Troy had put in the center of the table.

Troy looked at her intently. "What's wrong with him?"

Dani glanced at Kate again. Reassured that the little girl was still playing on the phone, she said, "He's always been a jerk. But today ..." Her voice dropped off. What could she say that wouldn't make her sound weak or like she was exaggerating? She shouldn't have brought it up in the first place.

Jackson's voice hardened. "What did he do today?"

"He grabbed my arm. I thought ..." She drew in a calming breath, then whispered, "For a minute there I thought he was going to um, force himself on me."

Both men exchanged looks, and Jackson, well, Jackson looked angrier than she'd ever seen him. Honestly, he was so steady and easygoing she hadn't even imagined he could get so angry. "Are you hurt?" he asked quietly.

She shook her head. "Um, as soon as I got free I grabbed my things and got out of there. I told him I wouldn't be back."

"Did you call the police?" Troy asked.

"The police? Um, no. Like I said, I got out of there. But it kind of shook me up. Mr. Moore went from kind of creepy to really creepy in a matter of ten seconds."

"Are you sure you're okay?" Troy asked, studying her carefully. "Do you need to go to the hospital or anything?"

Dani realized then that the guys thought she was fibbing about getting away. Raising her chin a bit, she said, "Guys, I promise, I'm fine. I'm sorry I brought it up."

"Where did he grab you, Dan?" Jackson asked.

She pointed to her upper left arm. "Here." Luckily, she had on a light sweater over her T-shirt.

"Let me see."

"Here? Um, I don't think so."

"I don't want to manhandle you, but I think I need to see, Dani."

Glancing at Troy, he nodded. "No one is looking. And it's just your arm, right?"

"Right." Realizing that if she refused to show her arm it would make even a bigger deal out of the incident, she slipped off one of the sides of the cardigan and edged it down her arm.

When she bared her arm, which was actually covered in bruises, Jackson sucked in a breath. After a mumbled curse, he helped her put back on her sweater. "He grabbed you hard. Are you sure he didn't touch you anywhere else? That you're all right?"

"I promise. I'm fine. I just need to calm down."

"I think we need to get this guy's name, Jack," Troy said.

"Yeah, I do, too," Jackson said quietly. "Now, who is it? His last name is Moore, you said?"

Oh, Lord. Had she actually said that? She really needed to get a hold of herself. "I'm not going to give you his name."

But instead of looking relaxed, Jackson looked even more upset. "Did he even pay you for working today?"

"No. I ran out of there. I mean, it wasn't like he was going to pull out his wallet and pay me anyway. He was pretty mad."

"You ran out of there," he repeated. Turning to Troy, Jackson said, "I'm thinking we need to pay this guy a visit."

"Absolutely," said Troy.

"No. I mean, I don't want you guys getting involved." Looking at Troy, too, she said, "Thank you both for caring, but it's over." She took a bite of her taco.

"It's not over, Dani."

"What's not over, Daddy?" Kate piped up.

Saved by a three-year-old! "I don't know, but my lunch is," Dani said as she stood up. "I've got to get over to my next house. Troy, it was nice to meet you."

"You too, Dani."

"Bye, Kate," she said as she gave the girl a hug.

"Let me walk you to your car. Troy, do you mind watching Kate?"

"Not at all." He stood up and held out his hand to Kate. "Let's throw away our trash and go look at the slide."

The moment they were out of earshot, she said, "Jackson, you make me wish I never said a thing."

"I'm glad you did." After a pause, he said, "So what was the guy's name?"

"I don't want you calling him or going over there."

"I'm going to find out. And I am going to talk to him."

"What are you going to do, hit him?"

"No. But I am going to make sure he knows that you aren't alone."

"Jackson," she whined.

He sighed next to her car. "What would Brian have done? Would he have simply just shrugged off the fact that some shit tried to force himself on you?"

She gasped. "I can't believe you are bringing up my *dead husband!* That's low."

Jackson didn't even look perturbed. "It's not low. I'm doing whatever I can to help a friend of mine. Now, give me the truth. What would Brian have done?"

She didn't even have to think about it. "Brian would've freaked out and gone to talk to him." Honestly, she figured he might have even gotten in a fight with the guy. "But that doesn't mean you need to do anything."

"I've been around men like that." Jackson frowned. "Not rapists, but guys who forget that there are rules, lines that men don't cross. And, what I want you to know, is that men like that don't make passes at women who they know have someone looking out for them. He pulled that shit because he knew you were a single woman with a kid to support."

Maybe she was weak or shaken up, or simply figured Jackson was right, but she nodded. "I know."

"Do you really want to think about how Jeremy would take this, knowing that some man tried to violate you today? Some man at his house that you were cleaning?"

"Don't you tell Jeremy a thing. He's got enough to worry about."

His gaze sharpened on her. "Then let me help you."

"Fine. His name is Reed Moore."

"He lives here in Bridgeport?"

"Yes. But—"

He cut her off. "Kay. Thanks, Dani."

"I don't feel good about this. I just want to forget it."

"I promise, you aren't going to forget it until he's dealt with. If you pretend it didn't happen, all that's going to happen is you're going to worry in the middle of the night."

She didn't know if he was right or wrong. Maybe she would dream about Reed grabbing her. Maybe she wouldn't. But she did have a feeling she was going to think about Jackson being determined to take care of her.

"Thanks," she said at last.

Pulling her into his arms, he held her close and kissed her temple. "Thanks for letting me help you."

"Will you call me later? I'm going to be worried about you."

"Don't worry. I'll be fine." After kissing her temple again, he said, "Good luck with your next house. I'll call you tonight."

She drove away thinking that his promise to call sure sounded like a promise of something more.

CHAPTER 16

FROM LES LARKE'S
*YOU, TOO, CAN HOST
A POKER TOURNEY:*

*On the other hand, the majority of your players
may have only come for the beer.*

"No judgments, but do you reckon we ought to do some thinking about this?" Troy asked as Jackson typed Reed Moore's address into his phone.

Jackson looked over at him. "What's there to think about? It seems fairly clear to me."

Troy leaned back in his chair. "Well, one, maybe we ought to remember that Dani didn't want us to get involved."

"Someone needs to."

Troy groaned. "Cookie …"

"No, I'm serious." Every time Jackson thought about what she told them, he saw red. "He said inappropriate things to her. He grabbed her arm hard enough to form bruises. Dani was afraid he was going to do a whole lot worse. I think that about covers it, don't you?"

Troy glanced over at Kate, who was playing with a pair of little boys on the jungle gym. "I'm not saying all that isn't bad, but he didn't actually hurt her."

"She was scared enough to run out of there, Troy. She works damn hard and has obviously been putting up with his crap for a while now. At the very least, she needs to get paid."

Troy sighed. "I agree. But maybe we need to get some reinforcements."

"Like who?"

"Oh, I don't know. Kurt. Ace." He grinned. "Ace would be good. He's still built like a wall and he constantly looks like he just rolled out of bed and is pissed off about it."

Though Jackson didn't disagree, he was a little offended that Troy didn't think he was man enough to handle some rich jerk on his own. "Ace does have a scary look about him, but I'm not showing up at this guy's house with a whole posse. I just want to talk to him."

"And you think he's going to give you the time of day?"

"What are you getting at? I'm not Ace's size, but I can still handle myself. And I might only be a bartender now, but I used to have a pretty decent job, Troy."

Troy blew out a breath. "Jeez. I ain't talking about your size or your job."

"What are you talking about then?"

"That the guy can just slam the door in your face."

Thinking about that, Jackson smiled. "Even if he does that, at least he'll know that someone is looking out for Dani."

"That's enough?"

Not really. Right now, what he really wanted to do was punch the guy hard enough to give him a couple of bruises of his own.

"If that's all that happens? I won't be happy, but at least I did something."

Since Troy still looked unhappy, Jackson realized that his buddy was in a much different place than he was. Troy had gone to college and been a college football star. Now he had a successful financial planning company and a lot of important clients. He probably couldn't afford to do anything that might ruin his hard-fought reputation.

"Hey, I'm sorry. It just occurred to me that this might be a little too redneck for you."

"Last I checked, we're both from Spartan."

"I know, but you've been here in Bridgeport for a while. You don't have to go with me."

Troy leaned forward. "You think I'm going to hang back and let you go on your own?"

"I'm trying to tell you that I wouldn't blame you if you did. This isn't your problem."

"Is Dani your problem?"

"Yeah. I think she is." Actually, he was sure of it.

"If some guy put his hands on Campbell and scared her, I wouldn't even still be here talking. When do you want to go?"

"Right now. Since Dani left that house about an hour ago, the guy is probably still there." Looking over at Kate, he realized that he didn't have anywhere to take her. Kurt, Ace, and their girlfriends were all at work.

At another time, he might have asked Gen to watch her for an hour, but Gen was embroiled in her whole Seth mess. Standing up, he said, "I'm going to have to leave Kate in the car while I handle this."

"I'll stay near the car so she doesn't get scared."

Feeling better about his plan—such that it was—Jackson stood up. "Let's do this, then."

Troy grinned. "I'll go get your girl."

After they gathered up Kate and loaded her up in his truck, Jackson clicked on the GPS and they headed out. Within five minutes, Kate was passed out in the back seat. Jackson was relieved about that. He actually didn't want to get in a fight with the guy, just wanted to make sure he knew he couldn't get away with treating Dani the way he did and then just go on with his life.

Beside him, Troy was texting like he was back in high school and had a hot date coming up.

"You doing work?"

"Heck, no. I'm texting Ace and Kurt and letting them know what we're doing. Figured they ought to know in case everything goes south."

"It won't."

"Just making sure someone else knows what we're doing."

Jackson rolled his eyes but knew he would've probably done the same thing if their positions were reversed. He was pretty riled up. It was good to have friends, and he had some of the best.

Five minutes later they pulled into the driveway of a nice home on the edge of Indian Hill, an affluent area just west of Bridgeport. The house was nice but nothing special. It looked like an average middle-class home.

"Huh," Troy said. "I was imagining something fancier."

"Me, too," Jackson replied as he got out. "I'll leave the car running for Kate."

"I'll stand out here. Let me know if you need me."

"Thanks." Not wanting to give what he was about to do another moment's thought, he strode to the front door and rang the bell. After thirty seconds or so, the door opened, and he was looking at a man about his height and weight, wearing an aqua-blue nylon T-shirt and black shorts. He also had frosted blond tips on his hair and had obviously gotten his eyebrows waxed.

"Yeah?"

Jackson hated him on sight. "Are you Reed Moore?"

"I am," he said impatiently. "You got a delivery for me or something?"

Suddenly, it was all Jackson could do to not grab the guy by the collar of his shiny shirt and slam him against the door. "I stopped by to talk to you about Dani Brown."

"My maid? What about her?"

"Your maid is my girlfriend," he ground out, not even caring that he was exaggerating his relationship with her a bit. "And she just told me about her morning with you."

The guy's expression tightened before it relaxed. "What about it?"

"I saw the bruises on her arm. She told me about your offer, too."

"So what? You decided to come over here and give me a piece of your mind?" His voice was mocking.

And it grated on Jackson's last nerve. Remembering that he had Kate in the car and reminding himself that this guy wasn't anything to him, he placed his left hand on the door frame and stepped closer. "I came over to get her pay for today."

"What? I paid her."

Now he was just getting plain mad. "I wouldn't start lying to me, Mr. Moore."

"Or what?" He gestured toward Troy. "You going to get your buddy over here to talk to me, too?"

Almost before he realized he was doing it, Jackson had the guy pinned against the door. "Or I'm going to make sure you're going to have a real good story to tell your wife when she gets home from work."

The guy whimpered. "I've got her money in the kitchen." After Jackson released him, he said, "I'll be right back."

Jackson smiled as he stepped inside. "We're going to go together."

"No. Wait. I mean, I have my wallet right here." Next thing Jackson knew, he was slipping three twenties into his palm. "Here."

He kept his palm out. "That's it? Are you sure? Because if Dani says you usually pay her more, I'm going to be back tonight."

"Fine. Here." He held out two more twenties.

Jackson stared at him, feeling nothing but contempt for the man. Then he turned away and started walking back to his truck.

"Wait! That's it?" Reed Moore called out.

"Yep," Jackson said. He didn't want to waste another word on the guy.

By the time he buckled his seat belt, Troy was laughing. "For a minute there, I thought you were going to lay one on that guy."

Now that they were driving back, Jackson grinned. "I almost did. He was a real jerk."

"You get Dani's money?"

"Oh, yeah." He chuckled softly as he quietly told Troy what happened. By the time he dropped Troy off at his truck, Kate woke up.

"Daddy, are we going home now?"

"Yep. But first we're going to pick up some ice cream and flowers for Miss Dani. We're going to take them over to her tonight."

"How come we're gonna do that? Because she's our friend?"

"Yep. Because she's our friend."

And because he was now sure that she was so much more.

* * *

Just after seven that night, Jackson had Kate by his side and they were knocking on Dani's door. They had their hands full, too. He'd wanted to do something for Dani and figured that flowers and ice cream might do the trick. Beth had always appreciated both.

Jeremy opened the door. "Hey, Jackson. Hey, wait. Are those for Mom?"

Kate stepped forward, holding a plastic Kroger bag in both of her hands. "Uh-huh. Hi, Jeremy!"

He smiled. "Hey, Kate." Looking back up at Jackson, the boy's voice was noticeably cooler. "What are the flowers for?"

"I thought she might like them," Jackson said, feeling strangely self-conscious. "Is she around?"

Jeremy was still looking at the flowers like they were squirming snakes. "Yeah." He turned. "Mom? Jackson's here!"

"And Kate! I'm here, too!" Kate called out.

Dani walked to the door. "Jeremy, why is everyone standing at the door? Let them inside."

"Hi, Miss Dani! We brought you flowers and ice cream," Katie said.

"You did?" she asked as Jeremy finally stepped backward and allowed Jackson in. After Dani gave Kate a hug and took the bag from her, she smiled tentatively at him. "What have you been doing?"

She looked so cute, Jackson allowed himself a moment to study her before replying. Tonight, she didn't have a lick of makeup on and her thick blond hair was pulled up in one of those messy buns women wore. She also happened to be wearing pink pajama bottoms decorated with penguins holding umbrellas and a red tank top. If he didn't know better, he would have thought she was about eighteen years old.

"Oh, nothing," he teased. "Kate and I just thought we'd do something nice for you. Here," he said, feeling awkward as hell. "I hope you like roses."

Dani held them to her chest. "I do. Thank you."

"Mom?" Jeremy said. "What's going on?"

"Miss Dani had a real bad day," Kate chirped. "My daddy wants to cheer her up."

"What happened, Mom?"

Dani bit her bottom lip. "Oh, nothing for you to worry about. I better go put these in water."

After she walked into the kitchen, Kate on her heels, Jeremy stared up at him. "What happened?"

Jackson was torn. Usually he would push off the question because it wasn't his place to answer, but there was something in the boy's expression that he knew not to ignore. "Your mom had some trouble at one of her houses today. I happened to see her right after, so it's been on my mind."

"I'm fine, Jeremy," Dani called out.

He walked right into the kitchen. "How come you didn't tell me you had a bad day?" Jeremy asked. "It must have been real bad if you got flowers and ice cream."

Dani put the flowers in a glass pitcher. "We'll talk about it later, okay? Now, let me speak to Jackson for a moment before he leaves." After Jeremy took Kate's hand and walked into the living room, she said, "I wish you wouldn't have said anything to him."

"I know, but he cares about you ... and he's not a little kid, Dani."

She sighed. "I guess you're right. So, do I even want to know what you did this afternoon? Did you go talk to Reed?"

He pulled out the five twenties from his back pocket and handed them to her. "I did. And I got your money."

She took the money but frowned at him. "Do I want to know what happened when you went over there?"

His instinct was to tell her no, but he realized that she also didn't need to be shielded. "All I did was let him know that you aren't alone in the world and that someone has your back."

Her brown eyes warmed. "You are something else, Jackson Koch."

Feeling that warm connection that seemed to increase every time they were together, he inclined his head. "I'll take that as a compliment. Now I'm gonna get on my way. I've got a Kate to put to bed."

After he gathered up his little girl in his arms, she walked him to the door. "I guess I'll see you soon?" Dani asked.

"Yes, ma'am." Then, because he couldn't help himself, he leaned over and pressed his lips to her brow. "Good night, Dan."

As they walked downstairs, Kate murmured, "I like Miss Dani and Jeremy."

"Me too, baby," he replied, realizing that he was no longer wondering if their friendship was about to change.

It already had.

CHAPTER 17

FROM LES LARKE'S
YOU, TOO, CAN HOST
A POKER TOURNEY:

*If the game is sure to be intense, it's good to
forewarn all newcomers that it's going to be a
serious game.*

"Mom, what's going on?" Jeremy asked as soon as they were alone
again.

Dani's stomach knotted. She'd known as soon as she saw his
expression about the flowers that they were going to have to have
a talk. She'd kind of hoped it would have been later, though. She
was still wrapping her head around the fact that Jackson had not
only taken on her problems as his own but had then gone out to
buy her flowers and a treat.

"Want to have some ice cream and we'll talk?"

He shrugged. "Sure."

After scooping them both generous portions of rocky road
into bowls, she sat down at the table. "What do you want to talk

about? Jackson and the flowers or what happened at work?"

He picked up his spoon. "Both."

Of course she wasn't going to get off easy! "All right then. Well, one of my clients made a pass at me today and when I, um, told him I wasn't interested, he got a little mad. I left without getting paid."

Jeremy frowned. "That's really bad."

"I know. The guy was a real jerk."

Taking another bite, he stared at her for a long moment. "Has that happened before?"

"What? Men making passes at me?" When he nodded, she shook her head. "No. This was the first time. Like I said, he was a real jerk. He's everything your father taught you never to be."

"How come Jackson knew about it? Did you call him?"

"No. I ended up grabbing something to eat from the taco truck near the park and ran into Jackson, Kate, and a friend of Jackson's. I told them about it."

"So Jackson went over there."

She sighed. "Even though I told him not to, he did." Hoping to finish up the sorry story, she said, "He did get the money the man owed me though, so I guess I'm glad Jackson did." She smiled as she took her last bite of the ice cream. "So, that's the story about that."

Jeremy didn't smile back. "Mom, would you have ever told me?"

"Probably." Like, maybe years from now. Maybe.

"When?" His eyes looked troubled.

"I don't know."

"I'm not a little kid anymore."

"I realize that, Jer. I just don't want you worrying about me. You've got enough to worry about with school and baseball."

After staring at her another long minute, he said, "I think Jackson likes you."

"I like him, too. We're friends." She pushed back her chair. "Would you like some more ice cream?"

"Mom, you know what I mean."

She sat back down. "I do know." Though she didn't want to discuss her love life with him, Dani knew that she owed it to Jeremy. "You're right," she said slowly. "I think he does like me in a romantic way."

"Do you like him that way, too?"

Here it was. "I'm not ready for anything serious to happen between us, but I think I might." She searched her son's face. "What do you think about that? Are you mad at me?"

"Does this mean you don't love Dad anymore?"

"You know I loved your father. I think we would've stayed married forever. But he isn't here any longer." Before he could respond to that, she added quickly, "Jeremy, just because I think I might like spending time with Jackson, nothing's going to change."

"Really?"

"Really. I'm not ready to get serious about another man yet. But, I will say that I think I'm starting to be ready to think about it happening one day. And, honey, Jackson feels the same way. Don't forget, he's been through his wife dying."

His mouth tightened as he stood up and rinsed off his bowl in the sink. Dani noticed that he was staring at the pitcher of flowers on the counter.

At last, he turned back to her. "I like Jackson, Mom. He … well, he's really nice."

"I think he is, too."

"And, he doesn't treat me like a little kid."

"I know he likes you, Jeremy. Not because you're my son, but because you're you."

"If you want to start dating him, I won't mind."

Fearing she might start crying, Dani nodded. "All right. Thank you for that." Walking to his side, she said, "I'm glad we talked. This was a good idea."

"I am fourteen, Mom."

"And that means?"

"I'm growing up. Next year I'll get my temps, and then I'll be driving. Then, before you know it, I'm going to be dating, too." He grinned.

Though she had a feeling he was right, the idea of him growing up so fast scared the daylights out of her. "If you don't mind, let's just get through the rest of eighth grade. I can't even think about you driving girls around."

He laughed as he walked down the hall to his room. "I can."

"Oh, brother," she moaned as she sat back down. Jeremy really was growing up. In more ways than one.

* * *

The next day, just as they were about to leave for baseball practice, they ran into Gen in the parking lot.

"Hey, Dani," she called out. "Hi, Jeremy."

As Jeremy raised a hand, Dani smiled at her and noticed that Gen wasn't alone. By her side was a very handsome dark-haired man in form-fitting jeans and cowboy boots. "Hi, Gen. I haven't seen you in a while. Have you been able to take one of those Calgon days?"

She grinned. "No, but I have been a little busy. This is Seth Parks. He's a friend of mine from back home in Lubbock."

"Nice to meet you," Dani said as Jeremy said the same thing.

Seth gestured to Jeremy's uniform. "On your way to a game?"

"Nah, just practice."

"What position do you play?" Seth asked.

"Catcher when I can. Shortstop, too."

"I always played first base," Seth said with a smile.

"First base is cool."

To Dani's amusement, Gen's expression turned a little dreamy. "Seth, I didn't know you played baseball growing up."

He tossed an arm over her shoulders. "That's because we're still getting to know each other again."

"Speaking of baseball, we better get going," Dani said. "Ready, Jeremy?"

"Yep." After telling Seth and Gen bye, he opened his door and got in. A couple of minutes later, when they were about halfway to the practice field, he started grinning.

"What's so funny?"

"Oh, I was just thinking that it looks like you and Jackson aren't the only adults starting to like each other."

Thinking about the sparks that were flowing between Gen and Seth, Dani started grinning, too. "You're right about that, buddy. There is definitely something going on between the two of them."

CHAPTER 18

FROM LES LARKE'S
YOU, TOO, CAN HOST
A POKER TOURNEY:

*Even in the most casual games, things can turn
on a dime. It's always a good idea to be prepared
for surprises.*

"Hey Mom, your phone's ringing!" Jeremy called out, even though the phone was sitting right there on the coffee table in front of them.

That was his new thing. Reinforcing the obvious. It cracked her up.

Not that she'd tell him that.

As the phone chimed again, Dani snatched it up. "I got it, Jeremy," she said with a laugh, just as she pushed the button to connect. "Hello?"

"Hey, Dani."

"Hey, Jackson. What's going on? Did you get called into work?"

Beside her, Jeremy tensed then sighed, looking resigned. For once, she didn't feel the need to chide him for it. After all, she was feeling the same way.

"No. Um, as a matter of fact, I wanted to know if you …" he hesitated. "I mean, if you and Jeremy wanted to come over to my buddy Kurt Holland's house."

She'd heard him talk about Kurt. He was one of Jackson's longtime friends from Spartan. But she had no idea what Kurt had to do with her. "Why?"

"Why?"

In the background, she could hear some other men's voices laughing. Suddenly, she felt like she was back in high school, getting prank called or something. She knew that wasn't the case, of course. Jackson wasn't like that.

But even though their friendship had moved to a new level after he'd gone to the Moores' house and gotten her money, it wasn't like they spent their free time together. "Does Kurt need something?"

"No. I mean, he's getting a group of people together. For a barbecue. Kids, too."

"Kids, too?" She saw Jeremy actively listening now.

"Yeah. I mean, absolutely. And not just little kids. Kurt has Sam who's fixin' to graduate. And his girl Kayla's coming over. Ace's boy Finn, Ace's girlfriend Meredith, and maybe a couple of their other friends will be there, too. It's a party."

He was asking her to a party. It had nothing to do with babysitting, but because they were friends. "And it's tonight?"

"Yeah. We were thinking everyone could start heading over here around six."

"At six." That was in three hours.

"Yeah." His voice was a little more tentative. "You know how guys are. We don't do a lot of planning. But their girlfriends are going to be here, too. So you won't be the only woman or anything."

She wouldn't be the only woman. It sounded like the other men were hooked up with someone. So … she would be his date. It had been so long, she was having to convince herself, she realized. Jackson was asking her out.

Kind of.

"Say yes, Mom," Jeremy whispered.

Though she was really glad Jeremy was now good with her dating Jackson, Dani still wasn't sure that she was ready to meet a bunch of Jackson's friends. "Jackson, should I bring something?" What could she bring, anyway?

"If you have some cookies or something already baked that would be great. If not, then don't worry about it. Just bring yourself and Jeremy."

"I could bring dessert." Mentally cataloging her pantry, she said, "I can definitely bring cookies."

"So you'll come?" He sounded real pleased.

Feeling almost jittery, she nodded. Then realized that he was probably waiting for a verbal answer. "Yes. I mean, Jeremy and I say yes."

While Jeremy fist-pumped the air, Jackson's voice warmed about a hundred degrees. "I'm so glad. Thank you."

"No need to thank me for saying yes to a barbecue party, Jackson. It sounds like fun." To her surprise, she meant it.

"Great. I'll text you Kurt's address. Looking forward to seeing you both."

After he disconnected, she stared at the phone for a moment, wondering what she'd just done. It wasn't that she didn't like barbecues or getting together with friends, it was that she hadn't done anything like it in years.

Not since Brian.

First it was because she hurt too much, then it was because she felt too self-conscious. Every other person she'd see would look at her in pity and then ask how she was doing. She'd grown to hate that question because she'd learned that it was a loaded one. People had expectations about widows. She was supposed to be in mourning. She wasn't supposed to be *okay*, though *better* was permitted. Never *good*, because for some reason, that meant that she wasn't sad that her husband had died.

After she got over that hurdle, she'd simply lost interest. It was easier to be with Jeremy. And then, of course, there was always work.

Now that three years had passed, she was in a strange situation again. Most people didn't ever ask about Brian. Shoot, most people had no idea she was a widow. All the people she used to do things with had either moved on to other friends or moved out of the area. A couple of her harshest critics had even gotten divorced. While she would have never held that against them, she'd discovered that surviving a broken marriage and a spouse's death didn't always mean the same things.

"Mom? Are we really gonna go?"

Pulling her head out of the clouds, she turned to him and smiled. "Yep. Jackson said that his friends Kurt and Ace will be there, and another man. They all have girlfriends."

Jeremy looked a little less excited. "Will Kate and I be the only kids?"

"No. Kurt has a little brother who he's raising named Sam. He's a high school senior. Ace has a son named Finn who's fifteen."

"I know who Finn Vance is." Jeremy's eyes brightened. "He's cool."

She reached out and ruffled his hair, though he was probably too old for it. "I'm glad you think so. Hopefully you'll like them."

"Are you going to make cookies?"

She got to her feet. "I am. Which means I better get busy."

"Chocolate chip and peanut butter?"

She smiled at the hopeful note in his voice. "Unfortunately, no. We're out of chocolate chips. I'm going to make sugar cookies with frosting."

"Those are good."

"Thanks. Do you want to help?"

"Um, no?"

She laughed. "No worries. I didn't think you would want to."

"I'm going to head out to the park for a little while."

"All right. Be careful."

He turned before she could see him rolling his eyes, which was probably a good thing. She didn't trust a bunch of teenagers hanging out in the park, which was ridiculous. She knew that. She made do with calling out, "Be back by a quarter after five. You need to shower."

"Mom."

"You'll need to shower."

"Fine." He grabbed a key and strode out the door, looking so old that she felt a lump form in her throat.

Luckily, she had a lot of cookies to bake and frost. No time to dwell.

***

When they arrived, right on time, there were only two other cars parked in the driveway. Dani took that as a good sign. She wasn't late, but she hadn't been the first to arrive either. She'd also texted Jackson when they'd left, hoping that he would read the text and be on the lookout for them.

As soon as she turned off the ignition, Jeremy had his door

open. "Be careful with the cookies." She'd put them on a big plate, not wanting to smudge the icing by stacking them."

"I got it, Mom."

Just as she was reaching for her purse in the back seat, she heard a door open and shut.

"Hey, Jeremy," Jackson said. "You bringing in some of your mom's amazing cookies?"

She was just getting out of the car in time to notice that Jeremy looked caught off guard by the praise. "They're just sugar cookies," he said with a shrug. "But yeah."

"They look fantastic to me." Jackson smiled at her over the car. "Thanks for coming."

"Thanks for inviting us." She walked around the car, noticing that Jackson was wearing a pair of faded khaki shorts and a worn green T-shirt proclaiming the wonders of the New River Gorge. His feet were bare. She forced herself to glance away before she started staring at the fine blond hair that covered his calves or the scar that marked his knee.

Instead, she smoothed the fabric of her rayon blouse. She was even gladder that she'd elected to wear a pair of new shorts, a loose flowy top, and her new silver sandals with the small heel. The outfit was pretty fancy for her, which just went to show how mundane her life had become. All she ever made time for anymore was work, Jeremy, and her online classes.

"Go get the front door for me, Jeremy," Jackson said as he waited for her to get to his side. The look he gave her was filled with appreciation. It even topped his happiness at seeing a container of sugar cookies. "You look pretty," he said quietly. "I like those shoes."

"Thanks." She knew she was probably smiling way too much, but she couldn't help but be glad that he'd noticed them. "I found them on the sale rack in a fancy boutique at the edge of Indian Hill."

He smiled. "Women and shoes," he said as he led her into the house. Her boy had the door open and was leaning against it, no doubt letting in a whole array of insects.

Just as she was about to tell him to close the door, Jackson said, "Jeremy, as you can probably tell, everyone is in the kitchen. Go on in. We'll be right behind you."

Jeremy took off without a backward glance. Just as she was about to chide him, Jackson reached out a hand to her. "Careful on these steps, now. They're uneven."

She took his hand before thinking to point out that she climbed steps all the time. Of course, as soon as her hand was snug against his, she forgot all about that. The truth was that it felt good to be fussed over and helped for a change.

"Thank you," she said when they were in Kurt's small entrance. She immediately felt his loss when their hands dropped.

Jackson smiled. "Come on, I'll introduce you to everyone."

Dani was relieved to see that everyone else was wearing shorts, too. The men dressed much like Jackson, and the women having gone to a little bit of effort to spruce up an otherwise casual outfit.

Jeremy had placed her plate on the narrow island. Dani came in just in time to see two teenage boys eyeing it with interest.

"Are those homemade?" A very handsome boy with blue eyes asked.

"Yes, they are," Dani said with way too much enthusiasm in her voice. "You're welcome to some, if you'd like." She'd stopped herself from asking if it was okay with his parents.

Jeremy shook his head. Obviously, she was ruining his attempts to look cool. Just as she wondered if she should say anything else, Jackson placed his hand on the middle of her back, anchoring her nerves.

"Everybody, this is Dani Brown and Jeremy. Dani, Jeremy, I'll start with the kids first. This is Sam," he said, pointing to the blue-eyed guy who'd asked about the cookies. "And that's his girlfriend, Kayla, and her sister, Brianna. Over there is Finn, and his neighbor Allison."

"Who's also his girlfriend," Sam grinned.

Finn, who looked like he could already play linebacker for a university, grinned. "Hey," he murmured.

"Finn," his father murmured. "Mind your manners, boy."

Finn straightened. "Nice to meet you, ma'am."

Allison, with her curly hair and light complexion, blushed but raised a hand. "Hi, Mrs. Brown."

"Hi, everyone," Dani said.

"Now, standing over by the fridge is Finn's dad, Ace, and his girl, Meredith." Jackson took a deep breath. "This here is an old buddy of mine from home, Troy, and his gal, Campbell. She's the one holding Kate. And finally, rounding out the group, is the couple who lives here, Kurt Holland and his fiancée, Emily Springer. Kurt is Sam's older brother."

"Hey, Dani," Troy said. "Good to see you again."

"Same. I mean, hi, everyone," Dani said. "Thank you for inviting us."

"I'm glad you're here," Kurt said. He had the same drawl as Jackson, but his voice was a little quieter. Maybe a little more gentle?

She smiled at him, then looked at Jackson. "I'm starting to learn that my new neighbor has more friends than I do around Bridgeport."

"That's hardly true," Jackson murmured. "This just happens to be my crew."

Meredith walked to her side and linked an arm through hers. "I felt the same way when I met Ace. These West Virginia guys stick together. Come on, there's some drinks and snacks on the back patio. Let's go sit down."

Watching Kurt and Emily pull trays out of the refrigerator, she hesitated. "Are you sure I can't help make something? Or I could carry a tray to the table or something."

Jackson answered before Meredith could. "We've got a slew of teenage boys here for that. You go relax, Dan."

Meredith smiled as she gestured toward a back door. "I promise, they've got this. Let's go sit down."

Dani followed Meredith out, thinking as she did that no woman should have such a perfect figure. She was slim and toned and had lots of auburn curls that somehow looked like they'd never heard of becoming frizzy in humidity.

The patio was really pretty. It had a stamped concrete surface, lots of high-end patio furniture, the kind she'd only seen in Front Gate catalogs, and a professional-looking grill. But the thing that drew her eyes were all the well-manicured bushes and flowers. "Wow, this is amazing out here."

Meredith nodded. "It's only when I see something like this that I remember that Kurt does own a landscaping business."

"I would spend as much time out here as I could."

"I think Emily does. She's a high school English teacher. Em's told me that she can feel her body relax as soon as she sits out here."

"I bet." Actually, she thought all of Kurt's house would do that to her. It looked homey and comfortable. Nothing too fancy, and it was uncluttered.

"Now, what can I get you to drink?" she asked as she poked around in a big tin bucket filled with ice and assorted bottles and cans. "We have beer, wine, soda, water ..." She looked around some more and then straightened, holding a plastic pitcher. "Oh! And it looks like we also have Arnold Palmers."

She loved that lemonade-tea mixture. "I'll have one of those."

"I'll have that too." Meredith smiled as she poured two glasses. "Campbell, do you want an Arnold Palmer?"

"Nope. I'm having a glass of rosé," she said, smiling at Dani. "Troy and I don't have any kids to look out for."

Dani thought Campbell, with her hourglass figure, perfectly curled hair, and darling navy sundress looked like a woman out of a sixties fashion magazine. Everything about her screamed beauty and old school. She made Dani feel frumpy in comparison.

The minute she sat down, though, she leaned back and kicked out her ankles. "I can't wait to get to know you, Dani. Troy said Jackson talks about you all the time."

"Oh, really?"

"Absolutely. So, tell us all about you."

Dani felt her smile turn strained as she prepared herself to share information about her job, being a widow, and living in an apartment. None of it was anything to be ashamed about.

But the problem was that all of it seemed to change people's opinion about her. Making her go from just being Dani, to Dani the widowed cleaning lady.

After taking a fortifying sip, she began, mentally preparing herself to answer a bunch questions about things she would rather not talk about.

CHAPTER 19

FROM LES LARKE'S
YOU, TOO, CAN HOST
A POKER TOURNEY:

*Remember, you don't have to have a poker table; a
dining room or kitchen table is perfectly fine. But
a "real" table does add to the party's ambiance.*

After Dani walked outside with Meredith and Campbell and the
teenagers took Kate and Jeremy over to check out the garage, Kurt
and Ace grinned at Jackson.

"You didn't say she was so beautiful, buddy," Kurt said. "And
what a sweetheart, baking cookies. She's a keeper, for sure."

Jackson groaned. "She's just a good friend. I told you that.
Whatever you do, don't embarrass her."

"I'm not going to embarrass her. But I'm not opposed to
giving you grief."

"I didn't sign up for that! You were supposed to help her out.
That's all. Remember, we're here because that boy of hers needs
some help."

"We haven't forgotten." Kurt smiled.

When Ace remained conspicuously silent, Jackson eyed him. "Don't tease her none. Okay?"

Ace held up his hands. "Settle down, buddy."

"Oh, guys, leave him alone," Emily said. "Jackson, I'm glad Dani came over. She seems really nice. Like someone I'd like to know." She looked over the island that was now filled with salads, hamburger and hot dog buns, and a baking sheet filled with hamburgers and hot dogs ready for the grill. "Now, you boys get busy grilling while I make sure she's doing okay."

"Any other things you want me to do, babe?" Kurt asked.

"Yes. Figure out how to talk to Dani about the tournament without freaking her out."

Even thinking about that made Jackson flinch. After Emily left the room, he said, "I told y'all the truth. She'll be upset and embarrassed if she thinks you think she is a charity case."

"You know what, let's go get it over with."

"Now?"

Ace nodded. "Kurt was thinking we'd wait, but you look stressed out. If you get any worse, then Dani is going to start worrying that she did something wrong and then her boy is going to get involved."

"She wouldn't think that." But would she?

"Come on, let's find out."

Before Jackson could stop him, Ace headed outside.

"Crap," he muttered.

"Come on, it will be all right," Troy said as he motioned him forward. "What matters is Dani is going to know you care about her and Jeremy. It could be worse."

Jackson secretly thought that there could be a whole lot more things that could happen, starting with Dani crying and ending with her never wanting to talk to him again.

But it looked like it was now all out of his hands.

* * *

The moment they got outside, Dani looked toward him. Her expression was sweet. Nice smile. Happy expression.

Even though this whole thing was his doing, he hated to remove it from her face.

"Hey, Dani. Um, the guys and I wanted to talk to you about something."

She looked from Troy to Ace to Kurt. Then at the girls and stiffened. "What's going on?"

"Nothing." Realizing that was probably a lie, he said, "I mean, nothing bad. We just wanted to talk to you about baseball."

"I don't know much about the game. You know that." She glanced at Campbell in an obvious plea for help.

Campbell didn't disappoint. "Troy, what's going on? We were having a nice conversation. Can't this wait?"

"No, honey."

"Huh?"

"Well, no. Seeing as this conversation was the reason we all got together," Troy answered.

Ace muttered something under his breath that was ripe enough that Jackson was glad Kate wasn't in earshot.

But he didn't have time to worry about that, because all he cared about what the expression that was on Dani's face. It was all hurt and confusion.

And, yes, a fair bit of irritation, too.

He didn't blame her one bit, either.

"Jackson, I think you better tell me what you have going on right now." Her voice was clipped.

He didn't have a choice. "Dani, it wasn't supposed to go this way."

"What wasn't?"

"Well, um, see I've been worried about Jeremy playing ball."

"Why? He's doing real good." She looked even more confused.

He didn't blame her for that, either. But how did he carefully broach the subject that they all wanted to help her without embarrassing her?

Kurt glanced at him. Shook his head like he was washing his hands of him, and then said, "Here's the deal, Dani. Jackson here has been real proud of your boy. He says he's the real deal and has a shot of doing something real good with his gifts."

Dani swallowed. "I know that." Turning to Jackson, she gave him a hurt look. "Are you thinking that I'm not taking good care of my son?"

"Of course not. You're a great mom. The best."

"Then I don't understand."

Before he could fumble around with his explanations, Ace stepped in. "Jackson here knows you aren't making a ton of money cleaning houses."

Dani stepped back. "I'm sorry?"

"He also knows that those select teams cost money." Ace glanced at Jackson and then at his fiancée. It was obvious he felt terrible. What a damn mess they were making the conversation.

And if he was feeling bad, well, then that made two of them.

Meredith intervened. "What are you boys doing?"

"We're trying to do a good deed, baby," Ace said.

"What is this good deed?" Dani said. "And please, for the love of Pete, just spit it out."

"We want to throw you a benefit poker game," Jackson said.

"A what?"

He started talking quickly. "The Bridgeport Social Club likes to hold a poker tournament for a good cause from time to time. I started thinking that Jeremy's baseball program would be just the thing all the guys would want to support."

155

Dani looked beyond hurt. "You came up with this crazy plan without me?"

"It wasn't like that."

"Buddy," Troy said.

She turned to Troy. "So, you're saying that it is?"

Troy had just gotten out a half-nod before Campbell placed her hand on his arm. "Don't."

"Honey, I promise, this is a good thing," he told her.

"Not this way. I can't believe you."

Dani looked from one of them to the next. With each new person she looked at, her expression became more tense and her face looked paler.

"I need to leave."

"Please don't," Emily said. She reached for Dani's hand, but Dani pulled it from her grasp. "I need to get Jeremy."

"Don't do that," Kurt said quickly. "Look, I know we sound like idiots and aren't explaining things real well, but that's because we don't explain things real well. I promise that our hearts are in the right place."

"I hope you feel real good about it then," she said as she edged farther away from him. "All I know is that I need to get out of here."

From the look she sent him, Jackson knew that she would no doubt never want to see any of them ever again. Stepping fast, hoping to bridge the gap, he said, "Danielle, I promise, it wasn't supposed to be like this."

"It wasn't? Now how, exactly, did you expect me to react when I heard I was going to be y'all's charity case."

"No one ever thought about you that way," Troy said. "We wanted to do something for Jeremy."

"Troy, stop talking," Campbell murmured. Turning to Dani, she said, "I know this is awkward, but I promise you, no one here wants to do something besides be your friend."

"As sweet as that sounds, I think we all know that that isn't exactly the truth."

"It's not a lie," Troy murmured.

Looking even more frustrated, Dani looked back at Jackson. "I don't know what you want me to say." Each word sounded like it was being pulled from her heart. "Jackson, coming out to a party like this was a big step for me. I came over here even though I only knew you."

"Everyone is really glad you did. They want to be your friends." Around him, he could practically feel their heads nod.

Dani glared at all of them. "Look, I'm trying to not take this out on all of you, but I don't know what to say. I guess I'm the first single mom you guys have ever met. Or, maybe I'm the first person you've gotten to know who doesn't live in a fancy house like this?"

"This isn't fancy."

"Not to you, Jackson. But it sure is to me. I've never owned a house. But, oh, yeah, you know that, because you've been paying me to watch your girl."

"I swear it wasn't like that."

"Just tell me where Jeremy is. Please."

"All right. I'll go get him."

"I'll … I'll be by the front door."

Emily rushed to her side. "Please don't go."

"But I don't see how I can stay. Can't you understand how I'm feeling?" she whispered. "I've been completely blindsided."

And … that was the problem. If the positions had been reversed, Jackson knew that he wouldn't have been able to look at any of them in the eye.

"I understand," he murmured. "I'll go find him right now."

Practically before he said the words, Dani had turned around and walked out the small side door in the fence.

He walked inside to find Jeremy and find a way to tell the kid that he'd just really upset his mother. No doubt, the boy would be both upset to leave and mad at him for being a jerk.

Jackson wouldn't blame him one bit either.

As Jackson walked down the hall, he wondered if there was anything he could possibly say to make things right.

Unfortunately, he had a feeling that answer was a big fat no.

CHAPTER 20

FROM LES LARKE'S
YOU, TOO, CAN HOST
A POKER TOURNEY:

If you plan to host more than once, consider
investing in a 500-chip set. Here are the usual
designations for each color: white is $5, blue is
$10, red is $20, and green is $40. Of course,
these amounts are just for show. No one ever
has to bet real money.

Standing on Kurt Holland's driveway, Dani was pretty sure she'd never been so embarrassed. She tried to recall some of the more uncomfortable moments in her life.

Maybe when she'd called Brian's parents two months after he'd died and had to ask for help with rent and clothes for Jeremy. Maybe when she'd had to ask the school for reduced lunch last year. Both of those experiences had been hard. But she didn't think even that little bit of pride swallowing had anything on what had just taken place.

At least the reduced lunch plan had been private. Well, for the most part. And she hadn't had to explain anything to the school district, just provide them proof that she wasn't making very much. That hadn't been hard—she had known exactly how little she was making.

For the most part, she'd been so relieved about the cut in price that she hadn't cared about what she had to do to make sure Jeremy ate well. The lunch ladies had treated Jeremy with dignity, as well. They didn't make the kids receiving help stand in the back of the line or anything.

And Brian's parents? Well, they'd acted like she was asking them to give up a limb, but his father had stopped by that very evening with an envelope of cash. And after telling her that they didn't have a lot of extra money, he assured her that it wasn't a loan, it was a gift. A one-time gift.

So, that had been awkward but not necessarily embarrassing. There had been a part of her that had wanted Brian's parents to know that their son hadn't been the best at planning for the future.

But this?

Well, this little episode had hurt like a knife. She'd thought Jackson had really liked her. He'd sure acted like it when he kissed her and gave her those warm hugs.

Then there was the fact that he'd marched over to the Moores' house and demanded she get her money. People didn't do things like that for just anyone. Not even good guys like Jackson.

She'd actually thought he liked her enough to introduce her to his friends. She'd actually been feeling pretty good about herself. Had thought that they'd become something more than just friends—that he'd found her attractive and saw something more in her than just a single mom with big dreams and small paychecks.

Obviously, she'd been wrong.

When she heard the door behind her open and shut, she turned in relief. Now she could get Jeremy and get going. He was likely going to be ticked and irritated with her, but she'd do her best to ignore his questions. He didn't need to know that all of this had been for his benefit.

But Jeremy wasn't walking toward her. Meredith was.

Dani braced herself. "Is Jeremy on his way?"

"Well, no."

She felt like stomping her foot in frustration. "All right. I'll go get him. Is he upstairs?"

"He's out in the back. But Dani, I don't think pulling him out of here and taking him home is a good idea."

"That isn't your call."

"I know. And you're right, it isn't. But, well, I was hoping we could talk for a few minutes."

"I don't want to sound like a bitch, but I don't think we have anything more to say."

"I'm sorry, but I think you're wrong." She pointed to a small park down the street, maybe a block away. "There's some park benches over there. We could talk. Please?"

"Did Jackson send you out here?"

"No. He knows I came out, but this wasn't his idea."

"You came out here on your own?"

"Yes. The guys convinced him to give me a chance." Her blue eyes widened. "Don't make me go back in there and tell them I failed."

At that moment, Dani didn't really care what Meredith and the guys were going to say to each other. But she wasn't in any hurry to go back in and pull out Jeremy.

"I'll go, but I feel like you all are playing a game or something," she admitted.

"I'm not playing a game, Dani. I thought we were just getting together as friends as well. I had no idea that the guys had talked about holding a poker tournament."

"I'm sorry." The hurt on Meredith's face was clear. Maybe

she couldn't fix what had happened between her and Jackson, but she could certainly fix what she'd just done to Meredith. "I think walking over to the bench and talking is a good idea. Obviously, I need to calm down."

"Let's walk, then."

As Dani walked beside Meredith, she became even more aware of how fit the woman was. She vaguely recalled Jackson once telling her that Ace's girlfriend owned the Shine Pilates studio. Obviously, she was a walking endorsement for the benefits of the program.

"I just remembered Jackson telling me about your studio. You teach Pilates?"

She smiled. "I do. I started my studio about a year ago. At first, I taught all the classes, now I even have two ladies who teach four or five classes a week. It's a lot of fun."

"That's wonderful."

"You know what? It really is. I love having an occupation that feeds my soul and my pocketbook."

"That's a blessing."

They sat down on the bench. "It really is. Ace and I talk about that all the time. He loves being a mechanic and now he manages a whole shop and spends his day repairing fancy cars. There's something for everyone, you know?"

"I guess there is."

"Jackson told me you are taking classes online?"

Dani scanned her face. She looked completely sincere. "I'm taking classes so I can open up my own daycare and preschool."

"Really? How far along are you?"

"Only four classes in, but that's four classes more than when I first started."

"Do you want to work for someone or a company or have your own place?"

"My own. I want to do things my way, you know?"

"I completely understand. That's why I have my own studio instead of managing a franchise or something."

Meredith was acting like they had a lot in common. Normally, Dani would have been so pleased to meet her and would have even asked her for some advice about one day starting her own business. But they weren't sitting there because she was a future entrepreneur.

"Listen, I appreciate you being so friendly, but I really don't think this is the right time to chat." She took a deep breath. "I need—"

"Jackson has been worried about you," she interrupted.

"What?"

"He came over to see Ace, Troy, and Kurt a couple of nights ago. You and Jeremy were all he talked about." Her eyes widened. "Dani, this wasn't about him feeling sorry for you or Jeremy or wanting to make you into a charity case. It was about him wanting to help you. Do you see the difference?"

"He never talked to me about this first."

"I'll tell you what happened. He came over and told the guys about how good a ball player Jeremy was. And about how you've been running yourself ragged trying to get him everywhere. That's when the guys started volunteering to help drive."

"They said they'd help drive Jeremy to his practices?"

Meredith's expression softened, like she was so glad that Dani was finally listening. "Yes. I think they would have started a schedule right then and there if Jackson had had your son's practice schedule in front of him."

"That's really nice of them." She leaned back against the bench's seat. "I'm kind of stunned. I mean, who would have thought?"

Meredith chuckled. "You don't get it, do you? These guys are special. They care about each other and they care about people who mean something to them." She looked off into the distance.

"I can promise you that if something happened with me or with my Pilates studio, Ace would have those guys over there in a heartbeat. And they'd go, too."

Turning slightly so she was facing Dani, Meredith said, "What I'm trying to say to you is that you are definitely reading something into Jackson's offer, but it's absolutely the wrong thing. No one feels sorry for you, Dani. What everyone feels is Jackson's feelings for you."

"We aren't actually a couple."

"Says who?"

"Um, says me. Says Jackson."

She shook her head. "That's not what he says."

"Meredith, we haven't even gone on a date." Though, they had certainly spent time together.

"Do you only get close to people on dates?"

"Of course not. But—"

"I thought you looked after little Kate, too."

"I do." She nodded. Maybe she had read too much into the guys' offer. Oh, it still made her uncomfortable—she didn't want Jeremy all the sudden known as the poor kid on the team.

But maybe she shouldn't have charged out of the room in an embarrassed snit. Maybe she should have thought about listening to Jackson instead of immediately thinking of the worst.

Finally answering Meredith's question, she said, "I've spent a lot of time with Kate. And even though he does pay me, maybe Jackson was trying to repay the favor."

Meredith sighed in relief. "I know he was." Reaching out to her, she pressed one slim hand on top of hers. "I know you don't know Ace, but believe me when I tell you that he's a stand-up guy. One of the best people I've ever met. There's no way he'd go out of his way to embarrass you. Neither would Kurt or Troy."

"I just thought that since Kurt lives in this nice house, maybe he wouldn't understand ..." Realizing how foolish she sounded, she shook her head instead of finishing her thought. "Never mind."

"None of these guys are from rich families, Dani. All of their dads were coal miners. There isn't a person in that house who is going to look down on you for worrying about paying bills or affording extras."

Boy, she'd really jumped the gun. Feeling even more embarrassed, she said, "I don't know what to do now. Do I go back inside?"

"I hope you will."

Before she lost her nerve, she stood up. "I'll apologize first thing. I'm ashamed that I got so worked up so quickly. I should have known better."

Standing up, too, Meredith rested a palm on her shoulder. "I wouldn't be too hard on yourself. The guys aren't the best with words. Come on, let's go in and get it over with."

"Thanks for coming out here. You didn't have to."

Meredith shook her head. "No, I think I did. Ace has been pretty worried about Jackson. He told me the other night that he was really glad that the two of you have become close."

"He said that?"

"Oh, yeah." Smiling softly, Meredith added, "He said you make Jackson happy. Happier than he's been in years."

"Jackson has made me happy, too." She realized that she was also happier now than she'd been in years.

"I'm so glad you said that. So, let's go fix this. If something happens to the two of you because of this, it's going to be terrible for everyone."

Walking by Meredith's side, Dani was stunned at how sincere the other woman was.

It seemed that she was already part of this group of close friends. To her surprise, she was so glad to be there, she didn't want to leave.

CHAPTER 21

FROM LES LARKE'S
*YOU, TOO, CAN HOST
A POKER TOURNEY:*

*It's also a good idea to have an extra deck of cards
on hand. Cards can get stained, damp, or even
bent from time to time. You might even want to
give participants the job of shuffling the new decks.*

Dani knew she had a lot of faults—for example, she was a little too sensitive about her current financial situation. But she'd never been afraid to apologize.

The moment she walked back into the kitchen, where Jackson was nursing a beer, Ace and the other guys were looking glum, and Emily and Campbell were playing with Kate, Dani started talking.

"Everyone, I'm really sorry. Ever since Brian died I've been struggling financially. It wasn't easy dealing with all his bills or having to admit to other people that we really were struggling." She looked down at her feet and then forced herself to continue. "Because of all that, I'm afraid I get sensitive whenever I can't

166

afford things for Jeremy." She heard her voice tremble. Realized everyone in the room heard it, too.

Kurt cleared his throat. "Dani, thanks, but there's no need ..."

She held up a hand. "No. Please let me finish." Taking a deep breath, she started talking faster. "When it comes to my son, I'm afraid I'm too sensitive to a fault."

"Don't know if that is possible, doll," Ace said. "Don't worry about it none."

"No, listen. I should have listened to what all of you had to say instead of running out of here." Looking at Jackson directly, she finished her little speech. "I hope you can forgive me."

Jackson walked right over to her and enfolded her in a hug. "Nothing to forgive, Dan. This is on me. As soon as I saw your expression, I knew I should've told you about our idea privately."

Oh, but his hug felt good—almost as sweet as his words. She leaned in, allowing herself to enjoy the feeling of being held, of being protected. And before she realized what she was doing, she tightened her arms around his middle, holding him close.

He kissed her brow. "That's right, honey," he said low enough for only her to hear. "You hold onto me, and I'll help you. Hold on tight."

After kissing her brow one more time, he released her.

She looked at his face. Saw something new there, something that was teasing at her own heart. Compassion, care, and a knowledge that there was something new between them. Or, maybe it had always been there. But it felt new.

And now she understood Meredith's expression when Dani'd said that she and Jackson were nothing more than friends. She knew now that was a lie. There was something real between them that wasn't like anything she'd experienced in a long time. Not since she'd first fallen in love with Brian.

Kurt pressed his hands together. "All right, y'all. I'm going to go finally put these burgers on before the boys revolt and take off to Burger King or something."

"Good. I'm starving," Troy said.

When everyone started working on supper again, Emily walked to Dani's side and gave her a little hug. "I'm glad you came back and gave us another chance."

"Me, too. I don't usually get so emotional. I'm so sorry."

Emily brushed off her apology with a shrug. "No reason to apologize. We're all friends here."

Dani realized that was now true.

* * *

Forty minutes later, after they'd all eaten burgers and hot dogs, potato salad, lettuce cups, and a whole lot of Dani's frosted sugar cookies, Jeremy appeared by her side.

She noticed that his eyes were bright and that he was wearing a relaxed smile she hadn't seen on his face lately. Well, not unless he was crouching behind home plate.

"You okay, Mom?"

She looked at him in surprise. "I'm fine. Why?"

"Oh, no reason. It's just that I haven't been around you much tonight."

She smiled at him. "I'm glad. That means you have been having a good time with all the kids." She searched his face. "You have, haven't you?"

"Yeah. Sam and Finn and their girlfriends have been really cool. They haven't even been acting like I'm younger than them."

"You're not that much younger than Finn, honey. Only by a year, right?"

"Yeah, but that doesn't matter a whole lot. He's in high school."

"I guess that is a big difference," she teased. "Anyway, don't worry about me. I'm fine."

"We going to stay for a while longer?"

Knowing that she still had to hear the guys' plans for the poker tournament, she nodded. "Probably another hour."

He grinned. "Cool."

"When I say it's time to go don't fight me, okay?"

"Yeah. I won't." After grabbing a soda from the tin bucket, he walked back over to the group of kids.

Unable to resist, Dani watched him walk over to them. Sam Holland was sitting on top of a brick-red retaining wall. His girlfriend, Kayla, was snuggled up next to him, practically sitting on his lap. Finn Vance and his girlfriend, Allison, were sitting together far less intimately. Though they were both talking nonstop. All of them grinned at Jeremy when he approached and sat down in the empty chair.

"He's doing all right, isn't he?" Jackson said, his voice soft.

"Yeah. I thought your friends' kids would be nice to him, but I didn't think they'd be so friendly. He's a little younger."

"Not that much. Just a year. Plus, they're good kids. Relaxed, too. Easy to get along with."

"Well, Jeremy's eating up their attention."

"He's a good kid too, Dani. I don't think they consider hanging out with him to be a hardship."

She was so glad about that. He had made a lot of good friends through baseball, but she wanted him to have friends who didn't care how well he batted or caught balls behind the plate. "Hey, speaking of kids, I just realized that it's been pretty quiet around here. Where's Kate?"

"She's inside the house, in Kurt and Emily's room watching *Frozen*. Again."

She laughed. "So she's just fine."

Jackson smiled big enough for both of his dimples to pop. "Yeah. I thought maybe Kate would want me to sit with her, but when I tried to talk to her while Elsa was singing she told me to 'Be quiet, Daddy.'"

"Enough said."

"Look, how about we sit down now and talk about the poker game?"

Steeling herself, she nodded. "Okay. Um, where do you want to go?"

"The guys thought we could go back to the living room. The kids just set up the firepit, so they won't be coming in anytime soon. They figured that would be the quietest place."

With a look of foreboding, she nodded and followed him back inside.

CHAPTER 22

FROM LES LARKE'S
YOU, TOO, CAN HOST
A POKER TOURNEY:

*It's always good to establish house rules before you
begin play. Think about how many chips each
player may begin with and when to raise blinds.*

Breathe, Dani reminded herself for at least the fifth time in three
minutes. *Try to look like you aren't embarrassed and horrified and
angry all at the same time.*

She doubted she succeeded though. The minute the other
women saw her face, their looks of happiness deflated.

The men eyed Jackson with concern. She could practically
feel his silent cues to them to not mess up.

Because that was what this was. A real mess.

Finally getting herself together, she steeled her shoulders and
shook her head. "Everyone, put those looks of concern away right
now. I'm fine."

Kurt darted a glance at Emily. "No offense, but I've learned the hard way that 'fine' doesn't really mean 'fine' when a woman says it. We don't have to do anything if you don't want."

He was giving her an out. If she told them that she didn't want to talk about auctions and baseball bills, they would nod, and change the subject.

Jackson would probably never try to lend her a helping hand ever again. She could go back to doing things on her own. Struggling in silence.

"Thank you for that, but to be real honest, if I keep being so pig-headed, I think the only thing that's going to benefit is my pride. I'd be real grateful to hear your plans."

Dani could practically feel all the worries that Jackson had been carrying slide off his shoulders.

Bracing herself, she glanced at Kurt. Ready to hear his plans. But to her surprise, it wasn't Kurt or Ace or even Jackson who started talking, but Emily.

"Dani, I don't know if you know this, but I've actually played poker with the guys." Looking over at Campbell, she smiled. "I mean, Campbell and I did."

"Camp beat our socks off," Troy muttered.

"No way. Really?"

"I'm pretty good at poker," Campbell said with a small smile. "My brother taught me to play when I was a little girl. I'll teach you, if you want."

"Um, maybe?" She'd never had any interest in poker, but if that's what it took to be a part of the group, she figured she could give it a try.

Emily laughed. "This isn't a test. You don't have to worry about playing Texas Hold'em if you don't want to. My point is that we've been to one of these poker games and I can tell you that the guys are nice guys. They aren't going to think anything about playing a tournament to raise money for your boy's fees."

"They want to do something like this," Troy said.

Ace nodded. "I promise, none of us in this room came from a lot of money. We've all felt the pinch. I have a son who played his share of peewee football, too. It didn't come cheap."

She exhaled. "Thank you all for telling me all this. I have to admit that I was taken aback. And I wasn't really a hundred percent on board, but I do want Jeremy to be able to play."

"And you need to take care of yourself, too, Dani," Jackson said quietly. "You can't do everything."

"So what's going to happen?"

"I'm going to set up a game and tell the players that it's a fifty dollar buy-in for charity. If we get twenty guys, that should help out with most of the bills."

That was a thousand dollars! "I couldn't accept that much. The baseball fees are only three hundred."

Now, wasn't that something? She wouldn't have ever imagined putting the words "only" and "three hundred" next to each other. She looked at the four men staring back at her, half expecting them to nod sheepishly.

But for some reason, not a one of them flinched.

"Hold on before you start refusing a good idea," Jackson said. "Didn't you tell me that playing for the Bats involved going to tournaments?"

"Well, yes."

"Then that means you're going to have to worry about gas, restaurants, and hotel rooms."

"Oh. I guess it does." Why hadn't she ever thought that "travel" might mean more than simply driving to Lexington or Columbus for the day?

Troy folded his arms over his chest. "Even if y'all are only staying at Motel Sixes, two nights can add up."

While she started mentally calculating hotel room prices, Ace chuckled. "Hell, Troy, these kids and their parents aren't staying there. They're at places with pools."

"Pools?" She quickly added another hundred and fifty to her estimates.

"And food." Jackson raised a brow. "And missed work."

She hadn't thought about that. If she was gone on Friday and Saturday nights, how was she going to help Jackson with Kate?

Feeling a little sick, she stood up. "I think I might have to tell Jeremy that it's not possible this year."

Campbell stood up, too. "Forgive me. I know you don't know me, but I think you're getting blinded by your worries. We're all sitting here, saying we want to help you."

"But you don't know me."

She lifted her chin. "Then, don't you think it's time we got to know each other?"

"Yes, of course. But it seems awfully one-sided ..." She bit her bottom lip. She sounded ungrateful. "You guys, it's not that I don't appreciate it. I do. It's just—"

"It's hard to accept so much generosity," Kurt finished.

"Well, yes." Even for Jeremy this felt like too much.

Jackson started laughing.

"What's so funny?"

"You are, Miss Dani. You've helped me time and again with Kate. How do you think I've been feeling?"

"That's different."

"Not really. It's only different because you aren't the one on the receiving end."

When she opened her mouth to protest, she couldn't think of a thing to say. Feeling sheepish, she looked at them all. "Jackson's right. Thank you."

Kurt clapped his hands. "Good. For a while there, I thought I was going to have to arm wrestle you."

Ace looked up from the screen of his phone that he'd been staring at for the last couple of seconds. "Next Saturday sound good?"

Troy nodded. "Yep. I'm in."

Kurt got out his phone and started thumbing through screens. "I'm going to announce it right now."

"What are you going to call the tournament, Kurt?" Emily asked.

"'Play for a Cause.' It's got a nice ring to it, don't you think?"

"What do you think, Dan?" Jackson murmured.

"I think ... well I think it sounds perfect." When she smiled at him, she realized that her smile was genuine. No matter what happened, she realized that she wasn't alone and that the others didn't think she was taking advantage of them. "I could bake cookies for the tournament, maybe?"

Emily winced. "Actually, most of the time, the guys—"

"Can't wait to have a couple of cookies," Kurt said quickly.

Dani laughed. "I'm pretty sure that isn't what Emily was going to say."

"That's fine with me, because I'm pretty sure she doesn't crave your baked goods like most of the men in my garage will. Bake lots of them."

She chuckled again, embarrassed. "Jackson—"

"Kurt didn't lie. I can promise if you bake those peanut butter ones with the milk-chocolate chips, guys are going to want to play all night."

* * *

Later that night, after they got back to their apartment complex and Jeremy was on the phone with his friends while Kate was fussing with her dolls, they stood outside Jackson's apartment. He was leaning outside his door, she was by his side, and though they'd just spent five hours in each other's company, Dani thought it felt like only five minutes had passed.

"Did you have a good time tonight?"

"I did. I mean, after I got over my freak-out and everything."

"How are you feeling now? Still freaking out?"

She paused, thinking about it. "You know what? I'm not. I don't know what happened, but I seem to be doing okay with everything. No, better than that. I've been really worried about telling Jeremy that he couldn't play."

"You were sure that was your only option, huh?"

She nodded. "I learned a while back that not having everything you want isn't fun but it's something we have to get used to … it's necessary to learn. But the thing of it is, I think Jeremy has already learned that lesson the hard way." Looking into his blue eyes, she said, "I'm not quite ready for him to learn that sometimes a person has to go without everything they need, too."

"Don't make him learn that lesson yet. I agree that it builds character, but it comes with a price, don't you think?"

Reluctantly, she nodded. She didn't want Jeremy to grow spoiled, but he was a long way from that.

"How about we simply be thankful that we have each other?"

She really was. What would her life be like if he hadn't entered it? "I'm glad we're friends."

He leaned down and gently pressed his lips to hers. "I think we're more than friends, Dani," he murmured as he brushed his lips against her jaw. "Don't you?"

She shivered. These sweet kisses might only be a sweet gesture of affection after an emotional afternoon. Or, maybe it was a reminder of all they'd shared. But even though that was the case, she couldn't help but notice how the faint scratch of scruff on his cheeks felt against her sensitive skin. Or the way his skin smelled faintly of whatever woodsy cologne he'd splashed on that morning.

"Dani?"

"Oh, sorry. My mind drifted." She cleared her throat. "I mean, I agree." Because he didn't lie. It was so good that they were friends.

But as she walked back upstairs to her own space, Dani found herself wondering if she actually wanted to figure out what they were.

She'd never imagined that she'd ever enter into a relationship again. But that suddenly seemed a little silly. Brian would have never expected such a thing.

Only his family did.

CHAPTER 23

FROM LES LARKE'S
YOU, TOO, CAN HOST A POKER TOURNEY:

Plan to have a discussion about poker etiquette, too.

"When are y'all coming back to visit?" Jackson's brother Grant asked for about the fifth time since they'd started talking. "Mom and Dad seem to think it's sooner than later."

Though he liked the idea of his family missing him and Kate, Jackson knew such a thing wasn't possible. "Yeah, that's not true. I don't have any plans to head home anytime soon."

"Are you sure about that?"

Grant's voice was quiet and measured. Much like it had always been. His older brother was steady and reliable and seemed to always go the way of least dissension. Grant could get along with anyone, at any time.

Jackson had always admired his brother's qualities. They'd sure made his mother happy and had served Grant well throughout most of his life.

But it didn't mean Grant always got his way—or that his little brother was ever going to adopt that same disposition.

No, Jackson was far more the type of man to deliver information bluntly. It was why he'd been a pretty good crew leader in the mines and it was why he'd had no problem grabbing Reed Moore's collar when he hadn't treated Dani right. "I'm real sure, Grant. I can't."

"Can't or won't?"

It was a fair question but just because it was fair it didn't make it any easier. "Both. I'm working most weekends, Grant. You know that."

"She's only three. Bring her home for a few days during the week."

Though he knew Grant's heart was in the right place, Jackson was beginning to get irritated. He shouldn't have to explain himself.

Trying to put his reasons into words, he said, "It's not just work. It's about other things, too."

"Such as?"

"Such as this move hasn't exactly been an easy adjustment. Not for me or Kate."

"Really? I thought it was going better."

"It is. Finally. And that's why I need to stay here. We don't need to be reminded of everything." Like Beth, for example. Or of how their lives used to be, back when he'd had a good job and Kate had been surrounded by loving relatives.

Grant scoffed. "You don't want to be reminded of Spartan. Wow, you're making your hometown sound like a real fine place. I can understand now why you hated to leave." Thick sarcasm laced his voice.

Jackson didn't blame him—but he was also uncomfortably aware that he wasn't all that sad to be gone anymore. There were times when his life in Spartan felt like it had belonged to a different man. With each passing day, Bridgeport felt more like home. There really wasn't anything more to say. He'd made his choice just as Grant had made his. "I'll call Mom and explain things again."

"You can do that, but you're gonna upset her."

"Then she's going to be sad because she's going to lose." Tired of talking about that, he said, "Now, tell me about you. You've been traveling, right?"

"Yeah." Pride edged into his brother's voice. "Jackson, you know, when we first got laid off, I was real suspicious of those government employees setting up shop in the old Kmart."

"Everyone was." It had felt like insult to injury to see welfare relief workers reaching out to all of them like they were refugees from Africa or something. Half the men he knew back in Spartan wouldn't even drive by the place, they acted so put out that their employment troubles were so well known. "I'm glad you talked to them. It sounds like it was the right decision."

He scoffed. "It wasn't like I had a choice. You know how Missy gets. She says there's pride and then there's being smart."

Jackson had always figured Grant's wife Missy could run a whole city if the town council gave her the opportunity. She was a forward thinker, always working, and didn't know the meaning of the words "can't" and "no." Her only soft spot was for her husband and kids. With them, she was all sweetness and light ... until she thought one of them needed a kick in the shin.

Thinking of Grant's packet of classes and training, Jackson said, "I couldn't believe it when you said you were going to start working for the power company."

"At first, I wasn't real sure I could do it. Climbing poles and working with electricity ain't for the faint of heart. But damned if I'm not enjoying it." Pure enthusiasm lit his voice. "And you wouldn't believe the money."

"It's that good?"

"Last month I made two grand over what I was making when Spartan Mine Number Nine laid me off."

"Two grand over?" His brother had been making good money in the mine. Real good.

"I know, right? Now, it's been hard, because everywhere the storms hit, I'm there, too. So I've been sleeping in motels and pulling ten- and twelve-hour shifts while Missy's had to pick up the slack at home. We're both dead on our feet half the time."

"But it's worth it."

"Heck, yeah. Missy was able to quit that stinkin' clerical job she hated and went back to being a mom and a housewife. She's happier and the kids are happier, too."

"I'm guessin' that means that you're happier, too."

"Well, yeah. When I'm home, Missy spoils me, tells me that she's proud of her husband. That right there makes me feel like I'm worth something."

"Grant, you always were worth something."

"Don't be getting all sappy on me. You know what I mean."

"I get it."

He paused. "You know, Jackson, could be that the reason you're having such a hard time is because you weren't meant to be out there in Ohio. Maybe God's simply trying to remind you that you're supposed to be doing something else."

Grant might have a point. As hard as that was to admit, Jackson realized that being a bartender wasn't anything that he was proud of. It was a good job. Just not for him. At least, he didn't think so.

"Hey, by your silence, I'm guessing I need to shut up."

"You don't need to shut up. I ... well I'm not ready to go back yet."

"All right. But, hey, if you want me to send you any literature."

"I'll call you."

"Okay. Sure." Grant's voice sounded deflated. Jackson didn't blame him. If their positions were reversed, he would have felt that exact same way, too.

"Thanks for calling."

"No problem. I'll call again. And you, pick up the damn phone and call Mom."

"I'll do it."

"Good." After a pause, Grant added, "You take care now, Jackson. Bye."

He hung up. Jackson hung up, too, feeling more melancholy than he had in a while. Every once in a while, he felt like hitting something. He didn't understand. His brother had Missy and four kids and now an even better paying job than before.

Grant was happy. Content. And he should be, too. He'd been living a charmed life and he was a faithful man who wasn't ashamed to both count his blessings and give thanks to the Lord for giving him such a bounty.

He deserved all of those blessings, too. He was a good man.

But, every once in a while, Jackson felt like asking God if He'd forgotten him. He wasn't perfect, but he'd sure tried to live a good life, too.

Why had he lost both his wife and his job? Why was he having to raise a sweet little girl on his own?

How come the only way he'd been able to handle those losses was to pull away from everything else he had? How come he was now serving people beer while his brother was making over double the money?

Some days, the disparity in their situations didn't make a lick of sense to him.

He hoped one day it would.

CHAPTER 24

FROM LES LARKE'S
YOU, TOO, CAN HOST
A POKER TOURNEY:

You can even make your own special house rules,
such as permitting players to have their cell
phones out or not.

A week had passed since Dani had sat in Kurt Holland's house and found herself nodding and agreeing to the poker tournament. But as far as all the changes that had taken place?

Well, it might as well have been a lifetime.

Something had happened that night to change practically everything in her social life. She now had plans.

Plans, as in social plans with Emily, Meredith, and Campbell. They texted her, called her, invited her out for coffee or walks, and even one of Meredith's free Pilates classes in her studio.

Campbell and Troy had even asked her and Jackson over for dinner, just like they were a real couple.

Which they were *not*.

Every time she thought about the awkward conversation they'd shared after Troy had called him and Campbell had called her she blushed outrageously. She was too old to be so giddy around a man.

But that didn't seem to make a difference to her heart. She'd been sure it was beating so fast that Jackson was going ask why her pulse was racing.

Luckily, he'd been working, and she'd already committed to watching Kate. If they'd both been free, she honestly didn't know what they would have done. It seemed to her that Jackson thought it was a good idea.

But even though she'd been taking very small steps into a social life, she had realized that a few hours of rest and relaxation was doing her a world of good. Her mind felt clearer and she was thinking about her day-care center again. Almost like now that she was taking time to rest instead of working for her goals, she was able to actually spend time figuring out how to make them happen.

Just as she was planning to sit on her little apartment balcony, her phone buzzed.

You coming?

Ugh. Another one of Meredith's free Pilates classes.

I don't know.

Come on. It will be fun.

Painful, yes. Difficult, yes. Fun … not yet.
Campbell texted again before she could respond.

It won't get fun until you go
enough to get better. Have to start
somewhere! Think of it that way.

185

Realizing that Campbell probably had a point, Dani pulled out a pair of black leggings and one of her more decent-looking T-shirts.

> I'll be right out. Save me a spot.

> We already have. Can't wait! This will be fun!

Shaking her head at Campbell's happy optimism, Dani quickly wrote a note for Jeremy, who would likely sleep for the next two hours, grabbed her keys, sunglasses, and phone, and hustled down the stairs.

Just as she was crossing the parking lot that her complex shared with many of the small businesses in the area, she spied Jackson's boss Gen again. Gen was leaning on the side of her Explorer and texting someone. She was wearing a frown and everything about her posture said she was frustrated.

There was something there that made Dani pause, and then make a decision. "Hey, Gen," she said as she got closer. "How are you?"

Gen looked up, focused and then dropped the hand that was holding the phone to her side. "Hey, Dani. What's going on?"

"I'm on my way to a Pilates class."

Gen wrinkled her nose. "A what?"

"I know. I thought the same thing when my friend Campbell first told me about it. It's an exercise class, kind of like yoga but not. Meredith Hunt teaches it. She offers a few free classes a month."

"Ah. Well, I hope you enjoy it."

This wasn't a great beginning, but she knew she had to push forward. "What are you doing now? You aren't going in to work already, are you?"

"I was half-thinking about it. I thought it was better to keep busy than ..." She stopped herself midsentence. "Why?"

"Well, I thought maybe you'd like to join me."

"Oh, Dani. I don't know." She looked down at her outfit. She was wearing a pair of black running shorts, a teal-colored sports bra and a white tank top over it. "I'm not really dressed for anything but running."

"For running or Pilates," Dani corrected. Seeing Gen waver, she smiled. "Come on. If you don't like it, you don't. But I'm thinking you might like it a lot." Boy, she hoped Campbell didn't hear her talking up the class! All she'd been doing ten minutes ago was trying to get out of going.

After staring at the screen of her cell phone again, Gen muttered something under her breath before exhaling. "All right, I'll go. I was going to meet Melissa at the bar to help with deliveries. Let me just let her know that I'll be in later." After she put her phone away, she looked back at Dani. "Okay. I'm set ... but I'm warning you, don't expect too much from me."

Dani chuckled. "Since I barely know what I'm doing, I won't. Come on. Campbell saved me a spot. We can get you one near us."

"You don't have to go to all that trouble."

"Sure we do," Dani joked. "I mean, we can't let you hang out in the back and sneak out."

Gen brushed a strand of hair away from her cheek. "Do you think I'd really do that?"

"Of course I do." She chuckled. "I know because I tried to do that my first time, too."

She shook her head. "You're something else, Dani. Always so positive."

"No, not always."

"Jackson seems to think you are."

"Jackson knows all my faults." Realizing that made it sound

like they were closer than they were, she amended her words. "I mean, Jackson has come to realize that I have just as many worries and grumpy moments as anyone else."

"It never seems that way. How come? Do you just hide them better?"

Dani shrugged. "What's going on? Do you have something you're worried about?"

"Maybe." After a couple of more steps, she grunted. "Is it that obvious?"

"No. I just saw you glaring at your phone. I figure it's either work and staffing problems or a man."

"It's a man all right."

Remembering tall, dark, and handsome Seth, Dani nodded. "When you're ready to talk about it, let me know."

Gen looked at her curiously. "You really mean that, don't you?"

Dani nodded. Part of her wanted to remind Gen that she'd lost her husband. That loss had put everything into perspective. But now, though that pain was very real and clear, it wasn't as sharp.

Now she had thoughts about Jackson as much as she ever had about Brian. It had come so gradually, she felt as if she'd had time to actually get used to the fact that she might not willingly be alone forever.

She didn't want to be a widow for the rest of her life.

CHAPTER 25

FROM LES LARKE'S
YOU, TOO, CAN HOST
A POKER TOURNEY:

Some days of the week are better than others for
a poker night. Saturday nights are sometimes
tough for guys who are married. Wednesday
night is usually reserved for church or school
functions. That's why I often suggest Thursday
night for a friendly game. By Thursday, most
people are ready for a fun night out.

It was a fact. She didn't like Pilates. It was too quiet, the move-ments were too controlled, and she didn't like laying down on some contraption. It made her feel vulnerable.

Then there was the fact that it was harder than it looked, and she kept messing up. That was another mark against it.

When Meredith, a way too cute instructor, told everyone to put something on the contraption called a long box, Gen was just about ready to bolt.

She was actually looking at the door longingly when Meredith walked up to her side and helped her put it on.

Okay, she placed the box on the machine for Gen, which meant Gen wasn't going to be able to go anywhere. "For what it's worth, it gets easier," Meredith said. "And when it does, then it becomes a lot more enjoyable. Then, next thing you know, you're going to love it."

Gen didn't think that was possible. After Meredith bent down to help Campbell, Gen muttered to herself. "Did I look that unhappy?"

"Oh, yeah," a woman to her left said.

Gen grimaced. "Sorry. I'm just a lot better at other sports like basketball or tennis. I'm finding these small moves frustrating." And harder than she thought they'd be.

"Don't be sorry for having an opinion," Meredith said. "There's no pressure here." Raising her voice, she called out the next set of instructions, which included sitting on that box like it was a horse.

Hoping she was looking a little less grumpy, Gen did what everyone else was doing. Then looked over at Dani.

Dani met her gaze and grinned. "You're doing good, Gen. I'm glad you came with me."

"You actually sound like you mean it."

"I do. I know we don't know each other very well, but it almost feels like I do, since Jackson talks about you all the time."

"Jackson is a good man."

Dani smiled. "I think so, too."

As Meredith continued out calling out instructions, Gen concentrated on keeping up. To her surprise, when it was over, she was sweaty, a little sore, and yet she felt much better. She hadn't thought about anything but keeping up with the rest of the women for the last hour.

Boy, maybe she needed these classes just to have a stress reliever.

"You work at the Corner Bar, don't you?" a brown-haired woman asked as she slipped on a loose knit top over her sports bra.

"I do. I also own it."

"No way. Good for you!"

"I don't know if that's a good thing or not," she said with an exaggerated grimace. "But I enjoy it."

Dani came up to their sides. "Gen, this is Emily Springer. Emily is the girlfriend of one of Jackson's buddies from West Virginia. Emily, this is Gen. Jackson works for her."

Emily smiled. "It's nice to meet you. Kurt and I stopped in there one evening before we went out to eat. It's really nice in there."

"I'm glad you gave it a try." When Meredith joined them, Gen said, "I really hope you will stop by soon. I'll buy you a drink. You deserve a treat for putting up with my grumpy self."

Meredith laughed. "You weren't so bad."

Emily groaned. "No offense, Gen, but for a moment there, I thought you were going to walk right out of here."

"That's because I was seriously contemplating it. It was hard, and I'm not flexible."

"I'm glad you didn't run off. That wouldn't have been good for my reputation," Meredith teased.

She liked the women. They were nice and didn't seem too high maintenance. "Seriously, I hope all of y'all will come by."

"I'm in," Emily said. "We should have a girls' night soon. Dan, Mer, what do you think?"

"I think it would be fun. If there's a night when Jackson isn't working, I could probably go. I watch Kate, you know."

Emily waved a hand. "We'll get Kurt's son and his girlfriend to watch Kate." With a wink, she said, "I kind of want to get the chance to ogle Jackson."

Gen almost spit out the sip of water she'd just taken. "If you came to ogle him, you'll have to get in line. Half the women in there flirt with him. It's hysterical."

Emily chuckled. "I'm happily engaged. I just couldn't help but tease Dani a little. Jackson Koch really is handsome."

"Does Jackson flirt back with all those women?" Dani asked. Suddenly looking horrified, she slapped a hand over her mouth. "Forget I asked that."

"He doesn't," Gen said, glad she wasn't lying. "I don't think I've seen him give any of those gals anything besides a faint smile."

Emily grinned at Meredith. "Now, I think we really need to plan a night out soon. I want to watch Jackson fend off women while flashing those dimples … and watch Dani here act like she doesn't care."

"I'll go with you girls, but I don't think I would be much fun," Meredith said slowly.

The three of them looked at her in confusion. "Why is that?" Dani asked.

"Because I'm pregnant."

"What? Oh my gosh!" Emily squealed and gave her a hug.

"Congratulations!" Dani said, hugging her too. "How far along are you?"

"Not very. And thanks. Ace and I … well, this wasn't planned. I'm still kind of in a daze about it, if you want to know the truth."

Oh, every word of that explanation stung. But even though it did, she wasn't going to let it show. "I'm happy for you," Gen said with a smile. "Congratulations."

"Thanks. We're pretty excited."

"Have you told Finn yet?" Emily asked.

"We did. He looked shocked but excited. He actually took the news better than I thought he would."

As they started talking about weddings and families, Gen felt like the walls were closing in. She didn't want to be jealous and didn't want Meredith's news to be another excuse for her to dwell about the baby she lost and how confusing things were with Seth.

"I hate to, um, do Pilates and run, but I've got to get out of here," she blurted, hoping she didn't sound as stressed as she felt. "The bar opens in two hours." They didn't need to know that Melissa had already planned to open for her.

"Oh, all right," Dani said as she gave her a quick hug. "Thanks for coming here with me."

"Yes, thanks for giving Pilates a try," Meredith added as Emily promised to see her soon.

Stepping outside, she felt the combination of relief and regret. She wished she didn't have so much baggage that she was constantly carrying around with her.

If only Seth hadn't come back. If only his being in town hadn't stirred up a bunch of pain and regrets … and made her think about things she didn't want to.

If only …

Oh, Lord.

If only he wasn't standing just outside the door looking at her—and looking just as good as ever. How could one man look so fine in just a pair of baggy shorts, old running shoes, and a faded, snug T-shirt?

"About time you stepped outside," he drawled. "I thought I was going to have to come in and get you."

"Why are you here?"

"I was about to step into the bar and ran into Melissa. She said you were over here taking a class. I thought I'd buy you a sandwich."

Grasping at straws, she said, "I should probably go help Melissa."

"She told me to tell you that she's fine. So, come on." Taking her hand, he gave a little tug.

And though she knew better, she allowed herself to be tugged along. Against her better judgment, she wanted to hear what he had to say.

CHAPTER 26

FROM LES LARKE'S
YOU, TOO, CAN HOST
A POKER TOURNEY:

*I suggest that you offer alternative activities for
players who go out early. Have a game on a nearby
TV or set up a "consolation table" for the losers.*

Seth figured he had less than three minutes to say something
good enough to keep Genevieve from walking away. He thought
quickly, realizing as he ran through topics in his head that he
really didn't know her anymore.

They'd been so in love. He'd thought they'd be together
forever. And now, a mere eighteen months later, Seth didn't even
know what she did besides work.

How did that happen?

He pointed to the deli about a block down the street. Called
Jamison's, it took up the whole floor of a small bungalow. Every-
thing was fresh inside, and the owners had been easy to talk to.
He'd discovered it two days ago when he'd been running.

"Is this place okay?"

"Jamison's? It's fine."

"If not, we can go someplace else."

She looked at him curiously. "You sound unsure. Why?"

Because he was unsure about pretty much everything when it came to them. "Oh, no reason."

"Really?"

It was becoming real clear that some things about her hadn't changed. Gen was a straight talker and she liked that in other people, too. "I just realized that I didn't know if you still ate bread. Or meat. Do you?"

She tilted her head up at him. "Do I eat bread and meat? What are you getting at?" Looking a little affronted, she said, "What do you think I eat now?"

He felt his neck flush. "I don't know. It's just that half the women I know are either vegan or gluten-free or keto or something. I started thinking that I didn't even know what kind of food you ate these days."

"As long as it tastes good, I eat just about anything."

He sighed in relief. "So sandwiches are fine."

"They're more than fine." She smiled. "They sound fantastic."

They walked across the street, then he held the door open when they entered.

Bree, the manager, looked up from behind the counter. "Hey, Gen." After a second, her eyes warmed. "And hey to you, too. Welcome back."

Gen's eyebrows rose. "Welcome back?"

"I was in here yesterday," he explained before smiling at the manager. "My name is Seth."

"Good to meet you. Are you two in here together?"

He felt Gen stiffen next to him, but he tried to not care. "We sure are."

"It's good to make a new friend." She waved a hand at the black chalkboard behind her. "We've got some specials today. Shrimp salad, carrot and kale soup, and French dips. A lot of our regular items, too."

"Carrot and Kale soup, Bree?" Gen asked. "That's pretty out there."

She shrugged. "A lot of people are on special diets now. I like to accommodate them."

Gen looked at Seth and chuckled. "We were just talking about that on the way over here. Seth was worried that I either didn't eat meat or I didn't eat bread."

"Now you know that whatever you do or don't eat, we can accommodate you here. We're a full-service deli."

"Looks like we came to the right place then," he murmured. "What would you like, Gen?"

She'd been staring hard at the chalkboard. "Just a turkey sandwich and some chips. Oh, and iced tea."

"I'll have the French dip with the salad and tea as well," he said as he pulled out his wallet. After he paid Bree, she motioned to the six empty tables.

"Take a seat and I'll bring out your orders in a few."

Even though there was only one other couple in the small café, he still wanted privacy. "How about over by the fireplace?" It was a fairly warm day, but the flickering fire cast a pretty glow. The Gen he knew used to like things like that.

She shrugged. "Sure. That's fine."

He followed her to the table, stopping himself just in time from pulling out her chair. This wasn't that kind of place, and Gen would probably be uncomfortable with the attention.

He did wait for her to sit down, then sat down across from her. She was sitting with her back straight and her expression slightly bored.

She was merely putting up with him.

Damn. It wasn't the response he had hoped for. Just as he was swallowing his disappointment, he reminded himself that he knew better than to expect too much. If they could have a civil conversation together, that would be an improvement.

"So, are you into Pilates now?"

"Hmm?"

"Pilates. Do you take a lot of classes there now?"

She wrinkled her nose. "Oh, gosh, no." Leaning back in her chair, she said, "Dani, who babysits for Jackson's daughter, saw me in the parking lot and asked me to go to the class."

"And you said yes?"

"Yep." Meeting his eyes directly for the first time, she said, "I know. It doesn't sound like me, does it?"

It didn't. Not at all. She'd always been a loner. Always better at talking about the weather with strangers than letting her guard down with other people. Especially other women.

"I'm glad you went and are making girlfriends. That's important." Of course, the moment the words were out of his mouth, he wished he could take them back. He sounded like Dr. Phil.

"Is it? I don't know." Her expression turned guarded again. "What about you? Are you any better than I was at making friends?"

"Probably not." He smiled slightly. "I've got a good excuse, though. I've known pretty much everybody in Lubbock my whole life. I haven't had much of the occasion to meet new people." Realizing how much he'd talked to Jackson and the customers when he'd bartended, he shrugged. "I've been doing all right here, though. So there is that."

She folded her arms over her chest. "I can't believe you're still here."

"I'm not going to leave until we get things settled between us."

"Seth, that isn't necessary."

"It is." He shrugged. "And since I aim to be here a little longer, I might end up meeting all kinds of people. It will be good for me."

Though she wasn't smiling, her eyes had lit up. "Maybe. Maybe not." Just as he thought she was going to turn silent again, she continued. "Jackson has a group of buddies from home. Believe it or not, they all moved here from a little town in West Virginia."

"Why did they do that?"

"At first, I thought they just kind of followed each other here, but now that I've gotten to know Jackson better, he told me that a lot of people they knew were affected by the mine closures."

"He used to mine, right?"

She nodded. "He was a crew supervisor. I don't think the others worked the mines, but their fathers did."

"Working in a mine has got to be difficult. Bet they're glad to be out of there."

"I thought that would be the case, but I think Jackson would return to that life in a heartbeat. I know he misses it."

"That's too bad for you, right?"

"Why would you say that?"

"You really like him. If he misses mining, he might go back to it."

She seemed to give that some thought. "No, I don't think he will. I'm under the impression that he's staying put."

"That's good. He's a good employee, right?"

"He's a good man but only an okay bartender." She smiled. "He's getting better, though. And, I guess he can manage all sorts of people. I keep giving him more and more responsibility, and he takes it all in stride. He's a great manager."

Bree's arrival with their sandwiches prevented him from replying.

"Here you go. One turkey for you, Gen, and the French dip for you, Seth."

The sandwiches looked amazing. "Thanks."

"You need anything else?" Bree looked from one to the other of them.

"I'm fine," Gen said.

"I'm good, too."

After Bree turned back around, Seth watched her take a bite of her sandwich then did the same with his own. Just as he was swallowing, she murmured, "I keep thinking about Jackson. Do … do you think it's easy to go back to being the person you used to be?"

Seth didn't even have to think about that. "No."

She raised her eyebrows. "Wow. You're certain."

"We all grow up. Grow old, too, I guess. Things change. Life happens. All of that influences a person's perspective, I think."

She nodded slowly as she chewed another bite. "I bet you're right. I've been here almost two years now. It's not that long but I've changed a ton."

"I know."

"I don't know if I ever could go back to being the girl I once was."

"Do you think you would want to be her?"

"Maybe." She brushed a lock of hair back behind her shoulder. "That girl was a little more optimistic about life. Maybe a little prettier."

She surely had been pretty two years ago. There had been a look of contentment in her eyes that he hadn't spied since he'd come to visit. But he couldn't say that the more guarded look was a bad thing. "You're still pretty. Still real pretty."

She rolled her eyes. "I don't know about that. All these late nights take their toll."

"I don't see it. To me, you look the same."

"I think you look about the same, too."

"I've got more gray hair."

"I noticed."

"It sucks to be starting to get gray at thirty-five, but whatever, you know? At least it's staying on my head."

She grinned as he took another bite of his sandwich. Then, she asked, "Why are we doing this?"

"Lunch, or everything?"

She put down the chip she'd been holding. "You know the answer. Everything. Why are you still here in Bridgeport?"

"I came here because of the baby." He refused to call what happened just *the miscarriage*. That word felt too distant for something that had affected them both so much. "But now? Now I realize that I not only lost a baby but you."

"We broke up a long time ago, Seth. Don't act like you haven't gone out with other women."

"I won't. I have gone out, but that doesn't mean any of those other women could fill the gap that you made in my life when you left. It's still there."

"What are you saying? That you want me back?"

"Maybe."

"Seth. Life doesn't work that way."

The tight control that he'd been holding close snapped. "How do you know? What if it does? What if the Lord decided that we weren't ready back then for each other?"

She looked stunned. After glancing at the counter where they ordered, she lowered her voice. "Are you thinking that we are ready to get back together now?"

"I think so."

"Even if we were, it still wouldn't work out."

She didn't realize it, but she'd just given him a grain of hope. "Why wouldn't it?" he asked softly.

"Because we live in two separate states. Because you're down in Lubbock. I'm here. In Ohio."

"I'm running my family's ranch. I can't move."

"Well, I'm running a bar that I own."

"Is that what you want to do for the rest of your life? Run a bar?"

"It's my job. It's what I do."

"You could always open a bar in Texas. Last time I checked, we drank beer and whiskey there, too."

She pushed her plate away. "Seth, thank you for lunch, but I think we need to agree that whatever we used to have is long gone. You need to get out of here and head back."

"If I leave now, I'm always going to feel like I didn't give us a real chance."

"But you did. You came to Bridgeport to find me. You did that."

"I came to Bridgeport with a thousand questions about why we used to argue so much. With a hundred reasons to be upset with you." More softly, he added, "I had a dozen excuses about why you owed me because I was so hurt."

"And now?"

"Now I can only think of one reason to stay here. You."

She sucked in a breath. "You can't do this."

"I'm afraid I can't do anything else. I want you back in my life, Genevieve Schuler. Even though it doesn't make sense and I shouldn't be so selfish, I absolutely want you to get to know me again. To learn to forgive me for being such a jerk."

"And then?"

"And then, I want you to sell your bar, move back to Lubbock, and realize that we were meant to be together."

"Is that all?"

"No. Then you're gonna live the rest of your life by my side."

She snapped her fingers. "Just like that?"

"No, not just like that," he said impatiently. "I know it's going to be difficult and frightening. I know our future is unsure and there's a lot of things that we need to get to know about each other."

After tossing a couple of bucks on the table, he stood up. "But, I also know that if I don't ask it will never happen. And if you don't even think about it, you're going to be tending bar by yourself, going to Pilates classes every now and then because you don't have anything else to do, and always, always living with the regret of never trying harder to hold on to the life we once had."

She gaped at him. "Seth ..."

"No, don't talk. Just listen to me. I don't know a whole hell of a lot of things, Gen, but I know that."

Not trusting himself to say another word to her, he walked to the trash can, threw the wrappings of his sandwich away, tipped his hat to Bree, and walked out the door.

He had no idea what was going to happen next, but he couldn't regret what had just happened.

Not when he'd seen the tears forming in her eyes. She felt something. His words had made that happen.

For now? That was enough.

CHAPTER 27

FROM LES LARKE'S
YOU, TOO, CAN HOST A POKER TOURNEY:

It's an uncomfortable topic to think about, but every once in a while, a fun, casual game can get out of hand. It's best to be prepared for that.

When had Dani laughed so much? It had probably been right around the last time she'd paid someone to watch Jeremy. Years. It had been years.

That meant it had been way too long.

"Are you sure you don't want an ice cream cone?" Jackson asked as they walked along the sidewalks of downtown Bridgeport, stopping to check out various boutiques and pubs. They were really just wasting time. They'd gone out to eat Italian food and now were walking off some of those carbs until it was time to meet their friends over at the Corner Bar.

"I couldn't eat another bite. But you can get one if you want."

Jackson hesitated in front of the cutest name for an ice cream shop ever, the Daily Scoop. It was in Bridgeport's old newspaper office and the owners had decorated the walls with framed front pages of the historic paper. "I better not."

"Afraid to lose some of your tips?" She was starting to have a really good time teasing him about all the women going to the bar just to look at him. Since he was one of the least flirty men she'd ever met, Dani knew he took the ladies' interest in stride instead of letting it go to his head.

"Ha, ha." He winked. "But maybe."

"I deserved that comment, didn't I?"

Wrapping his arm around her shoulders, he said, "No. But I now wish I never introduced you to Gen. I could have gone my whole life without you hearing her stories about all the flirty gals."

"I'm glad she told me." Taking a chance, she added, "It just goes to show you that I have good taste."

He stopped. "You really think that?"

She nodded. Realizing how important Jackson had become to her, she said, "I'm glad I found you."

He smiled slowly. "Me too, though I think it was more like I found you. I was the one who asked you to babysit Kate."

She giggled as they walked on, then stopped in front of another building, an old movie theater. It had stood empty for three years after it closed, and for a while people on the city council had even discussed demolishing it. Only a "Save the Carlyle" campaign had saved the building.

But even though it had been saved and money had gone into it to fix some of its basic needs, it had sat empty for months.

Now, however, white lights framed the windows, lights were shimmering inside, and in the windows were old-timey signs where movie posters had once been placed. "Look at this, Jackson! Someone finally moved in here."

"Dance with Me Dance Studio. Huh. I guess I better keep

this place in mind if Kate ever decides that she wants to take dance lessons."

Dani giggled. "Have you met your daughter? Of course she will. She's destined for ballet slippers."

Looking up at the building, his voice softened. "She would look real cute up on stage twirling around, wouldn't she?"

"Adorable." She slipped her fingers in his hand. "But I'm afraid this isn't that kind of place."

"What kind of dance place is it?"

After giving his hand a squeeze, she said, "I think it's a grown-up dance place."

"For women who want to take ballet?"

"No, for couples who want to dance like in *Dancing with the Stars*."

"Wow."

Lured by the music floating through the door, she said, "Let's go inside."

He didn't budge. "Dani, I don't think—"

"Oh, don't worry. It's not like I have money for dance lessons anyway. But can we just look inside? I really am curious about what it looks like. It was empty forever."

"You promise you won't suddenly make me sign up for salsa dancing or something?"

"I promise," she said with a smile. Though it was now apparent that he knew a lot more about dancing than he was letting on if he knew what salsa dancing was. "Come on."

Looking put-upon, Jackson opened the door and ushered her inside. As soon as the door closed, he let out a low whistle. "This place is awesome."

It really was. The walls had been painted a soft dove gray. Ornate trim painted a soft creamy white decorated all the windows and doors. Old-time movie and dance posters lined the hall, each one framed in a black metal frame. Velvet couches and chairs were placed in corners, each upholstered in rich jewel-toned fabric. And that same soothing music floated through each room.

Dani had never danced in her life and she wanted to slip on a pair of heels and twirl around.

"Have you seen enough?"

"Let's go in just a little further. No one seems to be around."

"May I help you?"

Turning abruptly, they came face-to-face with a dark-haired, slender woman on the tall side. She was easily five foot seven or eight. She was dressed in a form-fitting gray knit dress. It hugged her frame and flowed around her legs. She was wearing a pair of heels and had perfect makeup on. Dani thought she looked just as if she'd stepped out of *Dancing with the Stars* herself.

She was also staring at Jackson.

"Hi," Dani said with a smile. "I'm sorry to interrupt, but we were just walking by and noticed that someone had moved into the building."

An awkward second passed, then Dani noticed that Jackson was staring right back at the woman. "Jackson?"

"Shannon?" Jackson blurted, still staring.

Slowly the woman nodded. "Do I ... oh my gosh. Jackson Koch?" She swallowed, followed by a hesitant smile. "Jackson, is that really you?"

He grinned as he stepped over to her and gave her a hug. "Shannon, I can't believe it. What are you doing in Bridgeport?" After giving her another hug, he dropped his arms and stepped back by Dani's side.

"Living here." She laughed. "Starting a dance studio. What brings you to town?"

"Kate and I moved here a few months ago."

"We'll have to get together soon." Looking at Dani, she

blushed. "I mean, *all of us* should. I'm so sorry for my rudeness. I'm Shannon Murphy. I went to high school with Jackson here."

Before Dani could say a word, Jackson slipped an arm around her shoulders. "No, this is my fault. Shannon, this is my girlfriend, Dani Brown."

While she'd thought it would be scary to hear that word, it felt strangely comforting and warm. Like a good fit. Smiling brightly, Dani held out her hand. "If anyone should apologize, it's me. I forced Jackson to come inside."

"I'm glad you did. Would you like a tour? Do you dance?"

"Yes to the tour and no to dancing. I … well, I'm afraid I wouldn't even know how to do the two-step."

Shannon smiled. "Luckily, I have a cure for that. I give classes here. Y'all should sign up."

"Maybe another time, Shannon. We're pretty busy right now. Dani's son is playing baseball, so it seems just about every night is booked up."

"He's playing like you did," she said softly. "That's great."

The door opened, and two couples came inside. They looked to be in their forties and the men were wearing jeans and loafers and the women dresses much like Shannon's and heels.

Shannon smiled brightly at them. "Good evening. Y'all go right in." After they moved away, she said softly, "I guess we'll have to do that tour another time. But um, take my card. My number's on it. Y'all give me a call if you want to grab a coffee or something."

"I'll do that. Ace, Kurt Holland, and Troy are here in Bridgeport, too. They'd love to see you. We'll catch up. Winking, he added, "I'm sure they'll love to hear all what's been going on with Spartan High's former head cheerleader."

A new shadow entered her eyes. "That was a lifetime ago, wasn't it? Well, um, I better go. Nice to meet you, Dani. Bye."

She turned abruptly away.

"That was kind of strange, huh?" Jackson asked as he walked to the pile of cards and pocketed one.

"No, I think it was good. Something happened with that girl. I think she needs a friend. You should call her."

Kissing her brow, he murmured, "You really do have the best heart, Dani. I'm lucky to have you."

As they walked back out, Dani knew that she felt the same way about him. The exact same way.

CHAPTER 28

FROM LES LARKE'S
YOU, TOO, CAN HOST
A POKER TOURNEY:

*Not every family member is a good addition to
your monthly poker game. Remember, anytime
you mix gambling, drinking, and a good dose of
testosterone, trouble can ensue.*

Gen was out of sorts and Jackson was figuring that he'd had
just about enough. From the time they'd opened the doors that
afternoon, she'd been snapping orders at him like it was his fault
she was in such a bad mood. Kimmy had gotten yelled at for
wearing a shirt that Gen had deemed too low-cut. Poor Melissa
had gotten reamed for not taking a table's orders quick enough.

Even Brad at the door had gotten an earful for not checking
some regulars' IDs. It was only eleven o'clock, too. At this rate
none of them were going to make it through the night without
saying something back.

Jackson, for one, was nearing the end of his patience.

"You need to say something to her, Jackson," Kimmy said as

she loaded up a tray of drinks. "If she doesn't try to be a little nicer real soon, I swear I'm going to take off."

"You wouldn't leave me to pick up the slack, would you?"

"I might." She leaned both elbows on the bar, giving him a pretty good idea of why she wore those snug low-cut T-shirts. He wasn't interested in flirting with her, but even he would have taken a second look at her if he'd been simply there hanging out. She was a pretty thing, there was no denying that.

But that didn't mean he wasn't going to tease her a little bit. "Kimmy, if you run out of here and leave me to deal with Gen bitching about your work ethic, I'll reconsider picking up your hours when you go on vacation in two weeks."

"Oh, man. I need that vacation." Tossing her ponytail, she said, "All right, how about this, then? If she doesn't stop chewing on me in front of all the customers, I'm going to tell her what she can do with her advice."

"I'd settle for sticking a bar of Ivory soap in her mouth," Melissa grumbled as she approached the bar. "Two drafts, three Bud lights, and a Heineken."

Jackson started pouring drafts. "You still getting it too, Melissa?" Her complaints surprised him. The server was about three years older than him and a whole lot more experienced working at a bar. She'd had the patience of a saint with him his whole first week.

Melissa blew out a blast of hot air. "Oh, yeah. Gen has been evil. I don't know what's gotten up her butt, but I wish it would leave."

"Ouch." He placed all the beers on her tray. "Tab good?" He asked, checking at the table's bill.

"Yep. It's one of the guys' birthday. I overheard them say that one of their wives was going to pick them up in two hours."

As the door opened and another group of people entered,

Kimmy pushed back from the bar. "Looks like my night ain't over yet after all, Jack. Wish me luck."

"You don't need it. Thanks for not leaving me."

Melissa chuckled. "Don't worry, Jackson. There's no way either of us is going to do a thing to get on your bad side. We need you here too much."

Jackson grinned. "Nicest thing I've heard all night." Watching Melissa lift the tray and then navigate the way through the crowd, Jackson wiped down the counter. Two or three of the newcomers were heading his way. He'd bet a dollar they were going to sit at the bar with him.

"We've got a full bar here tonight, Koch. Your job is to serve drinks, not stand around and talk," Gen blurted as she joined him behind the counter.

Huh. Maybe Kimmy wasn't the one they had to worry about leaving early. "Why are you back here? Do you have an order for me?"

Her jaw tightened. "What is that supposed to mean?"

Wow. If anything, she'd gotten worse. From the periphery, he caught Kimmy's meaningful look. Damn. He really didn't want to get into this. "Nothing … except that you don't seem like yourself tonight."

"And how is that?"

"You're usually calmer. Less mean."

"Maybe you should stop worrying about me and start worrying about your own self."

"I will. As soon as I can do my job without worrying about you getting in my face about every little thing. Now, what's wrong?"

Just as it looked like she might actually tell him, the four empty seats filled up and Kimmy came with two tables' worth of drink orders. He and Gen shifted into work mode and began filling orders and methodically ringing up tickets.

By mutual agreement, he concentrated on Kimmy's orders while Gen poured bourbon and drafts for the two men and the woman who had sat down.

As Melissa approached, and then Kimmy came on her heels, Jackson didn't think about anything other than the job he'd been hired to do. By his side, Gen's posture eased as she settled into a rhythm. Little by little her mood lightened, and she started smiling more and even chatting a little bit with a couple of the regulars.

An hour passed. Then another. Both Kimmy and Melissa started smiling more as they all realized that as difficult as the night had been the tips were good and their wallets were going to be fuller.

By the time Gen called last call and the customers were filing out and Brad was calling Ubers, Jackson was only thinking about how long it was going to take him to mop the floors and wipe down the counters.

That was why when Gen finally answered his question, it caught him off guard.

"I had a great time with Seth today," she said, quietly. "That's what was wrong."

"If you had a good time, why are you in such a mood?"

"We talked a lot about some things we should have talked about months ago. He apologized, and I did, too."

He still wasn't following. But instead of asking another question, he said, "Beth and me used to do stuff like that." Forcing himself to think about their daily lives, and how things used to be, he added, "We had known each other so long that sometimes we took it for granted."

"How can you take that for granted?"

"We would assume the other person knew what we were thinking. Or that an apology was understood, not needed to be said." He shook his head, remembering one argument that had started out because he'd left his work clothes on the bathroom floor and it ended because she'd gone out and bought a new purse without telling him. "It was stupid, the things that we used to focus on."

"It's not stupid if it matters."

"You're exactly right. If it matters, then it's not stupid at all. But later, after she got sick and we had a little-bitty Kate? I started realizing that even some of the most 'important' things weren't really all that important."

"Do you think I should forgive Seth and move on?"

"We both know I can't answer that for you."

"But?"

"But, speaking from someone who would give a lot to be able to have one more day with Beth—I suggest you focus more on what you want. Seth in your life or out of it."

She bit down on her bottom lip. "That's the problem, Jackson. I'm pretty sure I want him in it."

He nodded. "Then accept that fact and move on."

"To hell with the consequences?" She raised an eyebrow.

He realized that she was offering him a challenge. That she was fairly sure he was full of it and didn't have any problem putting him back in his place.

But he knew for this, at least, he had the right words to say. "Honey, don't you see? Everything has consequences. Every single little thing."

She stared at him in shock.

Brad closed the door and locked it. "Bar's closed."

"Hallelujah," Kimmy muttered, taking off her apron and bringing her card and tips over to Gen.

Melissa did the same, looking exhausted. "What a night."

Gen took everything. "I'll have y'all's tips ready in ten minutes or so. You all did great tonight. Thanks for putting up with me."

Kimmy stayed silent, but Melissa said, "Are you feeling better now?"

"Yeah. I've been wrestling with something today, something that I wasn't sure I needed to do. But after talking to Jackson, I think I made my mind up."

"Glad I could help," Jackson walked around the bar. "Care to tell us about it?"

"Not yet. But when I'm ready to share, you'll be one of the first to know."

CHAPTER 29

FROM LES LARKE'S
YOU, TOO, CAN HOST A POKER TOURNEY:

If possible, choose your poker partners with care.
The last thing you want is for your uncle Joe to
turn into a rowdy, drunk buffoon.

Just like he'd done every time Jackson had ever sat in on a game, Kurt Holland stood up, lifted a bottle of Budweiser in the air, and announced, "The first rule of the Bridgeport Poker Tournament is that there aren't any rules."

While the guys at his table groaned, Kurt grinned. "Just be cool, okay? Play fair, have a good time, and remember that this time all our hard work is going to go for something better than just bragging rights."

Jackson smiled to himself as the guy on his right began dealing cards. This felt right. Everything about it did. Sure, everyone liked getting together, having a few beers, and having a good time. But there was a new sense of determination in the air.

All of them were glad to make a difference in a kid's life tonight.

As they started tossing in chips and betting, Vince, an older neighbor of Kurt's, looked around the table. "Anyone know who this kid is that we're helping?"

One of the guys sitting across from him replied. "All I know is it's a middle school boy who wants to play ball."

Vince frowned. "What kind of ball? Football?"

Jackson glanced his way. "Does it matter?"

"No. Not really, I guess. But aren't you curious? It would be nice to know who we're helping out."

"I heard it's baseball," Cameron Miller said. "And that the poor kid's mom is a maid."

"I hope he's a good kid," Vince said. "I'd like to know that our money is going for a good one."

That comment grated on his nerves. Before he took the time to think about it, Jackson said, "Every other time I've been here everyone's bet money for no other reason than they were glad to have something to do on a Saturday night. I don't know why the kid's character has to come into play now."

Two of the guys' eyebrows lifted.

"You know something we don't know, Jackson?" Cameron asked.

"No."

"Are you sure?" Vince asked. "You sound awfully defensive for a guy who is as in the dark as the rest of us."

"I'm not defensive. I'm just making a point that the boy's name is supposed to be kept out of it. I don't think we should start guessing who it is."

"That's fair enough," Cameron said as he picked up cards and dealt four of the guys another card.

Vince didn't look like he agreed, but he kept his silence. Something that Jackson was very glad about. He took another sip of his beer and settled in. Glad that the focus was finally off the mystery beneficiary and more on the actual game.

"Call," Cameron said.

More chips were tossed into the center and the cards were dealt. Finally, ten minutes later, there were only three of them still playing, Jackson, Vince, and a redheaded guy just out of college.

"Fold," the kid said.

"A pair of eights," Vince said.

"Three tens," Jackson said with a grin as the rest of the guys at the table groaned and tossed down their cards.

"You're on fire tonight. Looks like you're playing for a cause," Vince said as he pushed the pile of chips Jackson's way.

"I've just gotten lucky with the cards. You know how that goes."

Vince nodded as he grabbed a handful of pretzels from an open sack on the table. "I do, but you seem more focused than usual."

Jackson figured Vince wasn't wrong. He didn't care about winning tonight as much as making sure the games went well. "I guess I am."

As they stood up and walked around to their next tables, Vince held out his hand. "I hope you didn't take anything I said too personally, Jackson. I was just making conversation."

"No reason for me to take it personally," Jackson said.

Vince didn't look like he believed him, but Jackson didn't really care. All that mattered was that money was flowing and with a lot of luck, by the end of the night Dani was going to have something less to worry about.

As the games continued and the hour grew later, more and more of the guys opted out in the general game and either hung around to see who the night's winner was or played in the cash game. The donation jars that were scattered around the garage got fuller and fuller.

Jackson made it to the final table but had terrible cards and ended up getting out right away.

Ace, who was still playing, looked over at him and shrugged. "Sorry about that, buddy."

Jackson shrugged. He didn't care about himself, only about how much the tournament was going to help Dani. "Can't do anything about the cards."

As the game continued, he noticed that Kurt's garage was filling up with old chip bags, assorted cans and bottles, and a couple of ashtrays of cigar butts. Realizing he was too keyed up to sit still, he grabbed a black garbage bag from a back shelf and started cleaning up.

Just as he was taking a full bag to the trash can outside, Kurt walked up to him.

"Any reason you decided to start cleaning up?"

"Yeah. This place is a mess."

Kurt chuckled. "Yep. That about covers it." He held open the side door so Jackson could walk out. "Seriously, are you worried about how everything's going to go down?"

"A little bit. This means something to me, you know?"

"I know." Taking the bag from Jackson, he tossed it into the can and closed the lid. "I keep realizing I'd do most anything to make Em happy. Last week, I went to some Shakespeare play with her in downtown Cincinnati."

Jackson couldn't help but grin. "I didn't even know you knew who that guy was."

"I knew, though I couldn't have named one thing that the guy wrote."

"But you still went."

"Yep. Emily's a fan, which means I need to at least learn to appreciate the guy's work."

"What play did you see? *Romeo and Juliet?*"

"You know some of Shakespeare's work?"

Jackson laughed. "I'm not real smart but I know at least that."

"I don't know if I even knew that. We saw *The Taming of the Shrew*."

"What did you think?"

"The play sucked, but I thought it was a fitting symbol of how much I loved Em."

"Why? Did she hate it, too?"

"Hell, no. Em thought it was awesome. So I worked on keeping my mouth shut."

Liking the story, and how it had taken his mind off the game, Jackson said, "Beth would have said you got smart all the sudden."

Kurt slapped him on the back as he laughed. "Well, she would've been right."

CHAPTER 30

FROM LES LARKE'S
YOU, TOO, CAN HOST
A POKER TOURNEY:

Then there is the chance of having your big brother or busybody neighbor turn into a penny-pinching, angry drunk. And, I promise, it's always a possibility. You'd be surprised what can happen when people let their guard down.

You still up?

Blearily reading the text, Dani figured there were two ways to answer. Give Jackson the truth or type in the words that would make him happy.

I am. Everything okay?

Almost immediately, she saw the little black dots appear, signifying that he had read her text and was sending back a reply.

Really? That's good. I was afraid I
might have woken you up.

Glad she'd told him that little fib, Dani smiled at the screen
on her phone. She typed her response quickly.

Is the tournament finally over?

Yep. TG.

Well????? How did it go?

She was completely awake now and on pins and needles.

I'd rather tell you in person. Can
I stop by?

Two seconds later he sent off another quick note.

It's okay if you want to tell me no.

She grinned, loving both that he was anxious to see her and
that she was just as anxious to see him right away. After so many
months of feeling like an eighty-year-old woman suffering from
arthritis, it was nice to feel attractive and wanted again.

Of course, she might be swinging a bit far the other way now.
Sometimes she felt like she was turning more and more into a
teenage girl with every week they were together.

I'm sure. Come over.

Awesome. I'll be there in ten.

After she sent him a little thumbs-up emoji, she glanced at

the time. A quarter to two! It really was the middle of the night.

Quickly getting off the couch, she peeked in her bedroom to check on Kate. As expected, the little girl was still sound asleep in her bed. Her arms were thrown up above her head and her new *Scooby-Doo* pajamas were twisted around her torso. After pulling the blanket up a few inches, she peeked in on Jeremy.

He was flat on his stomach, arms and legs sprawled. Sound asleep, too.

She was relieved about that. He'd been up late playing some game on his Xbox. Because they didn't have anything planned until two the next day, she'd let him stay up as late as he'd wanted. She knew he stayed up until two every now and then. All the running he'd been doing for baseball must have taken its toll.

Now that she'd been assured that both kids were settled, she ran into the bathroom, ran a brush through her hair and rinsed her mouth. And, yes, swiped some lip gloss over her lips and analyzed her outfit. It was only leggings and a T-shirt. But for once it wasn't a stretched out old shirt of Brian's. It was a tunic she'd found at Old Navy on a clearance rack. She thought the deep rose color set off her skin tone and the V neckline made her rather flat chest look like there might be something there worth looking at. All in all, not too bad—considering she'd been sound asleep just a few minutes earlier.

His knock came just as she returned to the living room.

She didn't wait two seconds to open it.

Jackson was standing on the other side, looking more rumpled than she'd ever seen him, even after working nine hours at the pub. He was wearing a ratty pair of black gym shorts, a tight concert T-shirt, and a pair of thick tube socks and black tennis shoes. The outfit was bad enough that even Jeremy would've said Jackson looked ridiculous.

He also was wearing a smile so big, it verged on blinding. If he was a preschooler, she would have teased him, saying that he looked like the cat who swallowed the canary.

"Hey, you," she said as she waved him on in. "You sure are looking pleased with yourself."

He closed the door behind them. "If I'm lookin' pleased, that's because I am." Reaching into a back pocket, he pulled out a white envelope. "This, Ms. Brown, is for you."

It was a business-size white envelope that seemed especially thick. She was almost afraid to take it.

Just to be sure, she said, "Is this the money?"

Coming closer, he pressed it into her palm. "Of course, sweetheart."

His voice was gentle. That tone, combined with that new endearment, made her insides melt a little. But she still felt really awkward as she curved her hand around the packet. "How much is inside? Do you know?"

"I do." He took a breath, then said, "Dani, honey, there is fourteen hundred dollars in there."

She was so shocked, she almost dropped it. "Fourteen hundred? As in one thousand, four hundred dollars?"

His grin widened. "It's awesome, right? After Troy counted it up, Kurt and Ace and me were high-fiving everyone."

She thrust it back at him. "I can't accept this." She'd been hoping for a few hundred dollars and had even felt guilty taking that amount. This amount? Well, it felt almost sinful, considering it was just for baseball. There were other families in Bridgeport who were no doubt struggling to pay their utilities.

His blue eyes clouded in confusion. "Sure you can."

She shook her head. "No. This isn't right. I know we talked about maybe hitting a thousand, but I didn't expect even that much. Jackson, this is too much."

His smile widened. "People got excited, Dani. Guys who lost

in the tournament started betting crazy during the cash game when someone suggested they donate half their winnings."

Just the idea of people betting money like that for her made her uncomfortable. "But I didn't ask for anyone to do that."

His playful expression sobered. "Honey, you didn't ask for any of it. Neither did Jeremy, for that matter. That's what makes this whole thing so cool. It's a gift."

"But—"

Taking the envelope from her hand, he set it on the coffee table. "Come on. I think we ought to talk about this. Let's sit down."

"You have time for that?" Hating that she kept asking questions that were both inane and rude, she groaned. "I mean, it's late. I bet you're tired and want to go to bed."

Still staring at her intently, he said, "Believe it or not, I didn't have any other plans scheduled for two in the morning. I'm all yours."

"Oh, please."

"Stop fussing and come sit down," he repeated in that patient tone of voice he used with Kate when she was on the verge of a little-girl breakdown.

Just as he took a step forward, he sniffed the sleeve of his shirt. "But first, um, let me go wash up." Already walking toward her bathroom, he said, "You don't care if I use your bathroom, do you? I would go downstairs to my place to shower but that might take a while."

"I don't mind if you use my bathroom. And stop about the shower. You're fine."

"You may not think that when you get a good whiff of me. I smell like hell," he murmured as he walked toward the open door. "Boy, I need to get cleaned up. Damn."

Thinking about how comfortable he was acting, she had a

sudden vision of him stripping off his clothes. "Jackson, you aren't going to take a shower in my bathroom or anything are you?"

He paused to turn back at her. "Nah. I'm just gonna wash up a bit. You got an extra washcloth or something?"

"In the cabinet under the sink."

"Appreciate it." One of his dimples appeared. "I tell you what, it doesn't matter how cold it is outside, it always gets hot as hell in that garage. I'll be right out."

She smiled weakly as she sat down, staring at the envelope like it held a bomb inside it. And, maybe it did.

Fourteen hundred dollars was an enormous amount. There were so many things she could be doing with it besides pay for baseball games. Bills, car insurance, clothes for school. A trip to the grocery store that didn't involve twenty coupons and meat on sale.

Or, her guilty conscience reminded her, the money could go to someone who was actually in need. Someone hurt or homeless or in crisis.

Not this.

"Uh-oh. I don't think you've calmed down much."

"I was just thinking that it's wrong of me to take this. I mean, it's really nice and all, but unnecessary. It's just for baseball."

"Kurt and I didn't lie to anyone, Dani. Everyone knew what they were playing for and donating to." He sat down beside her. "Not your name or anything, but every player there knew the money was so a teenage boy and his mom could afford to be on a select baseball team."

Still staring at the envelope, she said, "What do you think?"

"Honey, you know what I think. I set it up." Reaching for her hand, he linked their fingers then pressed his lips to her fingertips sticking out. "Don't overthink things. It's done. Trust me, the best thing to do is accept the money and let Jeremy do his thing."

"I guess you're right." After all, how would she give the money back anyway? And what would she do about Jeremy and the team if she did give the money away? Keep working too much for too little pay?

"I'm glad you are seeing it my way." After squeezing her hand lightly again, he released it and rested an arm along the back of the couch behind her. "Now, tell me about your night. How was Kate?"

"It was terrific. Guess what? Kate likes doing puzzles. It's so cute."

"What? Isn't she a little young for that?"

"Oh, it's not a hundred-piece puzzle or anything. I have some wooden sets where preschoolers can put six or seven pieces together. She did great. She wanted to do the puzzle of circus animals again and again."

He looked pleased. "I knew she was smart! I bet not all three-year-olds can do that."

Boy, she loved seeing this proud-parent side of Jackson. It turned her to mush every single time. "She is pretty special. We also played with playdough and watched some television with Jeremy."

"Thanks again for watching her."

She shrugged off his thanks. "Now, how about you tell me why you are wearing that outfit. What's with those awful tube socks?"

Looking surprised, he looked down, "Dani, what are you talking about? These are awesome."

"They are thick white socks with red stripes on the end. You look like you're about to play basketball with Larry Bird in the seventies."

But instead of looking offended, Jackson seemed pleased. "I never thought of them like that. But that's awesome."

"So you've been wearing these around town and I just haven't ever seen them?"

"No, they're my lucky socks. I wear them only for poker."

"Did you win the tournament tonight?"

"Well, no. But I came in tenth place. And I won some money in the cash game, too."

"What about the T-shirt?"

"This? Oh, the guys and I went to their concert in Charleston back in '98. We usually have theme nights and tonight's was concerts."

She smiled at him. "That explains a lot of things."

"Like what?"

"Like the fact that it seems a little snug."

A new look appeared on his face. "Too tight, huh?"

Did she mind seeing his muscles a little more clearly than usual? Ah, no. "It's good. I don't mind."

He reached out and ran a finger along the ruffled collar of her V neck. "You look pretty."

"It's the middle of the night. I doubt I look anything but tired."

"Maybe we should try to put a different look on your face then." Before she could ask what he was talking about, he leaned in and brushed his lips against hers. Lightly. So sweetly.

When she reached out to steady herself, he kissed her again.

And then all she really wanted to do was hold on tight.

It had been so long. So long since she'd been held. Since she'd felt attractive. Since she'd been kissed.

He lifted his head slightly. Searched her face. "Okay?"

She liked that. Liked how he realized that this was new and was something she needed a moment to adjust to. But while her mind might be questioning every little thing in the morning, all the rest of her wanted to do was press close against him.

When she did just that, Jackson groaned and shifted them. Just like back in high school, she was lying on the couch and Jackson was propped above her. Tasting her neck, murmuring sweet things into her nape, doing things that made her pulse go a little faster and the rest of her sigh in relief.

Needing to touch him as much as he was touching her, she slid her hands under his shirt, felt the muscles of his back ripple under her searching fingers. His skin was smooth and warm. Felt like liquid velvet under her fingertips. With a moan, she reached for him with her other hand, then shifted so their mouths were meshed again.

Jackson's hands had started to roam as much as hers, and her back arched with a sigh when his fingers skimmed her rib cage, seeking her breast.

"Dani," he murmured after they shared another few minutes exploring each other. "We ought to stop."

Should they? She didn't see a reason why. She was an adult. So was he. And they were still fully clothed.

Well, more or less.

When he pulled away some more, she dropped her hands in frustration. It had been so sweet, and it had been so long. "Jackson?" She opened her eyes to see what she imagined was the same dreamy expression on his face that was probably on hers.

He got to his feet. "Dani, I'm sorry. Look, you're beautiful. You felt so good. But ..."

"But?" Please don't let him start saying something cheesy, like it was him and not her.

"But, well." He swallowed. "I just ..." He rubbed a hand over his face. "I just don't want to have regrets in the morning."

They'd barely gotten to second base, if they even called it that anymore. She'd been participating in everything they had been doing whole-heartedly, too.

Surely, he'd noticed?

She smiled slightly. "Do you really think we would ever regret making out a little?"

He looked down at his feet. "I don't know. Maybe?" When their eyes met again she realized that he wasn't being all sacrificing.

He was talking about himself.

"I know it's been two years since Beth died," he said haltingly. "But this is the first time I've kissed another woman." His cheeks reddened. "I know it's not cheating. I know it, and I love getting close to you. You're gorgeous, Dani. But—"

At last she got it. "But part of you feels like it is."

He nodded. "That. Plus, I like our friendship. I need it. When we finally do go to bed, I don't want it to be on your couch while our kids are sleeping in the other rooms. I want some privacy."

She laughed, suddenly imagining what hell would have broken loose if her light-sleeping son had stumbled out of his room on his way for more water and walked in on the two of them. "You're right. I don't know what got into me. I should have thought about that."

"No need to apologize. I'm the one who was lying on top of you." He grinned. "I would've never believed it, but I feel kind of awkward, like I almost got caught necking in my car." He closed his eyes. "Jeez, I'm out of practice."

"Luckily, that's something we can work on."

Smiling at her, he nodded. "Yeah. We absolutely can. I don't want to lose you."

"You haven't." Walking toward her bedroom, she said, "Are you ready for Kate?"

"Yep."

She waited in the small entryway while he walked into her bedroom and got his daughter. When he came out, Kate sprawled half over his shoulders and little legs clinging to him like a spider monkey, Dani opened the door. "Night, Jackson."

"Night, babe. Get some sleep."

She didn't bother answering him, just watched patiently as he walked to the landing and then disappeared down the stairs.

Just as she clicked the bolt shut and turned off the light, Jeremy stumbled out of his room. "Mom?" he asked as he walked to the kitchen.

"It's okay. Jackson just came to get Kate. He's gone now."

"'Kay," he mumbled as he turned on the sink.

After he got his drink of water and then disappeared back into his room, she picked up the envelope that they'd left on the coffee table, placed it on her dresser, then got ready for bed.

Jackson had absolutely saved the night. Ten minutes longer and clothes would have been off.

And her boy would have been greeted with a very different scene! Thank goodness for small favors and Jackson's cautiousness. She fell asleep smiling about that close call. They'd come so close to ruining one of the best nights she'd had in such a very long time.

And now she didn't even have to worry about paying for his fees! Her son was going to be so happy.

CHAPTER 31

FROM LES LARKE'S
YOU, TOO, CAN HOST
A POKER TOURNEY:

I'm often asked about why a group of guys would
want to hold a poker tournament in the first
place. My first response is always, why not?

Her bedroom door flew open with a bang. Jerking awake with a gasp, Dani stared at the intruder. And then panic set in.

"Jeremy? Honey, what's wrong? Are you hurt?" Seconds later, she realized that her fourteen-year-old wasn't upset or hurt. He was mad. Really mad.

With a glare, he held up his phone, displaying the screen like it was a poisonous snake. "How could you?"

"How could I what?" Turning to the side, she slid out of bed, bending down to pull her robe securely around her as she got to her feet.

"Make me into some kind of ... of ... pathetic kid." His voice was harsh and sounded ripped from his chest.

She'd done that? Dani kept her back to him as she tied the belt of her robe, needing a moment to figure out what the heck was going on with him. Jeremy was on the quiet side. He was patient with most people, and his father had ingrained in him a respect for her that had never—until now—crossed the line.

When she turned back to him, he was glaring at his phone and breathing heavy.

Dani knew he was either about to burst into tears or throw that phone at the wall.

Since she could never handle his tears—and she really couldn't afford a new phone for him—she knew she needed to calm him down, stat. "Hey, now. There's no need for you to get so excited," she said as patiently as she could. "Let me wake up and get a cup of coffee, and then we'll talk about things."

He raised his voice. "Mom, you don't even know what you're talking about."

"I know I don't like you talking to me in that tone. How about that?"

But instead of backing down, he held up his phone's screen again. "How about I don't like you making me into some kind of creepy charity case!" One angry tear slid down his cheek before he turned around. "How could you?"

She stared at his retreating back as those last words rang in her ears. *Charity case?*

She'd first thought that way, too. Hearing Jeremy say the same words hit very close to home.

Right then and there all of her worst fears came to the surface as she realized what had happened. Word had gotten out about last night's extremely successful poker tournament.

Fighting a new sense of dread, she reached on the bottom shelf of her bedside table and picked up both her glasses and her own phone. But she didn't see anything beyond the slightly flirty texts she and Jackson had exchanged last night after he'd told her the good news.

Though she knew she should probably delete the conversation in case Jeremy caught sight of it, she couldn't bring herself to do it. Even when she and Brian had been dating he'd never talk to her like that.

Like she was the last thing he ever wanted to think about before he fell asleep at night.

After doing her business in the bathroom, she walked directly to the coffee maker and pressed brew. Now that she had clean teeth, a rinsed face, and caffeine brewing, she was almost certain she was going to be able to face Jeremy's crisis. Maybe.

To her surprise, he wasn't standing in their small kitchen, impatiently waiting on her. No, he was standing out on their small balcony, texting.

Figuring he could wait a minute for her to drink her coffee, she poured a half cup, dosed it with milk, and drank it down as fast as she could.

The hot brew burned as it went down her throat. Finally waking her up and giving her the courage she needed to talk to her boy.

He didn't look up from his phone when she approached. Leaning against the doorway she studied him for a moment before speaking.

"I'm ready to talk now. Are you?"

"I don't even know what to say. You've ruined my life."

"We might as well sit down and talk about it, then. Standing here isn't helping."

"Fine." He brushed past her into the sitting area and plopped down in the center of the tan couch she'd bought brand new just a few years before.

Dani filled up her mug then walked over to join him. As she

did, an image flashed in her head, of the two of them sitting side by side in the center of it. Back then, her eleven-year-old Jeremy had acted like it was the fanciest, most comfortable couch ever created. She'd been feeling like she had finally turned the corner from Brian's death. As if she was finally going to survive on her own.

Though she knew that every moment couldn't feel so sweet, the fact that they were sitting back on it together, feeling everything opposite, was hard.

"Why don't you tell me what's been going on, son."

He stiffened. "You know, Mom."

"Well, I know my side of it. However, I'd rather hear your side right now." When he still didn't say anything, she tried again. "Please, Jeremy? I promise, I'm on your side here."

At last Jeremy held up the phone in his hand. "I started getting texts late last night. All about how half the guys' dads on the team were at Mr. Holland's house playing poker."

"Okay."

"At first, I kept wondering why I was supposed to care. I mean, everyone knows about Mr. Holland's poker games and the Bridgeport Social Club."

She took another sip of coffee to fortify herself. "But then?"

"But then Scott from the Bats texted everyone, saying that he heard the tournament was because of me."

"He said that?" She felt like everything inside of her was crushed.

"Yeah. He said a couple of dads had been telling their wives that last night's poker game wasn't just for fun, it was for a good cause."

"Oh, boy."

Jeremy continued, each word coming out stiff and full of pain. "Mom, everyone was talking about how there was a kid who had a lot of talent, but his mom didn't have a lot of money. His single, widowed mom."

She couldn't deny that pretty much summed up their situation. "And?"

"And then everyone figured out that the kid was me, Mom." He looked at her again, his brown eyes cloudy with pain.

"You're right. It is you. You don't have a lot of money, and I don't have a lot of money. Not enough to pay for select ball."

"So you started asking a bunch of guys to make me their charity case?" Before she could respond, he shook his head. "I can't believe you did this to me."

"I didn't do it. When we went over to Mr. Holland's house last week, Jackson told me that the guys wanted to do that for you."

"You mean *for you*. Jackson likes *you*, Mom."

"No, I mean for you." Setting her mug on the table next to the couch, Dani turned to face him. "I had no idea they'd planned it. It took me off guard, I can tell you that."

"But you still said okay."

Boy, he wasn't going to give her an inch. His indignation was starting to grate on her nerves, too. "I said okay after they talked to me about it. The guys were excited about it, Jeremy. None of them grew up rich and they all felt like it was a way of giving back. You know, like paying it forward."

"It's a stupid way for them to do it. You all ruined my life."

"I don't know what happened. They weren't supposed to use either your name or mine."

"Even if they didn't, everyone figured it out," Jeremy said bitterly. "You should have told me about this tournament, Mom."

"I realize that now. I guess I was just hoping that you would never know about it."

"I don't even understand why you felt we needed help. I mean, the fees weren't that bad. It was only a couple of hundred dollars, right?"

"It was more than that. You know I was working nonstop to pay for it. And I hadn't even thought about the traveling expenses. Jackson knew it was too much for me."

"You should have told me," he said again.

"But what could you have done?"

"Quit." His chin lifted. "You should've said I didn't need to be on the team."

She shook her head. "You deserve to be on the team. You like being on the team. It didn't make me feel real comfortable, but I can't deny that I'm glad you didn't have to quit."

"I'm going to quit now."

"You better not."

"All the guys are giving me crap. Saying that I'm not that good."

"Oh, for heaven's sakes. You really are. You know you are good. The coach tells you. Jackson said so, too."

"Here we go again. You trying to forget Dad. My life isn't all about Jackson, Mom."

Oh, that hurt. "Jeremy, I've been trying to understand your pain and embarrassment and give you your due. But you just crossed the line."

He had the gall to roll his eyes. "What line?"

"The line that means you need to watch your mouth when you speak to your mother," she said with as much control in her voice as she could grasp ahold of. "The point where you start talking about things that you don't know anything about."

"I know you are forgetting Dad."

"You know that isn't true. I still think about him every day."

He surged to his feet. "We both know that isn't true, Mom. You hardly talk about Dad anymore. It's all about Jackson and

Kate." His eyes flashed. "You've moved on, Mom. All you care about is yourself. And right now I'm really sick of it."

Before she could figure out how to respond to that, he headed toward the door.

"Jeremy, what are you doing?"

"I'm going to go get a job. I'll be back later."

Everything inside of her was screaming for him to come back and talk to her.

But instead she let him go.

Probably because there was a part of her that wondered if he had been right.

CHAPTER 32

FROM LES LARKE'S
YOU, TOO, CAN HOST
A POKER TOURNEY:

Besides the money factor, there are many reasons
why people like to attend a tournament. The best
reason might be camaraderie.

Seth had just gotten out of his car and was stretching for a quick three-mile run when he saw Jeremy Brown storm out of an apartment building nearby. Since he'd gone to the poker tournament the night before, the boy had been on his mind. Just as he was about to tell him congratulations, he noticed Jeremy looked beyond pissed off. Almost like he was about to explode.

When the kid stopped next to a light post and seemed to have trouble catching his breath, Seth knew he couldn't just ignore him. Someone needed to help. "Hey, are you okay?"

Straightening, the boy stared at him in confusion. "Seth?"

"Yeah. We met a couple of weeks ago in this very parking lot."

"I remember."

"Maybe you remember that I'm Gen Schuler's guy?" Seth figured he sounded kind of stupid, but he didn't want the kid to think he was some guy hanging out in the parking lot.

"Oh. Yeah. Hi." He stuffed his hands in the back pockets of his jeans and took a step away. Everything about the kid told Seth that he wanted to be anywhere but talking to him.

Seth didn't blame him and would have left him alone ... if he hadn't noticed that Jeremy's eyes were red from crying. "I was just getting ready to go for a run when I saw you tear out of that apartment building. Is everything okay? Hey, do you need a ride to a game or something?"

To Seth's surprise, the kid turned beet red. "I'm not going to play ball anymore."

Seth raised his eyebrows. "Um, you sure about that? Because I heard different last night."

"Oh yeah? Where?"

It was a fair question. He realized now that he was being pretty damn rude, too. Jeremy didn't know him, and Kurt Holland had said last night that they didn't want to divulge the name of the boy who they were all helping. Seth only knew who they were playing for because of Gen. Backpedaling, he said, "I don't know. Maybe Jackson?"

Jeremy's eyes narrowed, and a new tension rose between them. Seth knew why—the kid knew he was lying. "Never mind. I've got to go."

Seth knew he probably should let the kid go. They didn't know each other, and Seth had enough problems without making Jeremy's problems his, too.

But everything he and Gen had gone through lately had taught him a lot about communication. He'd learned that even bad news was better than silence.

And, truth be told, maybe he was viewing some of the same

hurt and confusion on Jeremy's face that he'd been feeling for the last couple of weeks. He couldn't just ignore that. "Look, I know you probably do have things to do. But give me a sec, okay?"

It was obvious that Jeremy was torn between the good manners that his momma taught him and walking off. "What do you want?"

"I just wanted you to know that if you want to share what's on your mind, I'm probably as good a person as any to share it with."

"Why would you say that?"

Suspicion was ripe in his tone, but the boy wasn't going anywhere. Seth took that as a positive sign.

Folding his arms over his chest, he replied, "Because you don't have to worry about me still liking you or not when we're done talking."

Jeremy's eyebrows rose. "Seriously?"

"Uh, yeah. Serious as a heart attack. You've obviously got something you're worried about. It's been my experience that means your problem is with someone close to you. Am I wrong?"

One second passed. Then two. "No."

"Well, then, what's wrong? And you might as well tell someone because I know from experience that keeping it inside can eat you up."

Jeremy looked around the parking lot, pausing a second or two at the door he exited. Finally, he nodded. "Fine. But do we have to talk here?"

"We can talk wherever you want. Where do you want to go?"

"The bike trail. It's just on the other side of these apartments. We won't be standing here in the middle of everything."

Or, Seth figured, in view of the apartment he just ran out of. "Lead the way."

Jeremy shook his head. "You sure got an accent. It's even thicker than Jackson's."

"That's 'cause Jackson hails from West Virginia. I'm from Texas, boy."

"I thought all of you would sound the same."

"If you think that, it's obvious that you need to travel a whole lot more. But, for the record, this is how we all sound."

The boy didn't say anything, but his lips twitched. Seth exhaled in relief as they started walking. They were making progress. After they crossed the pavement, he followed Jeremy when he turned left and started walking.

Immediately, they were surrounded by thick foliage. While most of the trees in the area were still gathering their leaves, the bushes and grasses lining both sides of the trail were already thick with new growth. The ground below them was damp. Though there were a couple of bike riders off in the distance, for the most part they were alone.

"This is awesome. Do you come here a lot?"

Jeremy shook his head. "Nah."

"So …"

"So, a bunch of people in town held a poker tournament last night to raise money for me."

"I know."

"You do?"

"Yeah. Jackson invited me to play."

"So you went?"

"I did. It was a good time."

Jeremy's hands clenched by his side. "Great."

Seth's heart hurt for him. "Hey, instead of telling me what I already know, why don't you share what I don't. What's been going on with you?"

"Fine. I don't have a dad. He's dead. I only got my mom

241

and she's not a fancy mom, okay? She's a maid." He eyed Seth again, practically daring him to joke about losing his dad and not having a lot of money.

Seth wouldn't dare do that. "All right. So, you've had your fair share of hardships."

"I wanted to get on a select baseball team, okay? The Bridgeport Bats."

"Sounds like a good opportunity."

"It was. And I was plenty good enough to get on it, too. But, well, it just costs a lot to be on it." Looking down at his feet, he mumbled, "I realized it, too, but I didn't care."

"'Cause you wanted to be on it. There's nothing wrong with that, Jeremy."

"Yeah. But I should have known better." He pursed his lips, then added, "My mom was working a ton and driving me around all the time and stressing about it so this group of guys, of men, decided to help her out."

"How come?"

"I just told you."

"No, you said that you were good. You wanted to play, and your mom was doing everything she could to make sure you could do that. You didn't say why these guys wanted to help you. You know, instead of some other kid." "Oh. Because one of them likes my mom."

"Jackson."

"Yeah."

"Huh. So because Jackson likes your mom and she was running herself ragged trying to make sure you could play on this expensive, special baseball team, he organized a poker tournament to raise money to help her out."

"Yeah." Jeremy nodded. "They did all this without talking to me about it, too."

"Ah."

"Yep. So, now you see why I'm pissed off."

"Sorry, but I don't," Seth said slowly. He paused, wondering if he was about to be too harsh, but decided to power on through. "Jeremy, I've liked a lot of women over the years. Never once did I decide to hold a poker tournament so I could get into her pants."

Jeremy stopped and gaped at him. "That's my mom. Don't talk about her like that."

"Then don't act like that's what happened," he retorted. "For you to act like that's what your mother was willing to do so you could play baseball is wrong. And so is acting like Jackson has nothing better to do than persuade a whole lot of grown men to give up their money and time for a kid they don't know."

Jeremy's hands clenched, and his expression looked pained as they continued walking.

Seth decided to keep quiet and let him stew for a while. He felt bad for the kid, but he would have felt worse for him if all evidence pointed to the fact that no one cared about him. It was obvious that a whole lot of people cared about him an awful lot.

After they walked another quarter mile or so, Jeremy said, "What do you think I should do?"

"I don't really know you. You sure as hell don't know me. I'm thinking that maybe my advice ain't going to mean much."

"It might not, but I still want to know what you think."

"Well then, here's what I think, and you can feel free to take it or leave it." He glanced down and met the boy's eyes. "You need to accept the fact that your mother loves you enough to work nonstop so you can play ball on the team that you deserve to play on. Then you need to accept the fact that Jackson cares for you both enough to try to help y'all out, and not by giving a handout, either."

"What do you mean by that?"

"I mean that a lot of people simply could've handed your momma a couple of hundreds and gone on with their lives. Jackson found a way to try to help y'all in a way that maybe you both could live with."

Jeremy nodded. "All right."

Seth paused, wondering if he was about to make a mistake, then dived in. "Finally, here's the hardest part."

"Yeah?"

"You're going to have to wrap your head around the fact that your mom and you don't have a lot of money for extras and that's just how it is. That's nothing to be ashamed of."

"The guys on the team are—"

"Going to know that your dad died and that your mother has to work really hard. There's only one thing you can do about it, and that's to give them something else to talk about."

"Which is?"

"Play baseball. Be so good that the other players won't care how you came to afford the hotel rooms and the uniforms. All they'll care about is whether or not you are pitching."

"Or catching. I'm a catcher."

"Does that mean you aren't going to pitch a fit and embarrass your mother and make all those guys who are feeling pretty good about themselves regret their decision?"

"I wasn't pitching a fit."

"But?"

The kid smiled. "But I'm going to play ball."

"Good."

"Hey, Seth?"

"Yeah?"

"I left my apartment so I could go get a job. Do you think I still should do that?" His voice was hesitant. Like he wanted to do the right thing, but he wasn't even sure what the right thing was anymore.

Boy, could he relate. Stepping carefully, he said, "Seems to me if you are going to school and playing on this fancy team and traveling during the season you aren't going to have a lot of extra time."

Jeremy's shoulders slumped. "I guess not."

"That said, I did hear that Kurt Holland has a landscaping business. Maybe when you go thank him you could see if he could give you some work from time to time."

"Do you really think he'd do that?"

"I think you won't know if he will or not if you don't ask."

"Yeah. I'll do that." He stopped then. "I think I better turn around and go see my mom."

"Sounds like a good idea."

After they turned and started walking back, Seth let his mind drift to everything that had kept him up last night. Gen and their argument. The way he'd assumed the worst. The pain that he'd spied in her eyes and the way she'd cried and he'd stood helplessly to the side because she didn't trust him anymore.

It had been obvious that he'd handled things the wrong way. But, like Jeremy, he'd been embarrassed that she'd seen the worst of him. He also had to face the fact that he was still going to make his fair share of mistakes … and because of that it was about time he started making his fair share of apologies.

It was time he worked harder to make things better.

"I'm real glad we talked, kid."

Jeremy glanced up at him. "My problems really mean that much to you?"

"No. It's just that you weren't the only one with some regrets on his mind this morning. I think I've been talking to myself as much as to you."

"Glad I could help."

Seth smiled the whole way back to the parking lot. Then he got into his truck and drove over to Gen's house. He was going to get through to her if it was the last thing he did.

Knowing how volatile her temper was, he realized he was going to have to do some hard thinking while he drove. He needed to come up with the right words or he was going to risk losing her forever.

CHAPTER 33

FROM LES LARKE'S
*YOU, TOO, CAN HOST
A POKER TOURNEY:*

*Maybe the best reason to host a poker game
is the simplest to understand. Everyone needs
some time to relax and unwind.*

Dani had picked up the phone three times to call Jackson and share
what had just happened with Jeremy. Each time, she'd set it back
down. It was still pretty early, and he was no doubt still sleeping or
taking care of Kate. The last thing he needed was for her to wake him
up or jar him out of his morning routine by crying on the phone.

But she'd rarely felt more alone. She sat down at her kitchen
table. Briefly considered calling her parents but knew they were
both probably asleep and wouldn't be of much help.

She thought about talking to Emily or Meredith, knowing
that since they were familiar with the Bridgeport Social Club they
might have a good idea of how to make the club's donation sound
better to a fourteen-year-old.

But those women didn't have children.

Closing her eyes, she inhaled, intending to speak to Brian like she usually did. Closing her eyes, speaking to his memory, and asking for his advice usually made her feel better. She'd probably talked to him like he was hovering over her shoulders a hundred times since his death, especially when it came to their son.

But for the first time, she didn't think either speaking to him up in Heaven or imagining his response was going to make her feel better.

Brian had never been one to accept help from anyone, and he hadn't been the best sounding board for figuring out how to solve a problem with Jeremy. Whether it was a matter of working on his multiplication tables or encouraging him to clean his room, Brian had been a firm believer in simply telling their boy what he wanted him to do and then assuming it would get done.

Forcing herself to shake off the last of her rose-colored memories of her husband, she made herself remember how he'd really been.

Unhelpful.

There. At last, she'd admitted it. Brian had often been unhelpful.

She'd loved Brian, but she'd often been upset with him, too. He was selfish. He didn't always think about how his actions affected other people. He'd rarely put Jeremy's needs or wishes first unless they coincided with his own. And when they had, he'd never had any problem with using that against her. Sometimes even in front of Jeremy, so she didn't have any choice but to give in.

Boy, she'd used to get so mad with him about that.

Instead of reaching out to anyone, Dani got up and wandered around her living room. Her mind a muddled mess, she rearranged books and picture frames that didn't need to be rearranged and dusted shelves that were already clean. Then, at last, she did the only thing that she could do. She prayed hard for some divine inspiration.

Fifteen minutes later, the door opened, and Jeremy walked in, looking far calmer and even a little bit embarrassed when he saw her standing in the living room reorganizing some old Disney DVDs.

"Hi."

After breathing in deep and saying a silent thank you to the Lord, she clumsily got to her feet. "Hey," she replied. "I ... I'm glad you're back." Standing stiffly, she waited for him to say something else. Hoped he would feel like talking.

Still looking awkward and embarrassed, Jeremy took off his sneakers, studied his shoes for a moment, then picked them up and set them against the wall. Finally, he walked over to her side. "Mom, I'm sorry I ran out of here. That wasn't cool."

It wasn't cool? Not only was that something of an understatement, she'd never heard him use that phrase in his life. "I was worried about you." Though she was anxious to ask where he'd gone for almost a whole hour, Dani settled for concentrating on what was important. "Are you okay?"

He nodded. "Yeah. I was really mad and was going to walk down to the bike trail to go for a run or something, when I met this man in the parking lot."

Oh, Lord. A lump formed in her throat before she reminded herself that one, he wasn't a little boy anymore and two, he was fine. "Who was the man? Do you know him?"

"His name is Seth. Seth Parks." He stepped forward. "Do you remember when we met him?"

She nodded her head slowly. "Did you?"

"Barely. Seth is Jackson's boss' friend."

"Jackson's mentioned him being Gen's boyfriend a time or two."

He shrugged. "Anyway, we started talking."

"You did?" She sat down on the couch and told herself to listen to what Jeremy had to say. If he was telling her about this Seth, then the conversation had meant something to him.

"I'm not sure why we started talking about everything, but I told him all about last night's poker game and how the money was for us." He glanced at her, then looked away. "I mean, for me."

"What did he say?"

"I couldn't believe it, but he was actually at that poker game."

"Really?"

He nodded. "He said Mr. Holland's garage was packed and that a lot of people were there."

Since Jeremy had paused again, Dani felt obligated to say something. "What a small world."

He shrugged. "Anyway, after I told him that I was mad about being a charity case, he told me that I was being a jerk."

Before she knew what she was doing, she got back to her feet. "That's hardly fair. That man doesn't even know you."

A hint of a smile played on his lips. "Mom. You don't even know what he said. And I surely was being a jerk to you, I reckon."

She sat back down. "I'm guessing he told you more about the poker tournament?"

"Yeah." He walked over and sat in the easy chair next to her. His voice turned soft. "Mom, he told me that all the guys were excited to have a reason to play for something other than just winning. And that they all had felt good about doing something for someone else. Seth even said that the men knew it was just for baseball, but they didn't care. They all acted like wanting to be on the Bats was cool." He paused, then blurted, "Do you think that's true?"

"I don't know what all the men think about the Bats, but I did hear from Jackson that the guys liked playing for a cause. It makes sense, I think. Everyone likes to help out someone who needs a hand. I always have." When he was staring at her hard, she said, "I think that's why I'm always baking people cakes and such. I don't have a lot of extra money, but a lot of people appreciate a cake made just for them. You know?"

"You make good cakes."

"You know what I meant, Jer. My point is that it's nice to do something for others. Like when you play with Kate but don't expect to get paid."

"I know what you meant."

Looking at him closely, she said, "What I didn't realize before this is that it's not always very easy to be the recipient of all that giving. It's hard to accept a gift without knowing how you can repay it."

"They gave you a lot of money, Mom. We can't repay it."

"You're right. I couldn't repay it easily at all. But, what I did realize this morning while you were gone is that there's something to be said for being a grateful recipient."

"Huh?"

"Saying 'no, thank you' and pushing away something that someone did for you is rude. It's like putting a chocolate cake that I worked hard to bake on a counter and never touching it. Or giving it right back, saying that you didn't want it."

"That would hurt your feelings."

"It would. Plus, it would make me feel bad because I thought I was doing something special." She scanned his face. "Do you understand?"

He nodded. "Yeah."

"All that aside, you're not a baby. You're fourteen and you've already had enough tests and hard times in your life. I'm not going to force you to accept something that you don't feel good about. What do you want to do, son?"

He sat up a little straighter and looked at her in the eye. "I'm going to keep playing ball for the Bats. I'm going to work hard and catch balls and prove to everyone that I deserve to be there. And, if any of the guys on the team gives me crap I'm not going to worry about it."

"That sounds like a plan."

"And … I want to go ask Mr. Holland if I can start working some for him. Not all the time, but when I have a weekend free or early in the mornings or something."

"Do you think you have time for that?"

"I think if it's important to me, I do."

He'd grown up. "All right. I can respect that."

"Can we go over to his house now and ask him?"

"It's still early. Plus, we should probably call."

"Mom, I'm afraid if I wait any longer I'm going to chicken out."

Though she still felt like it was a little rude to just go over there, Dani figured that Jeremy needed to be able to hold his head up right now. And that trumped everything. "Give me five minutes to put on some makeup."

His eyes brightened. "Really? You'll take me this morning?"

A dozen little encouraging phrases and comments floated through her head. All of them were typical mom things. But at the moment, she thought they all sounded a little wrong, a little bit too motherly.

So all she did was nod and smile before walking to her bathroom.

CHAPTER 34

FROM LES LARKE'S
YOU, TOO, CAN HOST
A POKER TOURNEY:

Believe it or not, some guys even use their time at
the poker table to talk business.

Almost a whole month had passed since they'd had the poker tournament for Jeremy and Dani. To Jackson's amazement, that one event, as difficult to accept for Jeremy as it had been, had broken down a lot of the barriers between him and Jackson.

And maybe, it had also broken down some of the barriers Dani had formed about dating again. She was more open with him, and with Jeremy and Kate about their relationship. Jackson realized that he had made the same strides. He'd stopped looking back and asking God and everyone who would listen why he'd had to lose his wife at such a young age, or why Kate had to grow up without a mother. Or why he'd had to lose the only job he'd ever wanted to have.

To his surprise, when he'd stopped missing what used to be, he'd allowed himself to think about what was possible. And that's when he'd realized that a whole lot still was possible for him.

Including love.

He knew they all needed more time to adjust, but Jackson knew what he wanted for his future. He wanted him and Kate and Dani and Jeremy to be a real family. He wanted to marry Dani one day. Maybe even have another child.

But he was in no hurry. For now, he was okay with helping Jeremy get to his games and giving Dani as much support as she needed in order to work on her degree. And as for work? Well, like everything else, he realized that once he'd stopped wishing for what wasn't, he was pretty darn grateful for what he had. The Corner Bar was a good place. He liked Melissa and Brad and the other staff members, too.

And Gen? Well, Gen was complicated and ornery and also really kind. She was also a good boss. He was good with bartending for her until something else came along that would suit him better.

And now that she was hot and heavy with her man Seth, she had given Jackson a raise and was leaving him in charge more and more, so she could see him.

All that was going through his head when he was wiping down the bar and listening to Gen and Kimmy banter back and forth about whether or not a certain B-list celebrity should have gotten that new tattoo on her wrist or not.

"You know I'm not against tattoos," Gen said. "All I'm saying is that if she wants to proclaim her love for Daveed, then she could've picked an easier place for it to be able to be removed."

"She won't ever want it removed. They're in love," Kimmy replied.

"Yeah. For now."

"Forever."

"Forever's a long time," Joel, one of their regulars murmured into his scotch.

"Amen to that," Gen said.

After Kimmy delivered a couple of glasses of merlot to a table of women, she popped out a hip. "I need three Rhinegeists on tap, Jack."

"Got it."

As he poured, Kimmy continued on. "Gen, the problem with you is that you don't believe in love."

"Of course I do. Have you not seen Seth?"

Melissa chuckled as she approached the bar. "Seth would make even me believe in love."

"You're married with two kids," Kimmy said.

"I know. I love Sean, too. But I'm just saying that Seth is hot, like tamale hot."

"I'm thinking we've talked this conversation into the ground."

"Probably. Sorry, Jackson." Smiling at him, she said, "I need a Bacardi and Coke, margarita, top shelf, and two Miller Lites."

"On it."

As he poured drinks and punched in the tickets, Gen came around to stand next to him. "You've been pretty quiet during our lively discussion, Jackson."

"Other than trying to shut it down?" he joked.

"You know what I mean."

"I'm not exactly certain who the starlet is who got that tattoo and I have no desire to ever think about Seth in any way at all."

"I'm sure he appreciates that, too."

"Do you have any tattoos, Jackson?" Kimmy asked.

"Nope."

"You didn't get one even when you were younger?"

"Nope, though I ain't opposed to them either. Beth and I

never talked about getting them." Setting a glass on Melissa's tray, he let himself try to imagine Beth in a tattoo parlor's chair. Nope. Couldn't do it. She didn't like needles even a little bit.

"Maybe you'll get Dani's name on you."

He grinned. "Maybe, though I don't reckon that she'd be all that excited about a tattoo. But if I do, I'll likely not choose my wrist."

"Where, on your heart?" Melissa teased.

"Heck no. I'd put it on my bicep or something and show it off."

Kimmy and Melissa laughed as they went back to the tables. Gen waved goodbye to Joel. Then sighed when they finally got a lull. "Whew. What a night, huh?"

"It's a good one. You've had a good crowd tonight."

"Moments like this, when the crowd is easy, and the girls are chatty and it's almost cool outside? It makes me think that I'm going to miss it here."

They were now standing side by side, staring at the crowd. He nudged her with his elbow. "Why would you miss it? Is Seth taking you on a trip soon?"

"No." She turned to look directly into his eyes. "I decided to move to Texas, Jackson."

"Yeah, right."

"No, I'm serious. Seth and I are serious. Real serious."

He stopped and stared at her. "Wow."

She laughed softly. "I'm thinking I caught you off guard."

"You would be thinking correctly." Though a bunch of questions were running through his head, the most pressing being what she was going to do with the bar, he forced himself to think about her. "I'm real happy for you. Truly."

She looked doubtful. "You don't think I'm making a mistake?"

"It's not my place to judge."

"But?"

"But I know that from the minute he walked in here it was obvious that he meant something to you." Remembering that first night that Seth had walked in, he smiled at her. "That first night, you wore an expression like a bomb had just gone off."

"I felt like it. I honestly thought I'd never see him again."

"After y'all talked and straightened everything out, you've been happy. Almost content."

Gen nodded. "That's how I feel. When Seth and I talked I realized that this bar isn't as special to me as I thought."

"Speaking from someone who knows a lot about losing someone I loved forever, I'd say that you're making the right choice."

"I'm glad you feel that way."

Their conversation was interrupted by a couple who joined them at the bar, then Melissa coming back around with another drink order. He and Gen filled the orders, washed the dirty glasses in the sink. He ran to the back to get another bottle of tequila.

When the rush eased up again, Gen said, "You haven't asked about the bar."

"I figure you'll tell me what you're going to do with it when you're ready."

"Well, I'm not quite ready to sell it yet, but I'm going to need a manager."

"Okay." He mentally exhaled. He wasn't about to lose his job.

"What do you think about that?"

"I think it's going to be fine. You've got a good customer base and some great employees, myself included."

She smiled broadly. "I can't tell you how happy I am to hear you say that."

"Don't think you need my approval, Gen."

"I'm saying that I'm happy you said that because I want you to manage this place."

"What?"

"What do you say?" Before he answered, she said, "Now, I know we'll have to come up with contracts and everything, but we'll take you off of hourly and put you on salary. Give you an insurance package, too."

"You're serious."

"Of course I am. I'm moving to Texas, Jackson. I've got to get things in order here."

"Are you sure that I'm the right person?"

"Positive."

"Hey, Jack. Give me a Bud."

"Sure thing," he told the customer, then rang up the bill and put it in front of him. The guy was a regular who didn't believe in running a tab.

"Even though I'll still own it, I'm not going to be one of those owners who's going to make you run everything by me," Gen said, her voice sounding more anxious. "You can make this place your own. Make changes. Hire, fire. Whatever you want."

"I appreciate that. Thanks."

"So ... do you need a couple of days?"

Did he? If he said yes, he was going to be a manager of a bar. That wasn't what he'd intended to be. Not ever.

But ... he couldn't exactly say that it wasn't a good fit. He liked Bridgeport, liked everyone there, and liked the idea of more responsibility. He'd be managing again.

It was also something that he and Dani were used to.

"I want to talk to Dani about it. Just to make sure."

Her eyes brightened. "Does that mean what I think it does?"

"I'm not saying a word."

She lifted her hands. "You're right. Sorry. Seth told me to not be pushy, but here I go again."

Spying Kimmy and Melissa walking toward them, he said, "Thank you, Gen. For you to think of me? It means a lot."

Her gaze warmed. "You're welcome, Cookie."

CHAPTER 35

FROM LES LARKE'S
YOU, TOO, CAN HOST
A POKER TOURNEY:

*Other men have told me that they've
found these few hours help relieve stress.*

Six Weeks Later

"I can't believe you're going to call the bar Gen's Place now," Troy said as Jackson unlocked the door and ushered him, Ace, and Kurt inside. "It's yours now, buddy."

"I know." And damn, he was still feeling that little burst of pride inside him every time he thought about owning his own restaurant and bar. He was his own boss now, finally in charge of his own future. "But I wouldn't have it if Gen hadn't hired me in the first place. And now that she's moving to Texas with Seth, she trusted me again to take the reins. I don't want to forget that."

"I'm thinking you probably never will," Kurt said. "She sold it to you for a song."

"Well, she and Seth are still investors. I just bought into it."

That was another reason he was naming the place after her. She would have made a lot more money if she'd sold to someone else.

"Where are the light switches?" Ace called out from the back.

"Under the cover. It looks like it's locked, but it isn't."

"Gotcha." Two seconds later, the place was lit with a soft glow. "Hey, everything looks real good."

"Thanks. Me and Jeremy have been cleaning for two days. Dani, too, from time to time."

"We would have helped you more if you'd called," Kurt said as he took a bar stool. "How come you didn't reach out?"

"Yeah," Troy said as he joined them. "Did you really think we wouldn't drop everything to help you?"

"I knew you would." Maybe that's why he hadn't called them. He didn't want to be another duty in their already tight schedules. Plus … well, there was another reason. "As corny as it sounds, I guess I wanted to do the majority of the work."

Kurt nodded. "Make it your own."

"It feels good." After the last couple of years he'd had, it had felt real good. Feeling more comfortable behind the bar than sitting on one of the stools, he walked through the opening and picked up a glass. "Anyone want a beer? I've got Rhinegeist on tap."

Ace smiled. "Sounds good, but you've gotta let us pay."

"Hell no."

"You won't make much money serving free alcohol."

"I'll charge you when I open in two days." He poured four glasses and passed the other three to his friends. Then, because it felt appropriate, he lifted his own. "Here's to y'all."

"And to Gen's Place," Troy said. "I wish you all the best, buddy. Nobody deserves something good to happen more than you."

"I appreciate that, though I have to tell you that I feel like I've been experiencing my own string of good luck lately."

"That you have," Ace said. "You've got Dani and Kate

261

and Jeremy." Winking, he added, "Practically your very own picture-perfect family."

Jackson knew Ace was teasing, but he kind of thought that really was the case. His Kate was near perfect, Jeremy was a boy any man would be proud of, and Dani? Well, Dani, in a lot of ways, had made him whole again. "I'm grateful for all of them."

Taking a sip of beer, he said, "Y'all, too. If not for y'all, I would still be sitting in Spartan feeling sorry for myself."

"Aww, you needed that time, Cookie. I'm just glad you came out here and decided to give Bridgeport a chance. A lot of people wouldn't," Kurt said. "A lot of people don't ever want to do anything different, no matter how bad things are."

Jackson knew Kurt was referring to his father, who had been so distraught over much of the same things that Jackson had been dealing with—the loss of a job and a wife—that he'd descended into depression. So much so, he was even willing to let his youngest son leave with Kurt.

He shrugged. "I can't speak for anyone else, but I guess I realized that things were better here. Kate was happy. Then, one day I woke up and realized that I was happy, too. And when that happened? I knew I wasn't going to give that up."

"You held on tight," Ace said.

Jackson wouldn't have phrased it that way, but he didn't disagree. "Yeah. I wasn't going to let that go easily."

Kurt leaned forward and rested. "So, you're happy. All of us are happy."

"And paired up like bookends." Troy grinned. "Are you really starting to think about who else needs to come out here?"

"No. Well, maybe."

Ace laughed. "Got anyone in mind?"

"No." Turning to Jackson, he said, "Who do you know in Spartan who needs to get on out?"

There wasn't anyone. All the rest of the guys had either found good work or were so settled in Spartan, there was no way they were going to want to move. But then, all of a sudden, Jackson thought of Shannon Murphy. "I know someone else who just moved here that might need our help getting settled."

"Another guy from Spartan's here?" Ace asked. "Who?"

"It's a woman. Shannon Murphy." Looking at his buddies, Jackson said, "Do any of y'all remember her?"

"I do," Ace said. "She was a cheerleader, right? And on the homecoming court."

"Dani and I ran into her a while back. She just opened that dance studio two blocks from here. Dance with Me."

"Are you sure she owns it?" Ace asked. "Last I heard Shannon got a job working at the hospital. And her family is great."

Kurt shook his head. "Um, maybe not so great. I just remembered that I heard she'd just found out she was adopted—and that she has two sisters who didn't fare as well as she did. Someone told me she was really struggling."

"She was close with one of my sisters," Ace said. "I'll stop by the dance studio and see how she's doing."

Jackson raised his eyebrows. "Just like that?"

"Oh, I'll play it cool," Ace replied. "I'll tell her about Meredith and the rest of us. Invite her to come over for supper one night soon. Reconnect with some old friends."

Jackson nodded slowly. "You know what? I think she might be up for that."

"I'll keep you posted about what happens," Ace said as he stood up. "Which reminds me. I told Finn and Mer I'd come home with everything to make a pot of chili. I better get on that."

One by one, they handed Jackson their glasses. He washed them and set them out to dry.

Kurt got up. "You getting out of here, too, Cookie, or staying?"

"I'm out, too." He didn't give them an explanation because he realized they didn't need one. They understood that he had people who were counting on him.

Just like he was counting on them, too.

EPILOGUE

FROM LES LARKE'S
YOU, TOO, CAN HOST
A POKER TOURNEY:

All those reasons aside, here's why I host poker
nights: because with me, it's never really been
just about the poker … it's always been about
everything else that comes with it. That, my friends,
is really all that matters at the end of the day.

Dani broke off their kiss with a breathless gasp. "Jackson, stop. We can't do this right now."

Her voice was husky, her eyes were bright, and that mouth that had drawn him to her from the start was slightly swollen. A pale pink flush highlighted her cheeks.

All in all, she looked much like he felt—happy, relaxed, and more than a little turned on. Holding her in his arms, Jackson tried to clear his mind enough to figure out what she was having trouble with. They were alone in her hotel room, both of their kids were occupied, and he hadn't done more than kiss her chastely in twenty-four hours. Surely, she'd missed him as much as he'd missed her.

Maybe she simply needed a little more reassurance.

"Sure we can, honey. All this is just right." He nipped at her neck, smoothed the slight sting with slow kisses. Murmured in her ear, "It's been so long, you've just forgotten how it's done." Leaning down, he claimed her mouth again. Smiled when she didn't hesitate before opening her lips to let him deepen the kiss.

Just like that, his body started humming—and started thinking of everything else they could be doing in an empty hotel room besides making out a little bit against a hotel room door.

When she moaned, it practically made him forget why he'd brought her up to her room in the first place. Practically.

And then he remembered. Yes, Dani Brown was gorgeous and very desirable, but that wasn't the real reason he'd brought her upstairs and into this room.

He'd also had some other plans that were getting put into play that very minute. Hopefully.

But had they been upstairs long enough? Maybe he needed to keep her occupied for a little while longer? He ran a hand down her spine, curved it around her hip, and pulled her closer. "You feel so good, Dan. Perfect."

After one last kiss, Dani pulled away with a low laugh. "Jackson, we've got to get out of here. Jeremy's going to come looking for us if we're not careful."

He knew Jeremy wasn't. "He's with all his buddies. He doesn't care where we are." Plus, Jeremy was in on the plans.

"He's going to care if we don't show up soon."

Her voice was breathless. Sounded almost like it had when they'd …

He forced his mind to get back on track.

Trying to sound aggravated, he murmured. "Are you sure we need to leave this room right this second? Because I know what's waiting for us downstairs."

"Me, too. Fifteen fourteen-year-olds, including my Jeremy; assorted siblings, including your Kate; and double the amount of parents. All of whom have probably realized that both of us were definitely not needed to retrieve one purse."

Actually, he'd needed to take her up here, otherwise she would have run up and back down in five minutes. "Everyone also knows that we're a new couple. They get it."

She chuckled as she walked in front of the mirror and started smoothing her hair and clothes. "If we don't get down there soon, they may understand too much. We need to hurry, Jackson."

He walked behind her and looped his hands around her middle, liking how they looked in the reflection. Pressing his lips to her head, he said, "I promise you, no matter what, no one is going to think we've been doing nothing but necking in here. We might as well prove them right."

"That won't do. Not today, it won't." Her pretty eyes met his in the mirror. "No way did we go to so much trouble to get Jeremy on the team just so they can think his momma is a floozy."

"Floozy?" He scoffed. "You're with your boyfriend, honey."

"Mothers have to go by different rules."

"I don't think so. And don't even call yourself that. Nobody calls anyone that anymore. Wait, is that even a word?"

"It is. And, despite women being all empowered and such, I promise you, where the conduct of teenage boys' mothers is concerned, it's firmly situated in the present day and not just in 1950."

Jackson thought about teasing her a bit, unbuttoning her shirt and asking if she could be his very own pinup model for a few moments, but he thought he might get his face slapped.

Besides, enough time had passed. It was time.

After kissing her temple once again, he dropped his hands and walked toward the door. "Let's get going then."

She picked up her purse—which had been the whole reason she'd run up to the room—and smiled brightly. "If it's any consolation, I miss you, too."

"Good." He loved how her cheeks were a little pink, probably from both his teasing her in front of the mirror and the memories they'd recently made when he'd taken her to bed a few weeks ago. The experience had been everything he'd hoped—and a whole lot better than he'd dared to imagine.

But one thing he hadn't thought about was how hard it was going to be to find any privacy with both of them crazy-busy, one four-year-old and one traveling baseball teenager. The way things were going, he might be able to sneak some time with her next month.

He held out his hand. "You know I'm only teasing you, right?"

"I know," she replied as she linked her fingers with his. "I have to say that I really am so glad that the kids seem to be handling us together okay."

"Me, too."

She kept talking as they kept walking. "And, who knows? Maybe one day, down the road, when we're ready …" Her voice trailed off.

"When we're ready?"

"Oh. I mean, you know. When we get more serious."

It was almost a crime to allow her to be so flustered. But it was also fun as hell. "When we get more serious, what?"

"Um, well, I was just thinking, maybe by that time, the kids will be on board with our relationship."

"You worried about Kate, honey? Because Kate loves you and has since you watched *Frozen* with her three times in a row."

"I guess I was thinking about Jeremy."

He'd been having a lot of conversations with that boy, and he felt good about where they were at. "He knows you love him, too, Dan." Resting his palm on the center of her back, he maneuvered her past the elevator to the stairs. "Let's go down this way."

Obviously distracted, she looked up at him as they started walking down. "You sound so confident."

"That's because I am. You should be, too." Down they went, four more steps. He moved to her side, because she kept looking up at him instead of where she was going.

"All right. I will." Still smiling at him, she said, "Now all we have to do is worry about tomorrow's championship game. If the Bats win, they'll win the whole thing."

"With your boy as their star catcher, too. It will be awesome."

Her smile got bigger. "I'm so proud of him."

"Me, too, honey. Now, slow down on these last two steps and watch where you're going."

"What?" She turned to look, and almost fell on her face.

Luckily, he grabbed her waist and prevented her from falling. "Careful, now. Everybody's watching."

"Jackson, there's got to be a hundred people down here."

"Thereabouts. Three more steps now."

She took another step but still didn't watch what she was doing. "Jackson Koch, what is going on?"

He leaned toward her. "I've got a little something planned for you." Pressing his lips to her temple, he whispered. "Do me a favor now and act surprised, 'kay?"

Just as she looked back at him, the whole room went crazy.

"Surprise!" Kate squealed at the top of her lungs as she came charging forward. The minute she did, the whole room burst into excited applause.

And there were a lot of people there.

Jackson grinned as he saw all the baseball folks, and Kurt, Troy, Ace, and their girlfriends. And Gen and Seth. Even Mrs. Burridge, Dani's Indian Hill client. So many people were there who cared about them.

"What's going on?"

The room suddenly quieted. It seemed he was up. "Well, I got to thinking that it was time to do something, and I know you. You would want to be surrounded by our kids, and the people who we love. So ..." He paused so he could kneel down on the floor in front of her.

She gasped, staring at him. "Jackson, you don't need to get on your knee ..."

"Yeah, I think I do. I promised myself if the Lord ever gave me another chance to fall in love, I wasn't going to mess it up. And I'm not. Danielle, give me that hand, honey."

Still looking shell-shocked, Dani placed it in front of her. Pleased that she didn't look upset and that her hand wasn't so much as quivering, Jackson leaned forward and kissed her fingers.

Then said quietly, "I believe in love, and I believe in second chances. Just as importantly, I believe in us, Dani. I love you, I love Jeremy, and Kate needs you as much as I do. Will you marry me?"

The whole room fell silent. Tears filled her eyes as she looked just beyond him. "Jeremy?"

"It's all good, Mom. Promise."

All of a sudden, the brightest smile he'd ever seen illuminated her face. "Yes, I'll marry you, Jackson."

Pulling the ring he'd bought two days ago out of his jeans pocket, he slid it on her finger.

Her eyes went wide. "You got me a ring?"

"That's usually how it's done, sweetheart," he said as he stood up.

She lifted her hand to stare at the ring, a half-carat diamond surrounded by pink sapphires. It looked delicate and feminine and impressive. Everything she was to him. "It's beautiful. I love it."

"I'm glad. Now, can I give you a kiss and a hug before this crowd of ours gets too restless?"

The moment she nodded, he claimed her lips again, then hugged her tight.

Then, as she giggled, he called out to the room. "Everybody, please meet Dani Brown, my fiancée."

"You're still holding her hand, Cookie!" Troy called out. "Are you ever going to let her go so we can give her a hug?"

Still staring at Dani, Jackson shook his head. "Nope. I'm going to hold on to her as tight as I can. I don't intend to ever let her go."

The End

Acknowledgments

When I began writing the first book in the Bridgeport Social Club, I had only a vague idea about a trio of novels featuring a bunch of guys trying to fit in. Never did I imagine that the books would be so well received. I'm so very grateful for that.

With all that in mind, I have many people to thank.

First is the incredible team at Blackstone Publishing. It's been an honor and a privilege to be one of their authors. Big thanks go out to both my editors Ember Hood and Vikki Warner for their guiding hands and encouragement. I felt that the three of us all worked together to make the books as good as they could be. I loved that.

Just as important to the series' success were Jeffrey Yamaguchi and Lauren Maturo. Their enthusiasm and skill made me want to work even harder, which says a lot! I'm indebted to them for sending me to the many conferences and appearances, setting up contests and promotions, and for doing all the things that authors dream about but rarely get the chance to experience.

Finally, I'm so grateful for the library sales team at Blackstone, especially Stephanie Hall. Stephanie has a way of making everyone feel like they're an old friend, which is a gift. I was so happy that she—and the rest of the team—put the word out about the books.

Closer to home, I'd like to thank my incredible agent Nicole Resciniti. She's been my biggest cheerleader and advocate. All writers should be so blessed to have an agent like Nicole.

I also owe a huge thank you to Seymour agent Lesley Sabga. Lesley went with me to signings, tutored me on Instagram, took more pictures and tweeted about them than I can count, and was a constant source of enthusiasm. Yes, Lesley just happens to be my daughter, but she's also been a tremendous amount of help.

Next I want to share another shout out of THANKS to Tony Westley, who started a poker club in our hometown and was the reason I began this series. Thank you, Tony!

I also am thankful for my husband, Tom, who patiently listens to my daily writing updates, now cooks more meals than I do, and always has a hug for me. I would be lost without you, Tom.

Finally, I want to take a moment to praise God for giving me the tools to write. With Him all things are possible. I really believe that.

Reader Questions

1. Both Jackson and Dani have had to start over after devastating circumstances. What were some of the challenges they faced? If you've ever had to "start over," either in a new job or a new relationship, what challenges did you face?

2. Jackson chose to move to Bridgeport instead of staying in Spartan near his family. Would you have done the same? Why or why not?

3. Dani has a close relationship with her son, Jeremy. How did you feel about the sacrifices that she made in order for him to play on the Bats baseball team?

4. Both Gen and Seth made a lot of mistakes in their past. Why do you think they were still able to get back together? What do you think will happen to them in the future?

5. How did you feel about the Bridgeport Social Club's benefit tournament?

6. If you've read more than one book in this series, what have you enjoyed about it? Who makes up your "social club"?

7. What characters, either in this novel or in the series, are you anxious to see again in a future book?

8. What do you "hold on tight" to in your life? Your faith? Family? Friends? Hope?